Praise for A

A Stolen Kiss by author Mindy S̶ Heart of the Amish series. It's a wonderful, fun, sweet, fast-paced read that is sure to captivate Amish romance cravers. Readers will love this endearing, inspiring, heart-warming story. I highly recommend!

–Lisa Jones Baker, bestselling author of *Promise at Pebble Creek* and The Hope Chest of Dreams series

Author Mindy Steele has become a premier writer of Amish Fiction. *A Stolen Kiss*, Steele's newest release, shows us in the best way possible what can happen when an Amish girl steals a kiss from an Amish man. Or did she? Heartwarming, funny, and full of "awww" moments, get to know LeEtta and Benuel, the couple that wasn't meant to be.

–Vicky Sluiter, author of *Oliver's Moving Day*

Another Wonderful Story of Love and Faith from Mindy Steele! What happens when you kiss a stranger just so your friends can't say you never have? That's what LeEtta and Ben are going to find out in Mindy's newest offering from "The Heart of the Amish" series, *"A Stolen Kiss"*. Fast paced and satisfying—just what I needed to make me smile!

–Anne Blackburne, Author of *Ruth's Ginger Snap Surprise* and *Mary's Calico Hope*

"Mindy Steele has an immense gift for turning a phrase and making her characters feel like beloved next-door neighbors you'd want to have over for a cup of cocoa. Settle into a comfy chair and enjoy the escape of Stolen Kisses, a heartfelt, inspiring, beautifully-written romance. Mindy is a rising star in Amish fiction."

–Jennifer Beckstrand, *USA Today* bestselling author of *The Amish Quiltmaker's Unattached Neighbor*

THE HEART *of* THE AMISH

A Stolen Kiss

MINDY STEELE

BARBOUR
PUBLISHING

Cover Design: Kirk DouPonce, DogEared Design

Published by Barbour Publishing, Inc., 1810 Barbour Drive, Uhrichsville, Ohio 44683, www.barbourbooks.com

Our mission is to inspire the world with the life-changing message of the Bible.

 Member of the
Evangelical Christian
Publishers Association

Printed in the United States of America.

DEDICATION

Blake and Tessa.
I don't know who kissed who first, but I love your story.

ACKNOWLEDGMENTS

To my husband for letting me talk
out all the scenes during ball games.

To Vicky Dali for hanging in there with
me during the grueling days.

To Becky for wanting this story.

*"For I know the plans I have for you," declares the LORD,
"plans to prosper you and not to harm you,
plans to give you hope and a future."*
JEREMIAH 29:11 NIV

Note to Readers

While I live near the Amish and have a great many Amish friends, this novel and its characters are completely fictional. No resemblance between the characters in this book and any real members of the Amish community is intended. My hope is to bring realism to these pages through research and familiarity. However, each community is different. Any inaccuracies of the Amish lifestyle are completely my own.

While I am truly dedicated to the inspirational romance genre, I strive to create characters and circumstances that are realistic but truly flawed. Life isn't a romance novel. It's complicated, hard, beautiful, and unpredictable; but with faith and perseverance, love always finds a way.

Mindy

GLOSSARY

ach: oh

aenti: aunt

boppli/bopplin: baby, babies

bruder: bother

bu/buwe: boy, boys

daed: dad

danke: thank you

dawdi: grandfather

dawdi haus: a small dwelling attached or unattached to the main family home, specifically for newlyweds or grandparents

dochter: daughter

dok: doctor

dummle: to hurry

Englisch/Englischer: a non-Amish person

fraa: wife

faul: lazy

ferhoodled: confused

freinden: friend

gegisch: silly

Gott: God

grosskind/grosskinner: grandchild, grandchildren

grossmammi: grandmother

gut: good

haus: house

hund: hound or dog

jah: yes

kaffi: coffee

kapp: prayer covering

kault: cold
kichlin: cookies
kinner: children
krank: sick or ill
kuche: cake
kumm: come
maed/maedel: girl, young woman
mamm/mammi: mom, grandmother
mann/menner: man, men
mariye: morning
mei: me
meinda: remember
nacht: night
naet: not
nee: no
nochber: neighbor
onkel: uncle
rumspringa: the time for young people to run around before baptism
schtupp: family room or sitting room
schwester: sister
sohn: son
vell: well
verra: very
wilkum: welcome
wunderbaar: wonderful
youngies: teenagers, youth

CHAPTER ONE

LeEtta Miller tried to roll her eyes as quietly as she could while *Mammi* Iola rambled on like a swoony teenager. Nothing was more embarrassing than standing in a hot kitchen with a dozen other women while your sixty-nine-year-old widowed grandmother spoke of her newest *special friend.*

"I thought you were sweet on Owen Schmit," Gemma Shetler quipped under a not-so-silent breath. The eighty-year-old had just celebrated her sixty-first anniversary and never skipped a chance to address Mammi Iola's unusual courting habits.

"I've yet to see him in a clean shirt," Mammi Iola replied shamelessly.

"A *fraa* could see to that," Gemma continued. "Such things as he has been in sore need of."

"We agree." Mammi Iola smiled unabashedly. "I do hope *Gott* wills him such as he needs, but. . ." With ease, she secured a lid on a bowl of macaroni salad. "I will not consider a man who can't wash and iron his own shirts."

Mammi Iola also didn't believe in marrying a man who couldn't cook, sweep a floor, or tie his own shoes without the need of assistance. At her age, that left scant few men to consider.

"Is your new interest someone we know?" the minister's fraa further quizzed.

LeEtta purposefully kept to the far end of the large kitchen.

Unfortunately, at twenty-two, she had impeccable hearing. These conversations were best avoided if at all possible. LeEtta would no doubt get the first-to-last detail of Mammi Iola's comings and goings when she took her grandmother for her weekly shopping. Mammi had no shame in sharing how her baked goods earned her sweet words and long looks.

"*Jah*, William Headings," Mammi Iola said with such romanticism that LeEtta almost found it endearing. *Almost.*

The name Headings was unfamiliar. Someone from a neighboring district perhaps. Mammi Iola found seeking a special friend outside of the community always worked best. That way when she found a flaw that she couldn't live with, she could avoid the rumor mill whispering all about her failed attempts.

"I'm surprised she hasn't pulled you into her search," LeEtta's friend Eunice muttered beside her.

"Not on account of her not trying," LeEtta replied.

"Perhaps now that you are older, you should consider a widower. You have few options left."

LeEtta's gaze shifted quickly to her friend. "I don't want to marry a widower." Those often came with a ready-made family. Though her friend was merely teasing, LeEtta was a tad envious of her elderly grandmother. Here she was of marrying age and had yet to secure even a long look. Well, Jonas Hostetler gave her many looks and winks and gawked to a point that LeEtta often hurried in the opposite direction—but he was only fifteen, and that didn't count.

Long looks sounded so appealing and a little frightening. Mammi clearly had no trouble getting them, even though she walked with a hitch in her hip and one brow much thinner than the other. Old women shouldn't be plucking their brows anyhow.

"His fraa has only just passed!" Cathreen Schwartz was as appalled with the conversation as LeEtta was, and for good reason. Didn't Bishop Schwartz just minutes ago preach about the importance of patiently waiting on God's direction? Mammi wasn't patient or concerned with being the center of attention. What she was doing was seeking a husband.

"Her funeral was last month." Mammi Iola leaned on the table as the conversation continued. "He's all alone without his fraa. We are to see over those, are we not? William is wonderfully fond of shoofly pie and he likes. . .color." Mammi Iola lifted her chin stubbornly. Her one blue shoelace drew several eyes downward. Her eyesight was not as good as it once was, despite her claim that she was ravaged with an onslaught of colorblindness. LeEtta knew better. She'd once read about the infirmity and found it was mostly a male setback, not subject to grandmothers who used fake diseases for attention.

"I think it's. . .good you are taking a second chance at love," *Dok* Stella remarked with a sly grin. Her rounded middle proved she too was an encourager of love at any age. Dok Stella was an herbal healer, the local midwife, and married to the bishop.

"*Danke*. A woman should not have to live alone all her days, but I won't tolerate a man who won't do his part."

Eunice giggled beside her. Clearly eavesdropping didn't concern her one bit. Why Mammi refused to move into a *dawdi haus,* where most aged grandparents lived close by family to be seen over, was beyond her. LeEtta could provide her daily companionship. LeEtta craved having someone to talk to more regularly. *Daed* wasn't much of a conversationalist and never enjoyed wasting words unnecessarily. Arlen Miller was of a stout position that a woman's place was in silence and in shadows. LeEtta didn't like silence, and shadows often gave her the willies.

LeEtta let out a sigh as she helped tidy the table. What she wouldn't give if her father treated her more like a helper than something fragile that might break under the slightest pressure. LeEtta wanted to do more than simply cook his meals. Although, she did need practice. Lots of it. Baking was a joy to learn, as each recipe took on a measure of delight to create. It was LeEtta's side dishes she struggled with most. Daed insisted she didn't need to explore with trying out new spices for what only needed but a pinch of salt, but LeEtta was sure she could make even the blandest green bean better by adding the right amount of garlic, red pepper, and bacon grease. It was a warm combination that he had yet to appreciate.

She'd serve better helping in the fields, she knew. A pot roast needed no one to watch over it, and she'd have less time on her hands to experiment. LeEtta made a mental note to argue the point at the next opportunity she had.

But first, she needed to find better ways of communicating with her father. Since he'd fallen off the grain-bin ladder two weeks ago, his quiet had grown unnervingly quieter. Surely he was concerned about the harvest. How was a man his age, with only one working arm, going to harvest all their corn when he struggled simply tending to the livestock? That's what she'd like to know.

It was no trouble feeding the cows, and she could hold the reins much easier with two smaller hands, could she not? Did he think that because she had grown up without a mother that she was incapable of doing what any *sohn* or *dochter* could? Or were her blue eyes and strawberry-blond hair reminders of what they had both lost?

"I can't believe this is our last Sunday together," Eunice said, pulling LeEtta back to the present. Two districts had swelled with the many blessings of growing families, causing a split recently. A small part of Cherry Grove and Miller's Creek would now become a new district. Growth was always a blessing. Unfortunately, Eunice would no longer live in the same district.

"But we will see each other often," LeEtta offered warmly as she watched Eunice collect her dessert container now that the fellowship meal was over. Her brownie container was empty, as expected. No one ever skipped trying one of Eunice's brownies.

"Did you see the cute newcomer sitting next to Jerry Hostetler?" Eunice leaned in closer and whispered in her left ear. "Gemma says he's visiting for the week. He sure is a looker."

LeEtta gave her friend an odd look. Eunice had a good eye, but she was also soon to marry Jerry and shouldn't even notice a handsome stranger. Of course, LeEtta had spotted the newcomer as soon as he exited the buggy with Eber and Mary Ropp. She wasn't blind. She was just terribly embarrassed to have a grandmother in a constant state of hunting for a life-end partner when LeEtta had not so much as taken a buggy ride home with a man.

"Jah, I saw him." LeEtta gathered her leftover dill relish and spicy mustard. No one appreciated the wonderful flavor of dill. One glass jar was only half-empty, and the other two were not even open. She glanced over at the sweet zucchini relish Linda Shetler always brought to complement a sandwich or hot dog. *Empty. Too many have a sweet tooth in Cherry Grove,* she scoffed.

"Just a visit?" Ellen Beechy had a voice as soft as a morning mist, and despite her terrible shyness, LeEtta always found her looks drew a few eyes her way.

"That's what I hear," Eunice replied.

"I think he is a looker too, but Chrissy Keim already has eyes for him." Ellen ducked her head as her cheeks turned an unearthly shade of crimson. Ellen was someone who knew the strains of being on the tip of gossip, seeing as her brother Alan had left his family after stealing a car and burning down a barn. She also knew what it was like to not have a mother. But Ellen had at least known her own *mamm* for a time. She had. . .memories. LeEtta had nothing but the reminder that her birthday was a day of sorrow.

LeEtta did find the visiting newcomer. . .well made, but she hadn't gotten a decent glimpse of him to decide if he truly was. She'd tried daring a peek during Minister Fender's short sermons, for curiosity always bested her. She had to shift into an awkward position, which she wasn't a fan of, peeking between the *kapps* of Mandy Schwartz and Chrissy Keim. It took a whole twenty minutes before they moved just enough for LeEtta to get a clear view of him across the long, narrow room that served as a cabinet shop during the week.

To her wonderment, their eyes met, and a sudden, inexplicable thrill washed over her. It was the same when she added her special summer salsa to plain old chili. It was as close to a long look as LeEtta had ever imagined.

He was handsome, with dark hair and eyes the color of mystery and suspense. She wondered if they were pure chocolate or possibly flaked with gold and greenery. The distance had left that up to mystery. LeEtta liked a good mystery. She had a collection currently hidden between linens in her keepsake chest so that when life got too quiet, she could always rely on characters to fill the silence around her.

The visiting newcomer would make a fine hero in any story, but no sooner had her pulse quickened and (her back straightened on her backless bench) than it dropped to a crawl when Chrissy Keim cautiously lifted a hand and waved in his direction. Of course, the handsome stranger was not looking at her but at two very single *maedels* who knew all about flirting and kissing and what attracted the opposite sex with their hair of summer wheat and sunshine. LeEtta was the last to know those things, and strawberries were only good picked fresh or served in a pie, not in hair.

But a girl could imagine, couldn't she? When you knew your life would be one of a spinster, since no one ever considered you anything more, having an imagination was a blessing.

"You should go say hello," Eunice insisted. Since it was the last Sunday, many of the folks she had known all her life would be together, and an extended fellowship meal and an evening of games and visiting were planned.

Teacher Kevin entered the kitchen, drawing eyes to him. "Anyone seen Willy Miller?" Kevin was terribly tall, with red hair and a beard, despite not being married. He wasn't the only man in Cherry Grove to do so after joining the church. Bishop Graber paid them no mind, as long as they didn't draw the wrong kind of attention to themselves.

"Last I saw him, he was outrunning Josh and Martin," Liz Eicher replied.

"It wonders me if that *bu* will not outrun a racehorse one day,"

Mammi Iola added. "I reckon you mean to have words with him on our last Sunday gathering." She lifted a stern brow, causing the always-stern teacher to shrink slightly. His deep, dark gaze turned LeEtta's way, and he frowned before walking out, leaving a gaggle of women to commence chattering behind him.

A hot late summer breeze kicked up outside and pushed through the screen windows of the Wickeys' brick home. "Are you still sore at him? You know he had no interest in you but only hoped for a new teacher's helper," Eunice said bluntly. "No sense in pouting over it."

LeEtta wasn't a pouter, but Teacher Kevin had left her with a sour stomach. He had sought her out right before school started up, sparking up talk about the importance of family and settling down. LeEtta presumed he might ask to court her. She didn't even mind that he was four years older, but instead of confessing an interest, he insisted that if she wasn't courting or considering marrying, she might want to become a teacher's helper and let other maedels focus on such things as finding husbands.

LeEtta wasn't a fan of school the first time. She made decent grades but was frowned upon plenty for being behind on other subjects, like boys. *Nee*, she would rather be a mother's helper and practice her cooking skills until she found flavors that brought life back to her father rather than return to school.

"God says to not dwell on yesterday, even though I'm not sure what He thinks of Jonas Hostetler." The fifteen-year-old had left another penned note on her front door this morning. At first, LeEtta found Jonas' infatuation sweet. But once she explained that seven years was an age gap she couldn't ignore, he had only persisted harder. He didn't even spell *violet* right in his simple poem.

"God loves us all, even Jonas," Eunice said on a fast breath. "He also says we are to be kind and welcoming to newcomers. You avoided him during the fellowship meal. He sat in your section."

"I'm kind to everyone," LeEtta defended. "I was trying to see over making fresh *kaffi*, but you know how Mammi Iola gets about kaffi."

All three nodded their heads in unison. Left unattended, Mammi Iola made her kaffi with the same technique as her homemade brown sugar syrup, and LeEtta wasn't about to make a fool of herself in front of others. If the newcomer wanted to meet her, he would.

"Perhaps you should be more like Iola," Eunice offered up. "I mean, she seems to have no trouble making friends, and I bet Iola's been kissed." Eunice giggled.

"She was married to my *dawdi*. Of course she's been kissed!" LeEtta narrowed her gaze. "We are not to seek attention, and one cannot be like someone else, but only themselves." The things that escaped her dear friend's lips tended to make LeEtta question how she managed to snag Jerry Hostetler at all. Then again, Eunice never had any difficulty turning heads. Perhaps being herself was the problem.

"Why doesn't one of you go ask his name?"

"And risk Jerry thinking I have sparks for another?" Eunice wiggled her brows.

"I couldn't walk up and speak to a stranger like that." Ellen's brows nearly touched when her expression grew grave. LeEtta wasn't as shy as Ellen, but she could never be as bold as Eunice.

"I bet Jonas would stop pestering you if you did," Eunice challenged, embedding an idea that did hold a certain appeal. Jonas was becoming a. . .problem. Just last week, LeEtta had to hide in the bulk storage room for a whole twenty minutes to avoid him.

It was a foolish idea. LeEtta wasn't about to approach a man. It was the kind of thing Mammi might try, but not her.

That was Eunice. Always pushing her. LeEtta let out an exasperated breath. Just because she'd never been kissed didn't mean anything. One day, she would be. Eventually she would marry, and there would be lots of kissing. She hoped.

"We've been talking," Eunice began, giving Ellen an encouraging look.

"Jah, we think you should meet my cousin Tyler from the next district." Ellen said it with such enthusiasm, LeEtta almost dropped one of her jars of relish.

"You want to set me up?" More embarrassing than being uninteresting was having your friends fix you up with someone.

"We can double date!"

"Nee, I will not be partnered up."

"Then you should introduce yourself to the newcomer. Really, LeEtta, the clock is ticking." Eunice gave her that look, the same one she often wore when she was about to bring embarrassment to LeEtta.

LeEtta heard no ticking, just a friend who thought her incapable of securing her own special friend. LeEtta wanted to remind Eunice she was plenty capable of that. There simply wasn't anyone who had caught her eye—or anyone who gave her a second look.

"I have to go." LeEtta quickly collected her things and moved to the back door. Perhaps she'd leave now, before Eunice embarrassed her. She'd say her so longs and walk home. Jah, it was a perfectly good day for walking but not one for talking to strangers. She'd rather go home with Daed and enjoy a quiet evening of him saying nothing and her having nothing to say.

"But you haven't even asked his name!" Ellen was in on it too.

"I can't think of anything worse than finding out his name," she told her friends over one shoulder. The faster she left, the better.

"LeEtta." Eunice's eyes widened.

"He's a stranger who hasn't visited his grandparents before. I mean, we've never seen him before. That says much about a person, ain't so?"

"LeEtta," Eunice repeated, but nothing she could say would convince LeEtta to boldly walk up to a man and introduce herself. Only Mammi Iola did that sort of thing.

LeEtta turned to leave and found herself staring at a wide breast of white. She lifted her gaze slowly and was met with dark eyes under two hiked brows. There wasn't a fleck of gold or dot of green in the eyes studying her intently.

"Excuse me."

His roguish tone sent a second shiver over her. So he was handsome up close too—and annoyed. LeEtta was speechless, embarrassed, and blocking the doorway. She slipped back inside and gave him a wide berth. He took it, walking into the kitchen without giving her a second look. She never got second looks. So why did it bother her so much now?

CHAPTER TWO

Benuel Ropp mentally grumbled as he stepped outside for a breath of fresh air. More than a hundred and sixty souls crammed into one overly warm building made for an unsavory mixture of sawdust, summer heat, and body odor.

Being a fresh face in a community that seemed to reserve the right to not give a care about progress told him his time here in Cherry Grove would be as miserable as he feared it would be, but he would endure it if that meant making enough money for a down payment on his own land.

In a sea of bad decisions, Ben was sure this time he had made the right one. He told his parents he would find his own way, but Ben secretly hoped that in his absence, Daed would change his recent decision. If Daed wanted to retire, then Ben was the one who should take over the family farm since he'd first shadowed him in the field. So why then did he give the land to his *bruder*?

Ben wasn't the only one surprised by Daed's choice. And each of his siblings had the same hope within them. *The family farm.*

They had been blessed with more land than most in the heavily populated area. It was a lot to see over. So why would his father leave it all in his bruder's hands? Even his sisters were heartbroken.

Lisa had been the most vocal, but Mary was no less disturbed that Sam had inherited every acre. His sisters had always harbored selfish streaks. Daed or Mamm had seen to it that they had everything they needed, yet they always begged for more. Ben was no whiner, nor was he a beggar, but the farm had been his dream since the first time he scooped seeds from a bucket and pushed them into cold spring earth with a tiny finger. He was amazed when green breached the earth, and he nursed every inch of the crop up to a harvest. Farming was in his blood, and now his plans were shattered. Sam didn't even like planting. He didn't like dirt. He liked cows. Stupid, dumb cows. It wouldn't surprise Ben in the least if he wasn't already planning to turn the barn into a dairy barn right now.

It was tradition for the last at home to receive the family farm, but being unwed with no home of his own, Ben knew he was first in line to assume the role. Daed was punishing him. Ben was certain of that. A punishment far too severe for something he didn't do. It wasn't Ben's fault that a man almost died. He'd only brought the shotgun. It was Caleb who missed the target and nearly delivered a fatal shot. No one was hurt. It was an accident. One which Ben was obviously still paying for.

How did he keep getting himself into these fixes? He should have never agreed to shoot targets with his friends, Caleb and Landis. Those two seemed to attract trouble like a ball of yarn in a room full of cats. Mamm was right about that, but did she not see that Sam made mistakes too? Ben couldn't ignore how Sam had fertilized too soon the weekend Daed had taken Ben to the farm-machinery auction. Not a rain cloud in sight. Thankfully, they had gotten home just in time to water all ninety acres before the crop burned to a crisp.

"Lord, let these next weeks go by swiftly," he prayed. He and God had not been on speaking terms for some time, so silence, of course, followed. Still, Ben had a reason for coming here. A man couldn't have anything of his own if he waited for handouts. Daed's own words. Well, Ben would make his way. Thankfully, Dawdi found him work with a local hog farmer in desperate need of help. Ben didn't like hogs, but he did like bacon and working outdoors, so he agreed. It was his only hope, considering he had put every dime he had earned over the years into the farm that was now his little brother's.

Ben would not return unless he had enough for a down payment on a small piece of land he knew would soon be up for sale. The owner promised he wasn't ready to move until spring. So Ben had time to add to the small amount of cash in his pocket now.

His own farm. That's why he was here, in the middle of nowhere, sitting through a three-hour service and staying focused while his dawdi glanced his way often for signs of a rebellious nature.

Ben kept his gaze trained on the minister and the bishop. He hadn't even laughed when two little boys at the end of one bench started playing thumb war. One little guy really knew how to swivel himself into a win.

Only once had he dared scan the room. He noted two maedels trying to gain his attention, but Ben wasn't here to make friends. Friends only let you down. He was there for a purpose. At least that was what he told himself until, just beyond a clutch of kapps and parted hair, a hint of strawberry-kissed hair caught his eye. She was a small woman. Her innocent curiosity of him surprising as their gazes met. She was lovely.

She leaned out, noting him looking her way, and for one brief moment Ben forgot all about how quickly one could be betrayed or that he was in another community on the hottest September he'd ever known. Suddenly, a hand lifted, a flirtatious wave from someone in front of her, and Ben quickly averted his gaze. He would not let himself get distracted. He had to stay focused.

Even so, Ben found himself searching for the woman with wide, pale-blue eyes and red-blond hair during the fellowship meal. Twice, he spotted her doting over an older man and keeping two silver kaffi dispensers full. By all assumptions, Ben guessed the stern-looking man was her father. The red beard was a strong indicator of such. A young boy shadowed her close by, and judging by her frustration, Ben guessed he was a younger bruder. Some families were knitted into tight knots. His own sister, Mary, often did the same when they were *youngies*, he thought with a smile.

Once the fellowship meal was finished, folks continued to mill about instead of heading home. Ben shouldered a few introductions. He had hoped to meet Shepard Eversole, his new employer. Unfortunately, Ben quickly learned that Shepard had just married and was taking a honeymoon somewhere down in Tennessee.

"I'd hoped to meet him today," Ben told his grandfather.

"We can go see Shep tomorrow when he's back home. Best you go see if your mammi can use help packing up," Eber Ropp said. At his grandfather's request, Ben aimed for the house. Just as he reached the kitchen door, it swung open, barely missing his face. A surprised, small figure of a woman stood in its wake. *Strawberry blond.* He couldn't help but grin a little. Maybe saying hi wouldn't hurt.

"I can't think of anything worse than finding out his name." She spoke to two other women behind her. One met Ben's gaze, and her eyes bulged.

"LeEtta." Her friend warned, but it seemed little stopped the pretty *maed* from speaking whatever was on her mind.

She shoved a tight fist onto her hip. Ben lifted a brow.

"He's a stranger who hasn't visited his grandparents before. I mean, we've never seen him before. That says much about a person, ain't so?"

Ben's brows drew tighter. She didn't know him, yet she had already made a fast judgment of him. Then she turned and smacked right into him. Looking down, it took all Ben could do to keep his temper and not lose his head. She was prettier up close, making his grimace lose a bit of its tightness. Wide-eyed, Ben could see her working up an audible reply to her earlier statement. He gave her no time to take back her comments but slipped into the room where his mammi would be waiting. This LeEtta, as they called her, was a pretty face, but she had a sour opinion of others.

Ben loaded his mammi's things into the buggy as eyes followed his every move. He had spent enough time under the sharp eye of his father. If folks were simply going to make a day of it, he'd find a path and escape a few hours.

"Don't you want to stay?" Mammi asked. Her pale eyes glinted in a love only his mother had ever shown him.

"It would do you good to make *freinden* that aren't into mischief." Eber Ropp had a stern voice and a sharp gaze. From the moment Ben arrived, his dawdi insisted Ben was making a terrible mistake. This time, Ben was certain the mistake had been his father's.

"I have friends," Ben replied. In truth, he hadn't any. At least not anymore. Not after Caleb and Landis tried putting all the blame on him.

"*Naet* friends at all." Eber narrowed one eye, leaving the larger one to drill him with unspoken words. Ben backed away. It was no use arguing with his elder. Ben knew he'd not win anyway.

"Fine, but I might take a quick walk. See the lay of things here." Upon his grandfather's nod, Ben took off in the opposite direction of the crowd. He had never liked crowds.

Two new families had moved in recently. The Schwartz family was from Indiana, a young couple with three little *kinner*. By all appearances, they seemed happy to be here, but LeEtta couldn't help notice that each time the kinner smiled, it looked manufactured. LeEtta had spent enough time being a mother's helper to know when a child was overwhelmed, and a flood of new faces had certainly overwhelmed these three.

Lester Milford was from the neighboring community of Miller's Creek. He'd just finished building a machine shop on Hummingbird Lane, and as a single daed, had already reached out in hopes LeEtta would be available if he ever needed help with his son.

"*Ach*, LeEtta often helps with kinner too young for school'n," Mammi Iola went on.

"I'd only require help if the need arises. My sister-in-law often sees over him for me, but now that I've moved farther away, it's good to know someone could come if called upon," Lester said.

"Of course, I'd be happy to help." LeEtta gave the dark-haired child a warm smile. He was a fresh image of his father. LeEtta loved any time spent with God's little blessings. Perhaps one day God would see fit to bless her too.

"Well then, I see this is a *gut* arrangement. Don't you, LeEtta?" Mammi Iola shot her a cunning grin.

"Jah, if you'll excuse me." LeEtta quickly made her leave, not giving her mammi any fresh fodder to think LeEtta was interested in a widow nearly thirty. What was so wrong with her that no one had faith that God would deliver her match?

Shouldering her bag of jarred relish and mustard, she slipped around the side of the cabinet shop. She was plenty capable of waiting on the Lord. She simply wished He would consider a match for her a little quicker.

Basketball games were starting, as well as a game of kickball among some of the younger school-aged boys. No one paid her any mind as she moved toward the Wickeys' back pasture.

"Where are you going?"

LeEtta let out a high-pitched squeak at the sound of Jonas Hostetler's voice. She should have known *he* was paying attention. She was invisible to nearly all the men of Cherry Grove, with exception of this one.

Turning, she tried not to address the unusual grin on Jonas' face. He and his twin, Joe, tended to be a bit unusual, which is why she had only seen over them for sweet Joanie Hostetler once out of pity all those years ago. Having eight sons and not one daughter surely was difficult.

"Hi, Jonas." LeEtta collected herself.

"Aren't you *kumm*'n to watch me play?"

"I'm sure you will play well, but I'm not staying to watch anyone in particular." It was best he understood she had no interest in him. "I have. . .somewhere to be right now." LeEtta wasn't prone to lying, but she did have plans to breathe in as much fresh air and summer beauty as she could find—and as far away from Mammi Iola and widowers as she could get.

"Where? Your daed already left. I could give you a ride home. It will only take a minute to hitch *mei* buggy." The desperation in his voice pinched her heart. LeEtta didn't like upsetting others, but it couldn't be helped. Not when it came to Jonas. He clearly had hopes she'd notice him.

"Danke, but I don't need a ride home. Daed knows where I'm going. I need to go so I can check in on him soon. You should go before your bruder notices you missing. Perhaps Martha May will be hoping to watch you play. I think she looked very pretty today, didn't you?" LeEtta smiled. She probably shouldn't have mentioned Martha May, diverting his attention, but she had noticed the young girl stare often at the twins.

"I don't see Martha May. I see you." His eyes narrowed stubbornly.

"Excuse me. I don't want to be late. Have a good day." It was best to put some distance between herself and the determined young man. If only someone her own age had equal determination, her friends might not think she was immature.

LeEtta moved swiftly toward the beaten trail running from pasture to forest. By buggy, it was a good three miles home, but the worn-down path shortened the distance. The sun and breeze were working as a team, making it a fine day for walking.

From a line of cedars and wire fencing, the view shifted from pasture to rolling hills underneath swollen clouds. She loved the view from here, seeing homesteads and farms from a vantage height. The nearby orchard sprawled over the uneven landscape, disappearing into the yonder. Her lips curved into a smile. The blooms had all fallen, but full branches reached out, giving their bounty room to grow. Over a hundred trees were planted by the newcomer for his wife. What a gift of his love.

Had that been why their farm was covered with so many rosebushes? LeEtta often wondered if love had started what now spiraled out of control, but it was hard to imagine her father ever being romantic. Perhaps her yearning for such was inherited from her mother. She shuddered to think she was as hopeless about love as Mammi Iola. LeEtta would never go to such lengths for love.

Thoughts of her mother filled her heart. It was hard to bring someone to mind when no memory was there to encourage it. Did Mamm even like roses? Did she know she had a child aching to know her? Would she have loved mashed potatoes with garlic powder and cream cheese instead of plain ol' salt and milk?

Daed never spoke of the woman who brought her into this world, and it didn't seem proper to ask Mammi Iola. Surely losing a dochter was a terrible thing to endure.

Over the next rise, she paused near a patch of milkweed. Butterflies floated from bulging pod heads to bursting blooms. She sat in the grass, content to linger. Who didn't have time for butterflies? If she returned home too soon, Daed would ask if something was wrong, knowing a woman her age should be visiting with friends. If she returned too late, he'd think her friends were more important than their quiet life. Being an adult was terribly troubling.

Buttermilk Branch Creek twisted in parallel with the narrow, packed earth and scant gravel road. From this height, LeEtta could trace each bend in the road and enjoy the abundance of summer's near end. A hot breeze kicked up, a reminder that rain was sorely needed.

The harvest would be upon them soon, late October or November if the weather held. What if Daed wasn't fully healed, as the doctors insisted he might not be? LeEtta couldn't see how he would work the corn picker and team with one arm, let alone work the gravity wagons and elevator, filling grain bins. He struggled daily to feed the cattle and no longer could lift a hammer to work on building houses with Ervin Graber's crew.

Standing, she collected her bag and bid the wild things farewell before stepping over the low-lying fence separating parcels. She aimed west into the sun, where the creek emptied into the lake. It was too far yet to see from here, but home was there, just beyond the next hill.

She reached the pesky brambles. If there was a way around them, she'd not found it yet. Perhaps she could convince the owners to mow them down, but then birds and small critters would suffer, so she decided not to mention it.

"Ouch!" Two new scratches to add to her almost healed ones.

"Who's there?"

LeEtta instantly froze in the awkwardness of trying to free herself and the sound of another. She had never crossed paths with anyone along this path before. Twigs snapped, and footfalls drew closer. She let out a hostaged breath when the newcomer came into view and to an abrupt halt.

"Hi."

"Hiya," LeEtta offered in return. If he hadn't just scared the freckles off of her, she'd have freed herself by now.

"You lost, or are you following me?" He hiked a brow, but she noted a glint of teasing there.

"I live here, so I am not lost. Are you?" LeEtta put a foot on the thick, relentless briar and made another attempt to free herself, but his laugh unbalanced her. No one liked being laughed at. "And why would I follow you? I'm walking home. This is the path I often take." She worked her leg over the bend of the cane, but it held tight, digging into her socks. She'd have a fresh mark to nurse once she got home.

"You live...nearby?" He watched her predicament with amusement and a faintly different accent. It suited his pleasant features.

Although she wasn't in the habit of telling strangers where she lived, LeEtta knew all good questions deserved an answer. "Just past the creek, jah." She offered a smile and gave her dress another tug. Mustard and relish jars clacked against one another in her carry bag. "It's quicker to walk than take the buggy, and it's such a fine day, ain't so?" she rambled.

"I'm—I'm LeEtta Miller." She yanked herself loose and strained to gain her balance. A sudden waft of sweet vinegar pickled the air, and she closed her eyes. Surely she hadn't broken one of the jars. Had she not just sewn the bag up from its last tear? Oh, her sewing skills needed as much work as her cooking ones.

"You're leaking," the newcomer pointed.

"Ach, well, I'm certain none will mind." This close, he was even more handsome. His nose was a little round on one side and pointy on the other. She didn't mind flaws, especially when they looked good on a person. "Few appreciate condiments as much as I do."

One side of his lips hitched. A reflection of summer wore on his nose, proof he worked without a hat often. "Benuel," he said.

"Benuel?" She blinked.

"Benuel Ropp, and I too like a good relish and all the condiments." He winked, unsettling her.

He was clearly not sore at her comment from earlier and knew the relish was her contribution to the fellowship meal today. *Benuel.* Not really an heroic name, but it fit the man's wide-shoulder stance. His chin narrowed to a point, but it wasn't pointing. Not like Teacher Kevin's. His dark hair was cut shorter than the men of Cherry Grove, but she suspected some communities were leaner on rules than others. Eunice had once told her about a community in Indiana who wore pink. LeEtta always liked pink, the color of spring phlox over the rocky hillside behind her home.

His eyes held a mystery and a playfulness. Eyes told much about a person, did they not? His were the color of walnuts, with matching brows. His left brow hiked naturally, making him look in a constant state of either playfulness or judgment.

"I'm sure your grandparents are enjoying your visit. It's kind of you to spend time with them." She was fishing, but she had never known Eber and Mary to have family come visiting, only that they traveled to Ohio to see their son at Christmas.

"Kind, huh?" He stepped closer and offered her a hand. When their fingers touched, LeEtta was certain she might melt right there.

CHAPTER THREE

Ben turned to face the landscape. "It's pretty from up here. I started walking to see more and sort of kept going."

"Don't you want to meet everyone?" Surely he had better things to do than stand here with her. "This evening is the youth gathering. I'm certain everyone will be happy for you to join them. They sing for one hour and then play baseball or basketball. Do you play?"

"I'm too old for playing games," he said as if taking offense. LeEtta would never purposefully offend anyone.

"Are you going to the youth gathering?" His observation made her cheeks warm. LeEtta could never admit to her reasons for not attending or that she'd be walking home in the dark if she did attend.

"I'm twenty-two," she said as if that was reason enough. Some friends her age still attended. The rest were married with *bopplin* of their own. She'd not visit that thought on such a fine day as this one.

"And I was not born with long legs." She laughed, looking down at her feet. "I have much better things to do than lose at basketball." She moved to his side and ignored the fact she didn't even meet his shoulders.

"This is one of my favorite views, aside from our farm. I love every inch of it," she continued. "Down there, that's the Bontragers'. He's from Indiana and likes landscaping. He has a whole crew now!" Wasn't landscaping such a fine word? Though the land here needed no further indulgence as Gott had a way of dropping seeds and creating beauty.

"Over there." She turned, then peered back to see if Ben was even looking. Of course he was. Cherry Grove was beautiful from this height. "That's the hill. Bishop Graber lives there. In winter, everyone sleighs the hill because it's one of the few places where you won't plow into a fence or end up on the road or in a pond. If you reach the top and turn down the lane, the Hooleys have a cherry farm."

"Cherry farm," he repeated.

Good. LeEtta worried her rambling was going to scare him off. This was the longest any man had remained in her company.

"I saw plenty of farms. Corn and beans, but I missed that one, I guess."

"Jah, the whole community is plenty rich in farming, unless you travel beyond the lake. Daed says it all turns to clay from there." His frown said he agreed with Daed that clay was not good ground either. "We've recently split, so I reckon we still have good soil, and they don't now." She waved a hand west.

"Split? And you still have so many members?"

"Nee, this was the last Sunday before it is so. We will all still gather plenty, but if you're here come the next service, you'll have more elbow room at the table."

He laughed.

No one ever thought her jokes were funny. He had a nice laugh, which only spurred her smile to widen naturally.

"I certainly like my space at a table. Change is good, I reckon." He looked out once more and inhaled a deep breath of hot, dry air like a man starved for it.

Perhaps change was what brought him for a visit. Currently, LeEtta was hoping the winds of change had finally reached her. Perhaps he would stay a while. He was observant, not too chatty, and didn't mind talking to a rambler on a thorny hillside. LeEtta wondered if he frowned on reading. "Of course, I will miss my closest friend, Eunice. She and I won't see each other as often." Which means she'd have less time to fret over LeEtta's nonexistent love life.

LeEtta began walking along the hoof-rutted trail, and surprisingly, he followed. "Do you know anyone here besides Mary and Eber?"

"You."

"Will you be staying in Cherry Grove for long?" She continued to stammer and prod at the same time. His plans were none of her business, but she was having a nice walk, and how else did you learn about a person if you didn't ask?

"I sure hope not," he said so bluntly that LeEtta stiffened. "May I walk you home?"

He was blunt to a point, yet wanted to spend more time with her. Giddiness bloomed inside her chest, but she worked to keep it contained. Eunice insisted men didn't like giddy or chatty or smart maedels. Maybe LeEtta should not be taking advice from her best friend, because clearly, this handsome newcomer didn't mind at all.

"Jah, I'd like that," she said, studying his expression intently. "But. . .what if you get lost returning?" He didn't know the area.

"Getting lost is the least of my concerns," he said flatly. "Which way?"

LeEtta suddenly felt just like every other woman. Perhaps Gott had delivered Ben here especially for her. Maybe he would fall in love with the landscape too and not be so hurried to leave. That was too many maybes to ponder while watching your footing.

When they reached the farm, Ben's eyes traveled over the landscape, stopping to take in the slanted barn door that had suffered from a storm. The roof needed painting, and pastures were in desperate need of rain as fat, black cattle grazed on thicker patches nearest the creek.

"This is a nice farm." He sounded surprised. LeEtta didn't know if it was nice, not with so many things needing to be tended to, but she did always imagine its potential, such as a freshly painted barn and lambs playing on leaning hillsides, and found she couldn't agree more.

"It has many needs. My daed is Arlen Miller. He fell recently, and his arm is of no use to him right now. I just hope it is healed by the harvest." He probably didn't want to hear about that.

"I'm sorry to hear that." His eyes said he truly was.

"Danke. I'm sure if he had a sohn, he'd worry less. I try to help, but Daed can be smothery at times when it comes to what I should do." Ben probably agreed with Daed's philosophy of women not working the fields.

"Sometimes, being a son gets you little as well." Something in the way he said it tugged at LeEtta's tender heart. "I'm sure others will help him. It is our way," he added.

"Jah, but it isn't his. Daed is of the mind that he can do it all. He thinks it's a burden to trouble others when they have farms to tend to as well."

"A man doesn't like to ask for help." Her father would agree, but LeEtta was of the mind that everyone needed help with something. Currently, she wondered what Ben needed help with. Though he looked sturdy enough, something in his quick replies told her he just might.

"Neither does a woman, yet we all need help from time to time." Like how to bake chicken so it's not poisonous or how to take out a hem when you've grown two inches.

"I find it better to rely on myself. Safer that way." The way his jaw tightened, LeEtta feared she had spoiled their visit together. She didn't want this day to end. She couldn't wait to tell Eunice and Ellen that Ben walked her home. At least now she wouldn't have to be paired up with Ellen's cousin.

Beyond corn stretching eight feet toward heaven was the pond. She often found herself sitting on the high bank, feet dangling over the edges during the dry season. During the last charge of rain, water breached the old pipe buried in its northern corner to remove the flowing excess, burdening the pond walls.

"If you are in no hurry. . ." She swallowed. It wasn't proper to ask a man to stick around, was it?

"I'm in no hurry." He laughed.

"Gut." She tugged on his shirt sleeve, pulling him forward. "You should see the pond. It's not big enough to skip a stone for more than five skips, but I've caught the Hostetlers stealing bass from it the size of your forearm."

They slipped into the corn, a sea of stalks drying under the summer sun. When they emerged out the other side, the pond came into view. "The cattle and horses have worn down the far bank, all but over here." LeEtta motioned to a spot just under a leaning apple tree, its green fruit weighing down the thin, knobby branches over the water. Animals had picked clean what they could reach from the bank. Much like life, it was empty where a person stood on dry land, and all the fruit was just out of reach.

Ben's gaze traveled to the edges of the water. He was slightly out of breath. She shouldn't have hurried them here. When his gaze moved heavenward, where clouds hung low beneath timid blue skies, he let out a breath.

"I used to sit under them and try to spot different shapes."

"I still do that," he admitted, floating her a kind smile. "Kumm, let's see what we can find." He sat near the tree where shade was provided. LeEtta hesitated. She had been so excited to spend more time with him that she hadn't fully considered that he might want to spend time with her too. Would he stay long enough for friendship to bloom? He sat and patted the ground. "It's not damp." He grinned, causing her nerves to tingle delightfully. "It might even be fun to see what we see."

Fun. Mammi Iola told her she should seek more of that out, did she not? Eunice had tried a handful of times to encourage her to be more fun, but she wasn't fun. Her quiet life was about tending to her daed, seeing her flock looked after, and watching others' kinner. Her life was not fun at all, not in the least little bit, leaving long moments of quiet needing filled. That's why she kept so many books under the quilt in her chest. They had been an escape from the quiet everyday, but now they were putting all kinds of improper notions in her head. Like kissing.

LeEtta sat, tucking her dress skirts neatly around her bent legs.

Her heart beat a little nervously. Was this how Eunice felt the first time Jerry had taken her on a walk?

Ben leaned back on his elbows, eyes to the sky. "A turtle."

Craning her neck back as far as it would go, she saw it: four feet, the round shell with a head peeking out, and the tail trying to stay attached under a soft breeze. Soon she spotted a horse head and then two faces staring at one another. She laid back, her kapp resting on a soft bed of early fallen leaves, as she continued to search the heavens for more. They laid there for a spell, talking about childhood summers and spotting new shapes. Jah, LeEtta had never known such fun.

"I've never met a woman who didn't mind talking about clouds and ponds."

"Ach, I do talk too much, don't I?" Eunice had warned her that chatty was not an admirable trait, but LeEtta couldn't help it. Ben was an easy listener, and after twenty years of quiet, she had plenty to say. "I reckon I could have worse habits, like chewing with my mouth open or falling over pebbles. We can just lie here and watch the clouds." And that would be enough, she thought happily.

"Nee, I like that you do. This is the most fun I've had in years." A smile bloomed over his lips and put a twinkle in his eye. He was getting to know her.

"Me too," she admitted. His gaze remained on her, and finally LeEtta knew what it felt like not to be rejected.

"I'm only here for a short time."

"Like the clouds."

"Jah, like the clouds." His eyes held her close, like a touch. He tucked an arm under his head and turned toward her as if he could see beyond what made her, seeking turtles in the clouds.

The way he was looking at her was something she hoped he would do again and again. Her eyes traveled to his lips, the way one side hiked slightly higher. What would it be like to kiss a man worthy of kissing? He wasn't staying, she measured. Her friends would no longer remind her of all she had lacked if she did.

He blinked, clearly feeling the same magnetic tug that had come over her.

"LeEtta..." He swallowed. "I usually don't watch clouds with pretty women." Clouds ceased parading across the sky as time stilled to hear the sound of two fast-moving heartbeats. Her name on his lips did something strange to her. She hadn't a clue what came over her, but the need to not ignore it was stronger still.

"You think I'm pretty?"

"I think you are...beautiful."

Spurred by words she had never heard before, LeEtta threw caution to the wind and did the last thing either of them expected. Her lips crashed into his in eager appreciation and immature spontaneity. Her heart seized in her foolish desire not to miss this one thing all her friends knew. It wasn't the lovely moment she had long envisioned. Not until his rigid body moved in closer to hers. Suddenly, a hand cradled her head in safe regard.

All those nerves and fears slipped away in a touch that pushed her emotions into new and unfamiliar territory. The contact and careful touch he was showing her was strange. This was as close to love as she may ever know. If she were standing, she'd float off the ground for sure and certain.

In a stolen moment, she'd received a memory that would follow her for the rest of her days. For a few short seconds, LeEtta knew what it felt like to be...wanted.

Ben knew the moment he spotted her that there was an attraction. Nothing could come of their friendship, of course, but he desperately needed her sunshine. A rise of caution squeezed his chest every time she looked up at him with those blue eyes.

Perhaps he shouldn't have flirted, but she was pretty. Beautiful. Pretty was for flowers and spring rains on eager fields. Her cheeks had warmed at the compliment, creating a faster beat in his chest. She was a rare weed, capable of smothering out a healthy plant or keeping away any threats to it. He liked her humor and how at ease she made him feel. She made him smile, and when was the last time Ben had laughed out loud?

A breeze fingered the strands of her fine hair, and all his burdens vanished underneath the dirt. Reaching out, he touched one of her kapp strings. Something flickered in her eyes—raw, new, and eager. She was beautiful, though that shouldn't matter, but it was not something easy to ignore. Not when she looked at him as if he had just offered her a cloud of her very own to shape.

She was innocent and sweet, and he had no business even watching clouds with her. Then she shocked him when she crashed her lips into his. He stiffened, but only briefly. She tasted like warm summer lemonade, sunrises, and new life. He cradled her small head tenderly, deepening the kiss. Shamefully, he'd known his share of secret kisses, but he suspected she didn't. Not the innocent, vulnerable woman he had just discovered. She melted into him like wax below the flame, and for one short moment under a perfect sky, his troubles melted too.

"This is why you have been ignoring me!"

LeEtta shoved back quickly and sprang to her feet. Ben slowly stood beside her as she touched her kapp, probably to see it was still there. Her lips were swollen. At least he had kissed her well, he thought before raking his eye toward the young man wearing disdain on his face. LeEtta shivered despite the heat of summer and what had been forged between them. Maybe he should have been more tender, but a man not prepared did not always think right.

"Jonas, it's not what you think."

Actually, it was, Ben nearly spoke, slanting her a brow. Before he could respond to either of them, the young man lowered his head and attacked. Ben stepped in front of LeEtta and readied for the impact. Jonas was still thin with boyhood, but his anger added to his strength.

"Kumm now," Ben tried to discourage him, latching hold and wrapping two large arms around the flailing youth. It was not their way to be physical, but clearly the young man was in a fit of rage. "Don't hurt yourself." Now it made sense, Ben collected. The youngie had sparks for LeEtta. Ben didn't blame him. She was worthy of a man forgetting his place.

"Boyfriend?" He looked to LeEtta once more.

"He's fifteen!" LeEtta gave him a sharp look before turning to Jonas again. "Jonas, please. We can never let our tempers best us. Now if Ben lets loose of ya, will you stop this?"

The bu resisted, but even he knew Ben had him in a spot, and finally he nodded. Ben loosened his hold, and Jonas stumbled forward, his chest heaving. Ben bent to retrieve his hat and offered it back to him. Jonas simply stared at him for a time before swiping it out of his hand.

"Jonas—" LeEtta began.

"I thought—"Jonas said. "I've been kind to you. Helping your daed with his horses, delivering seed right to your door! I gave you chickens!"

"Jah, you have been kind, for certain, but..."

"Yet you'd rather let this stranger touch you!"

Shame rose in her cheeks in crimson waves.

"Your daed will be disappointed when he finds out." It was a threat.

Ben felt his own temper rise. "I don't think this was worthy of speaking to her father about."

"But *you* have taken advantage of her. I would never do that. You should go back to where you came from before someone makes you," Jonas snapped in reply before turning and running away.

"A long temper and a short fuse is not a good mix," Ben recited words his father once offered to him.

"I'm so sorry, Ben. I should have never..."

"We both had a part in it." He grinned.

"I've never kissed anyone before," she admitted. "It was wrong of me, and I didn't want mei freinden fixing me up, and..."

Ben flinched. Her friends were fixing her up, and she wanted no part in it. A young bu was now dealing with his first of many heart-breaks the world would dish out to him, and Ben couldn't help but

wonder why she chose him to give her first kiss to. If she only knew him. What a waste, to spend so much...on him.

"I should go." She nervously gathered her wits and ran in the opposite direction, leaving Ben standing behind at the edge of a cornfield with the crows to keep him company.

CHAPTER FOUR

Shepard Eversole finally returned to Cherry Grove. Ben was eager to start work, and these last few days had him concerned the older man had forgotten he requested a new hire. Keeping busy was no hardship. Not with his grandfather needing so many things tended to. Ben helped where he could, mending fences until his shoulders ached. Paint was still splattered on his trousers from painting the fences, but he couldn't keep his focus, not with that kiss lingering in his mind as it was.

It was another mark against him, but hopefully, the smitten boy simply went home, nursing his heart in silence, and didn't tell anyone. Ben didn't want to think what his grandfather would have to say if he thought Ben had taken advantage of another. Which he hadn't. LeEtta had kissed him. He wasn't complaining. Kisses like that could be life-changing, but Ben had plans that didn't include strawberry-sweet maedels. He simply had to avoid any other mishaps while he was here. He had to focus on saving as much as he could, enough for the down payment. It was best to forget about LeEtta Miller.

Not since Sunday had he ventured beyond the old split-rail fence, with the exception of wrangling two piglets that could root under heavy wire fencing like a starved weasel. Ben had cleaned every inch of the old barn's concrete floors littered by the season and a half-dozen piglets. Dawdi was much like Sam in that way. It was plain to see that Eber Ropp had a heart for the four-legged. Not Ben. It was the earth Ben found that nourished his soul. Where he found sanctuary when life sided against him. Where a man could plant a seed and see it harvested. Sadly, his own father didn't think so.

Once the first drop of rain fell, he focused more on staying dry than painting. Mammi had him replacing the flooring in the washroom. It was sorely needed, and it kept a man's head dry.

"Be sure to measure twice."

"And cut once." Ben winked at his grandfather. Age and time had made it hard for Dawdi to bend a knee on a hard floor.

When the sun broke through the clouds on Thursday morning, Ben was eager to seek out the hog farmer. The faster he earned a wage, the quicker he could go back to Ohio.

He swallowed his breakfast in earnest. "I'd like to head out to speak to Shepard today and maybe check out the store nearby. Pick up a few things." Eber Ropp was a man who took the time to think before he spoke, but sometimes he took longer than Ben wished he would. Two more bites of oatmeal. Ben waited.

"You are asking to take the buggy?" Dawdi lifted his gaze above his cup and took a slow drink.

"I am." Ben saw no sense in purchasing his own. After all, he had so little already and no interest in living in Kentucky longer than necessary.

"But you have forgotten how to do so?"

"May I borrow the buggy?"

"Jah, and you can pick up more paint while you're gone," Eber said. His suspenders looked worn. Nearly as much as the wide shoulders Ben remembered so well. His grandfather had been a tall man, but time and hard work had bent him. Gravity did the rest.

"I reckon if you hope to keep from making your folks worry, you best see to making a living somewhere."

Ben had no intention of making his family worry. What he had was every intention to own his own place since Sam was given his inheritance. Ben thought his grandfather understood his plight when he'd called to say he knew of someone hiring.

"I don't mean to make anyone worry. You know I've had my heart set on keeping the farm going."

"I also know you tend to rush into a decision. Like making freinden with those *buwe* up there," Eber pointed his fork in Ben's direction.

Ben lowered his gaze in response to the reprimand. Of course his grandparents knew every mistake he made. Mamm often sought Mammi's advice over the years when she was beside herself. Perhaps he hadn't always made the best decisions. He had been caught drinking when he was sixteen, but everyone did that at least once. Sam may not have, but Ben had plenty of friends who did.

There was that run-in with the local wildlife officer. At seventeen, Ben had to pay fines for fishing without a license, but he hadn't even asked his parents to help him. That was only two offenses, not even worthy of the elders showing up at his parents' door.

Not until. . .

Bowman Jackson. The crusty neighbor had no fondness for the Amish or patience with young folk. His complaints over the years had worn Ben's parents down, but the fact was that his land was the quickest way to Caleb's.

Ben pushed his plate to the side. He had taken responsibility for his part, but Dawdi was right—Ben hadn't been very wise in who he gave his trust to. Caleb had always been right there, every time trouble came knocking. Even that day. They were only target practicing since hunting season was just days away; but when Caleb nearly hit the elderly man with a bullet, all those little mistakes, those complaints of crossing property without permission, had turned into one big problem.

A man could have died.

That was a year ago. Ben had worked hard to put the incident behind him. He had endured months of his father's silence and his mother's sorrowful looks. "I don't need any friends." Not anymore. A person couldn't count on others to do the right thing. "Just enough money to buy my own farm."

"You can work alongside your bruder instead of putting up fences between you." He wasn't the one who had built the fence between him and his younger brother. Sam accepted the farm. That was plenty for Ben to know where he stood in his family. *His family.*

"A man must make his own way when his way is no longer there."

"A man must trust Gott and his father's decision." Eber glared at him as if Ben had not trusted either. He had. That was the problem. He had trusted those closest to him, and where had that gotten him?

"I'll be busy making pickles today, but I could use some more flour if you're willing," Mammi quickly interrupted. "It's cheaper at the bulk store. Only thirty-one dollars a bag."

"I'd be happy to see to it." Ben floated her a grateful smile for shutting down the topic he knew they would revisit soon.

"And hinges," Dawdi added. "Those stall doors can't go unfinished." He lifted both brows, a lector without as many words.

"Of course. I can get some oil for the barn door too. I'm sure your neighbors hear you every time you enter and leave." Ben finished his plate, not leaving even the oatmeal he normally would ignore.

"Let me write down the directions so you don't get lost. The roads can be a trick, and you haven't been here since you were a bu." Mammi got up from the table and sought out a pen and small notebook. It wasn't his fault his parents didn't like to travel. She quickly jotted down directions and handed them to him before moving to clear dishes from the table.

"I'm glad I'm here now," Ben offered. Why hadn't his parents visited more? Surely Daed would want to know Mammi was limping slightly and napping in the afternoon. Did he know Dawdi struggled to hold a hammer? Ben decided right then that maybe he should take a stroll to the end of the drive where the phone shanty rested. Calling home and letting his folks know all was well might be a good idea.

"Don't waste the day. Shep might have you feeding hogs by morning, and we have stall doors to mend and old paint to brush off. Your mammi has been wanting this house painted for years."

Dawdi's tone never changed, which made it hard to tell if he was being sarcastic, stern, or simply engaging in everyday talk. Ben didn't mind painting the house, but did he hear a scolding in there?

If the past was the past, then why did it never stay there? A man changed plenty in a year. Ben had never shucked a chore in his life. How could a handful of mistakes really make them forget he was the same little boy who packed in wood without being asked and hitched the buggy before anyone else aimed to?

Pushing aside any such unsettling thoughts, Ben hurried to hitch his grandfather's horse and venture beyond freshly painted fencing and the smell of Mammi's pickling spices.

Going by Mammi's scribbles and lines, her best attempt at a map, Cherry Grove looked like a crooked stick with too many branches. He pocketed the paper and pulled onto the paved road. He knew to take a quick right on Hickory Hill and keep going until he passed the bishop's horse farm. The problem was that Ben didn't know where the bishop's home was. How did he know a bishop's house from any other?

A sudden vision of LeEtta sprang to mind. Her lopsided kapp, her twinkling eyes, and her small finger pointing over a hill to an orchard. "She said the bishop lived above that," Ben reminded himself. One walk, and she had given him better bearings of the area than Mammi had living here all her life. Ben searched out the high hill meant for safe sledding.

The sun felt warm against his shoulders, and he thought about the woman again. His smile weakened. It was best not to let a pretty face change his focus. He would be leaving as soon as he could. "Hopefully before Sam spends all my savings in milkers," he quipped.

Hickory Hill was not much of a hill at all, just gentle rises and lamblike falls. At a mailbox marked GLICK, he noted the long fields of corn and a sign for homemade furniture. Cottage shops made up much of the area. Ben liked to see so many embracing what they were good at. Nearly all his friends either built homes or worked for someone who did.

"Well, ol' fella, it seems we are heading the right way." The horse paid him no mind, having the same laid-back demeanor as Eber Ropp. Horses did tend to do that, getting comfortable with the pace their owner set.

Mammi had said to turn left on a side road cutting into the next paved road. He would know it by the white horse standing under a large oak. "Now where is the horse?" he questioned, searching, just as common sense gripped him like a slap to the back of the head, spurring a laugh out of him.

"A white horse under an oak!" Ben spouted. What were the chances that Ben would see a white horse under an oak that would take him onto Cattail Crossing, as Mammi insisted? Horses didn't very well stand still all day, every day. She might be a better cook than Mamm, but her directional abilities needed practice.

"And who named these roads?" That's what he'd like to know. Veering left on an unmarked road, Ben hoped for the best when he spotted an unusually large oak with arms stretching over two separate pastoral fences. Surely he was as lost as a man in the wilderness, but forty days out here would be no hardship. The land mimicked home in such a way that he didn't feel so far away. Its quaintness held a charm for a weary traveler with so much baggage.

It only took ten minutes for the Hostetler house to come into view. The three-story home stood out among the string of short erected barns scattered about. On a hillside surrounded by white, flimsy fencing, he noticed hundreds of chickens, providing evidence that the Hostetlers were chicken farmers as well as the owners of the Amish hardware store.

Ben parked next to a red pickup truck, secured the reins on a post nearby, and strolled inside the old, faded metal building. A strong stench of grain and molasses met him immediately. It took his eyes a few minutes to adjust to the dim lighting before noting the two tall figures standing with the owner of the truck. One turned his way.

"Be with ya in a minute."

Ben nodded and browsed the aisles. He strolled past metal shelves of tools, buckets of nails, and screws. Near the end of the first aisle, he spotted a variety of hinges.

"You're Eber and Mary's grandson." It wasn't a question. The lanky man walked with a slight limp and was about Ben's age.

"Jah. I'm repairing a few stall doors. Do you have any hinges bigger than these?"

"Next aisle." He waved him forward.

"I'm Jerry. That's Leo up there." He pointed. Both men sported a bit of hair on their faces, indicating they were already married. Ben would have thought about LeEtta again if not for the door opening and another man walking in. Ben did a double take. As sure as clouds lived in the heavens, he was seeing double.

Sensing his confusion, Jerry chuckled. "Jah, I'm a twin. Only Jeremiah is shorter and barely three minutes older."

"Nice to meet ya." Ben offered both men a hand.

"Mamm actually liked twins so much that she had a second pair," Jerry added.

"That's because she was trying to improve on us." Jeremiah laughed. "You can call me Jerm. Most do."

"You need more than hinges?"

"Paint. Dawdi wants to paint the house next."

"We can fix you up with that too. Bet Eber is sure glad you showed up. That house has been needing a few things for a spell," Jerry added. All three brothers had light hair and dark eyes. Ben paid for his things, and they all began loading paint cans into the buggy. A light breeze kicked up, moving clouds quicker now over the landscape. Ben noted a small pond nearby.

"You fish that?" He liked to fish, but since getting caught without a license, Ben hadn't drowned a single worm.

"Nee, ain't got much in it with these two about. Say, if you are sticking around. . ." Leo pressed.

"I'm staying for a couple months. See to painting the house and so forth." It was no one's business that he came to work at a pig farm as a means to find his own way.

"That's gut," Jerm said. "We plan to go fishing on Saturday. You should come."

"That is, if we aren't strapped to chores because this one thought it funny to hide LeRoy Miller's buggy while he was courting."

"I wasn't the only one," Jerry said, then burst into laughter. "It took him two days to find it in old Widow Eicher's shed. He had to drive his future father-in-law's two-seater home. Talk about embarrassing."

Ben laughed too. "Danke for the invite." Folks were friendlier here. Most families back home were close-knit and large enough that they seldom needed to venture next door for a simple chat.

"I'd need to get my license." Lesson learned, he thought, until both men laughed.

"Nee, you don't."

Ben prickled. Perhaps the twins were more like Caleb and Landis.

"It's not that kind of fishing." Leo adjusted his hat a little higher. "You two know better than to test a man's patience." He extended a hand. "It's a harvest of sorts."

A harvest?

"A friend of ours has a fish farm on the other side of the valley. He usually clears out his stock in late fall, but he got himself a big order. We like to lend a hand helping with the nets and seines, and there's plenty to eat afterward."

"Never harvested fish before without a line."

"Can you swim, in case one of the big ones pulls you under?" Jerry teased.

"I can swim, and I haven't met a fish yet to best me."

"Kumm, let me write down directions. You can meet up with us Saturday. Matthias will be glad you're coming."

He'd made fast friends with the three men, and they liked fishing. Perhaps God was tossing a bit of mercy his way, making his time here more bearable. When Ben reached his buggy, two more Hostetlers appeared around the corner. Although they looked nothing alike, these two had to be the twins he'd heard about. Ben recognized the one on the left immediately.

"Thought you'd be gone by now," Jonas said.

"We haven't been properly introduced. My name is Ben." He offered both boys a smile and extended his hand. Neither took it. Ben remembered his own stubborn youth, when a man sat at the peak of boyhood.

Jonas crossed his arms over his chest, disagreeably. Ben hoped to clear the air between them. "Your family has a nice shop here." Moving to the side of the buggy, Ben climbed in.

"Go on, Joe," Jonas instructed his twin. When Joe shut the door behind him, the boy spoke again. "You don't belong here."

"I agree," Ben said.

"Then go." Jonas motioned as if to dismiss Ben. "And don't be thinking of taking anything with you that belongs to me."

With that, the young boy stomped inside and slammed the hardwood door, leaving Ben scratching his head. He'd been accused of a lot of things in his *rumspringa* years, but never a thief. Young fella was going to learn some hard lessons soon, Ben predicted.

Two wrong turns and two hours later, Ben shook the hand of Shepard Eversole. He appreciated the firm handshake, a sign the deal was made.

"Let me show you about." Shep had insisted Ben call him Shep. They had agreed on a fair wage, and though Ben wanted to work as many hours as Shep would give him, his workweek would only include five days. Shep insisted that the weekends were reserved for teaching his new stepsons how to run the farm.

Pigs were noisy and smelly, but Shep took great pride in three hundred hogs in various stages. His eyes glinted strongly of a man who loved his work. Daed did that when he spoke of tobacco, corn, or soybeans. As Ben walked both long barns with low ceilings and concrete floors, learning what was expected of him, he was certain that if his brother were here to see how low he would go to earn his own place, he'd be laughing.

CHAPTER FIVE

LeEtta was of the mind that rain was one of God's greatest gifts, unless it came in sheets and buckets and lasted for four straight days.

"But no winter shall last forever," she affirmed, smiling up at the sun, thankful it had chased off every cloud in the sky today.

She called to Posey in the pasture. The old mare raised her head, eager to come. Thursday was LeEtta's favorite day of the week. Not because it was a shopping day, though she did enjoy browsing the new material selections at Frannie Shetler's material shop. It was her favorite because she could spend time with her grandmother, even if it included listening about what dish she would be gifting to any recent widowers.

"Let me hitch her up for you." Daed opened the gate and let Posey pass through. The bulk of the blue cast bulged from underneath his cut sleeve. Since the focus was on his elbow, shattered as they said it was, his arm had to remain at a slight bend, making him look as if he were in a constant state of rubbing his stomach. LeEtta mentally reminded herself to learn how to sew him new shirts soon. The doctor insisted he'd only be laid up a few weeks.

"I haven't needed help hitching her since I was nine, but danke." She worked the horse back between the shafts and began the familiar process of working leather over horseflesh and securing it.

"You're still sore at me." He stepped forward and took over the chore. She could have hitched the buggy quicker, but his stubbornness always took over. LeEtta was sore. She had only tried to muck out the stalls a few evenings ago to help him. Was it not her duty to help?

"You know the doctor said it will take longer for you to heal than most. That break wasn't a good one." Extra rods and pins were holding everything together. "If you keep on using it so often, it will never heal."

"Jah, you are right." He stepped back and frowned. Looking at her, his pale eyes grew weary. He was working too hard. That was plain to see. He'd also carried a forlorn expression all her life, proof that some breaks never heal, especially where the heart was concerned.

"I can do more than hitch a buggy too," she reminded him.

"LeEtta, you must see it. I am a man, and I am your father."

She gave him a perplexed look. Was that not exactly why he should be letting her help?

"There is little I know to spare for you. I cannot be a mamm, teaching you the things you should know, but I can be a gut daed, seeing you are cared for."

As the wind picked up and tossed his beard to the side, LeEtta's heart melted. She was plenty capable of caring for herself. She never expected him to teach her womanly things, but she had never heard him share his feelings before. Relief washed over, knowing his true thoughts. For as hard as it was to be raised without a mamm, it was harder yet to lose one's wife.

"You are a good father," LeEtta said, pressing a kiss to his cheek. "And I have never been without."

"You've missed much, I'm afraid," he said as he checked Posey's neck-rein, pad, and trace for sturdiness. Posey knew the routine when his hands worked her instead of LeEtta's, and she remained perfectly still.

"I've learned much from others. Mammi Iola taught me to never ride my scooter beyond Cattail Crossing." The narrow road was a chore to navigate. Either the ruts made it dangerous or, when new gravel was laid, the pieces were so large that a person could break their neck.

"Frannie helps me sew my own dresses." Though LeEtta hated that she had to lean on Frannie anytime she needed a new one. "I can bake well enough, I reckon, thanks to working at the bakery before becoming a mother's helper." LeEtta was glad when Daed had insisted she find different work. The bakery owner had a habit of inserting herself into a person's private life. LeEtta adored her and had learned so much in the kitchen in her two summers there; but she had agreed with her father when the local matchmaker couldn't even find her a match that it was best to be helpful to young mudders. LeEtta loved kinner and found herself attached so quickly. She looked forward to watching the Schwartz kinner next week while their mamm went for a doctor visit. Maybe she would discover the mystery behind all those fake smiles.

"I reckon Hazel is a fine baker to learn from," he said, holding the reins as he turned to look at her. "But she'd have you married if I let you stay, and you were too young yet."

"I'm not now," LeEtta replied and watched the fact cause his brow to twitch.

"All in Gott's time," he said. "You'll make a fine fraa. . .someday."

If he only knew what a horrible daughter she was, kissing Ben—a mere stranger—so abruptly, he would not think well of her at all. "Perhaps, but there's nothing I have been deprived of, except being of help to you. You have no fraa, and I have no husband. We only have each other, so please let me help you."

"It's not your place to plow fields and put hay up," he said and kicked at the ground.

"Mandy Schwartz can mow a field faster than her bruders, and just last week, I know you saw young Mary Rose cutting grass for her folks when we visited with Mammi." LeEtta would be thrilled to let Posey have more time out of the pasture.

"You are my dochter and have no need to be working like a sohn."

LeEtta took up the reins and climbed into the buggy. Was there ever a man more stubborn? She thought not. "You should have had a sohn. For that I'm sorry, but I'm here and plenty capable of helping you muck a stall—and certainly to harness my own horse."

Chin up, LeEtta held his gaze. She loved her father, but sometimes he couldn't see the simple way around a problem.

"Best get on now. Iola isn't one for waiting long."

End of discussion.

Seething all the way to Farrows Creek and her grandmother's quaint little house, LeEtta whispered a prayer for her father. . .and one for patience for herself.

As she often was, Mammi Iola stood eagerly waiting on the small concrete porch bare of flowers or even a hummingbird feeder. LeEtta had offered to plant her flowers and hang one, but Mammi Iola insisted the upkeep was unnecessary and it bothered her allergies. LeEtta had never known her to be allergic to anything.

"Thought you had your head in a book and forgot me," Mammi Iola jested as she settled beside her. They went to the next house on the right. LeEtta purchased two more spools of thread. She wondered if Frannie had a pattern she could follow for Daed's shirts, then worried sewing might prove too difficult to do alone and decided to ask another time. It was hard asking others how to do something that every other maed in the community already knew how to do.

"It was kind of Frannie to send that apple fry pie for Arlen. He has a hankering for them often."

"I can make them too, you know," LeEtta said sorely as Posey clomped along the blacktop along Cherry Grove. "He wouldn't even let me harness Posey this morning without fussing. I don't know why he treats me like a *boppli*."

"He treats you like his dochter. Arlen was much the same with Laura."

"So he didn't let Mamm out of the house or harness a buggy either?" LeEtta brought Posey to a slow trot and clamped her lips tight. She shouldn't have spoken the thought out loud.

"Don't be disrespectful. He does his best."

"I don't mean to be disrespectful, but you know, if he keeps using that arm like he does, he might never heal fully."

"Gott is the healer of all things, even stubborn fathers. Arlen never

had *schwester*, and his folks were a quiet lot. Nothing like us Grabers,"
she laughed. "A man who knows so little about women does not know
all their needs or what fills their heads."

Thankfully Daed didn't know all the thoughts that filled her head.
She knew her parents had only been married three short years. Daed
spoke nothing of their courtship or of when they first felt sparks for
each other. She thought of Ben and the sparks he'd ignited touching
her hand, the heat and lightning he'd caused after. Were sparks and
lightning normal? Did they come when strangers met, the unknowing
of another, or when something more was present?

"How did they meet?" They passed the greenhouse, and LeEtta
spotted Colleen bent over a row of tomatoes. She rose, waved, and
went back to picking tomatoes.

"Arlen had kumm to visit his cousins, if I *meinda* correctly. He was
running away from a bad courtship with another."

"Daed courted another?" LeEtta tried to imagine her father courting
at all, but she couldn't even muster up a faint picture of it. He was still
handsome and strong, but his short words and permanent frown had
earned him no looks from available women. She had always been confused about why he had never considered remarrying and having more
children. Widows often remarried and built a larger family. Perhaps
that was why Mammi Iola was having such difficulty finding a match
at her age. Did love have a time limit? She hoped not.

"He did. There was a wedding at Aaron and Lena Grabers'." She
turned to LeEtta. "This was long before Aaron's passing and Bishop
Hershberger leaving."

LeEtta knew Lena, the bishop's mamm, but only had old memories of the former bishop who walked with a cane and had over a
dozen kinner.

"Your mamm had always had a look to her, and many tried for
her attention, but I knew the moment she offered him a chicken leg
that she was smitten."

Love over chicken. LeEtta found a smile emerging at the thought.

Could love bloom over cloud watching?

"Laura always wanted a farm and kinner." Mammi turned to the landscape, letting out a heavy sigh.

"I'm sorry, Mammi. I shouldn't have asked. I know it is hard for you."

"Nee. I never want to stop thinking or talking of her. I remain quiet for Arlen's sake, but your mamm is worth remembering. She had dreamed of you since she was just a child playing with dolls. I even knew what to name you because she had chosen it. . .long before."

LeEtta warmed at the idea she had once been someone's dream. Someone's want. More often than not, she felt she was a burden to others, always asking questions about how to do something, then failing at it. "But I never knew her, so I only miss what I never knew. You miss her. It wasn't fair of me to bring it up."

"You may talk with me about Laura anytime. She would have much, I think, to say to you now that you are of an age to seek a husband."

LeEtta squeezed the reins tighter, her secret kiss bubbling inside her. If only she could shout it out loud for all to hear, she would get fewer pitiful looks than she did.

"Eunice and Ellen want to fix me up with Ellen's cousin." LeEtta rolled her eyes.

"You never know where it might lead. I made asparagus-and-cauliflower casserole once, and Owen still thinks to give me second looks."

"I don't want to be paired up with Ellen's cousin." And asparagus-and-cauliflower casserole didn't sound one bit romantic.

"We could double date," Mammi winked.

"I don't want someone to date me because he was asked to." That would be terribly embarrassing. "What would Mamm have said if I asked her how one goes about seeking a husband?" LeEtta was desperate to know what wise words her mother would bestow on her. Did she know how to get through to Daed? Would she think Ben Ropp a possible prospect despite him living elsewhere? LeEtta quickly pushed the idea of Ben away. He was only visiting and was probably now back in Ohio, trying to forget the bold maed who kissed him.

"Laura would say, If you want a new future, best be finding you a husband."

"I think that's what you would say." LeEtta tilted her a grin. "Mammi, there is no one here I'm interested in." Most of the men of Cherry Grove were either courting already or had no interest in her... that way. There was the handsome newcomer, but how was anything to bloom with someone determined to let weeds grow?

"Perhaps you should stop looking here. You could go visit your cousins in Havenlee."

LeEtta had only been to Indiana once, and she had been too young to remember what her cousins Belinda and Tabitha even looked like. But a spontaneous trip did hold a certain appeal. She'd have to imagine it, for there was no way she could leave Daed alone. He needed her, even if he didn't know it.

"If Gott wants me to marry, then He will see it so."

"If you wait for Him to drop a man on your doorstep, then you will be disappointed. He wants us to do a bit of the work too. I know you don't stick around those youth gatherings since you were asked to teach."

"How did you know that?"

"Teacher Kevin has an *onkel* in Walnut Ridge. He likes to talk... with his mouth full." Mammi groaned. "I'll never bake another cranberry bread again, but he is charming."

"Mammi Iola!" LeEtta couldn't believe Mammi had yet another suitor. "Who is he? How did you meet?"

"Well, he ran into me." She grinned, never minding sharing a single romantic encounter with her granddaughter. "Almost gave me a concussion. So he asked to buy me lunch. It was only right I accept. I could have been killed."

LeEtta stared at her grandmother in awe. What was her secret? How did she simply find special friends so easily? LeEtta had literally thrown herself at a stranger.

"You have to take charge of your life and not just sit at home waiting for it to find you." Mammi thrust a fist in the air playfully.

"Sometimes, even that doesn't work." LeEtta blew out a breath. "Not all of us can find an interest as easily as you."

"I don't see why not. You could have three if you want them. A woman needs to know who is best suited for her—without spoiling her reputation, of course."

"Of course," LeEtta said, sinking down in the seat. Hopefully, Jonas wouldn't speak of it. As it was, LeEtta didn't need another embarrassing mark on her reputation. "What about William Headings? I heard you speaking of him on Sunday." LeEtta pulled Posey to a stop at the end of the road and looked about for fast-moving cars before pulling out.

"Ach, William is a kind sort, with many things to offer a woman, but he cannot carry a tune if his life depends on it. I'm afraid my search continues. Widow Yoder is a terrible gossip, but Gott knows what plans He has for me. The right man is out there. He just hasn't found me yet."

Mammi's positive attitude made LeEtta want to be positive too. Perhaps she could take life by the reins and not simply wait for Gott to do it for her. Had she not already proved herself capable of securing at least a kiss? If it was a mindset that made life sweeter, LeEtta would certainly consider changing hers.

"I hope when I get old—older, I'm just like you." LeEtta parked the buggy in front of the bulk store and helped her grandmother out. "I need to see if Verna has ordered the cheese yet. Daed won't eat a single vegetable if I don't put cheese in it."

"Hiding a good thing under a bad thing will not do anything at all."

"Like ignoring an interest because he can't sing?"

"Now you are learning something that might lead you to a happy life."

While Mammi filled her short list, LeEtta collected a cartful and made her way down the last aisle, where freezer meats and cold foods were lined along a concrete wall. Behind one of the five glass doors in the refrigerated section, she spotted the long cheese blocks and put three in her cart before slipping to the book section.

It was a scant collection, mostly used books others had offered up to keep this part of the store from being removed. There were always a few Linda Byler books. No one ever frowned on reading those, but LeEtta had read every Linda Byler book there was. Scanning beyond horse books and children's stories, she began flipping through the pages of a plain yellow book with the title *The Pineapple Quilt* on the front. Suddenly, the hairs on the back of her neck lifted in awareness.

LeEtta glanced toward the corner where stacks of straw hats were piled on a table. She looked over her shoulder, noting Mammi Iola in deep conversation with Verna, the bulk store owner, over a shelf of homemade greeting cards. When she turned back to the shelf of books, she was startled and jumped back to find Jonas Hostetler standing there, leaning on the shelf, watching her.

"Jonas! You gave me a fright." LeEtta clutched her chest.

"I didn't mean to. You looked like you were fully into the book. I could purchase it for you. . .as a gift."

LeEtta quickly set the book back down and gripped her cart. "Nee, thank you. I've no time to read that one anyway. Have a gut day." She hurried to the front of the store, thankful Mammi Iola was ready herself. LeEtta quickly paid for her cheese and ushered Mammi Iola out the door.

"That was the quickest I've ever gotten you out of there." Mammi lifted a questioning brow.

"I don't want to dawdle. We still have to go to town for the rest of our groceries, jah?" LeEtta stowed her grocery bags and quickly climbed into the seat.

A buggy veered into the parking lot, catching both women's attention. LeEtta felt her heart thunder at the sight of the man holding the reins. *He's still here!*

Ben recognized her too, throwing up a hand in greeting. He made quick work of pulling alongside her and climbing out. She had hoped to see him again, but then again, she hoped he was a few hundred miles away too. LeEtta could feel her cheeks burning immediately as thoughts of their last encounter filled her head.

"Hi," Ben said approaching.

"Hi." LeEtta looked toward the door, and sure enough, Jonas was stepping out. LeEtta gave him a pleading look in hopes he didn't cause a scene right there in the parking lot with her overly romantic grandmother taking it all in.

"Ben, this is my grandmother, Iola Graber."

He tipped his hat in a gentlemanly fashion. LeEtta had always read about men doing that, but she had yet to see one consider the gesture.

"It's good to see you." His eyes smiled long before his lips did.

One more glance forward, and LeEtta knew she had to leave. "You too, but we are aiming for town. I wish I could stay and chat, but we best be going." Her eyes shifted anxiously toward the front door again. Jonas' frown deepened, as if he had any right to tell her who she could speak with.

"So long, Ben. Have a nice day." Her words croaked out like a frog.

With eagerness, LeEtta wheeled the buggy back and around and hurried onto the main road. The only good thing about the whole uneasy encounter was that Ben looked disappointed that she left so quickly. It wouldn't be so bad if he was staying, but he wasn't.

"Well, that looks like the kind of chance I had hoped for you," Mammi Iola said as they pulled back onto the blacktop.

CHAPTER SIX

LeEtta knew nothing of motherhood, but she did know that when all was quiet, it was best to see if *all* was all right. The Schwartz kinner were too quiet. She quickly made peanut butter sandwiches with a spoonful of grape jelly, cut them for small fingers before putting them on a plate, and hurried outside. They had to be hungry, considering they hadn't touched a thing at breakfast.

Six-year-old Anna Mary attended the nearby school, but four-year-old Laverna and three-year-old Bethie both played with a puzzle on the front porch, not so much as daring to step foot into the grassy yard.

LeEtta never had met two kinner so content with doing or saying absolutely nothing. Perhaps they were worried over their mamm, given whatever ailed her to see a doctor so often. Perhaps they just preferred the quiet.

LeEtta had tried all kinds of ways to spur something resembling joy in the girls. They frowned at her singing and her cheesy eggs. They looked at her as if she sprouted two heads when she suggested a game of hide-and-seek. It was only when LeEtta found a stack of puzzles packed in a box that the girls showed some interest. LeEtta decided to sit them outside on the porch, where the sun could reach them, to work on the puzzle of two kittens and tangled yarn. Hopefully, the sun could inspire them as it often did LeEtta on gloomy days.

A dusty black car pulled into the driveway. LeEtta noted Driver

Dan behind the wheel. When Anna Jay stepped out, LeEtta looked at the girls. "Your mamm is home." *Nothing.* Puzzles were not that fun, she silently measured.

"I see you are enjoying the fresh air today," Anna Jay worked her way up the porch steps, her black bonnet matching two perfectly aligned brows and her parted hair. In summer months, LeEtta's brows tended to fade so much she looked as if she had let Mammi Iola pluck them clean.

"I thought a snack might suit them, but I'm afraid I have yet to find what likes they have." LeEtta wasn't sure how anyone could mess up peanut butter and jelly. She looked at the girls and the untouched sandwiches beside them and shrugged.

"They are picky like their daed," Anna Jay said. "I often struggle with that myself." She walked with lighter steps, as if a great weight had somehow been taken from her. LeEtta hadn't pried by asking if she was in the family way or suffering from a terrible illness. Still, despite the smile, her eyes remained as dull as a burned, fallen oak leaf.

"I didn't mean to take so long," the young mother said almost shamefully.

"I enjoyed getting to know them, and next time you need me, we'll be less strangers than before," LeEtta offered with a hint of positivity. Anna Jay may be suffering with something that dulled her smiles, but she had three kinner. Three blessings gifted by Gott. One would think she'd smile all the time at such blessings as that.

"The move has been hard on them. Not seeing their *grossmammi* is the hardest still. Anna Mary has yet to adjust to school. She cries every morning not to go."

"It will pass." LeEtta remembered those first days. She had cried too, but her father's kind words of encouragement helped the transition pass quickly. "If you'd like, I can come back and take them for a nature walk tomorrow." *Foolish.* Their mamm was plenty capable of taking the kinner on a walk. LeEtta only wanted to get to know the kinner better so she knew what needs they had.

"That would be kind of you. I have—" Anna Jay bit her lip. "I have a health issue. Nothing to fret terribly over, but I will be seeing a woman each week for it. Would you be available on Wednesdays?"

"I am," LeEtta said happily. The money would be useful, and the more time spent with the kinner, the better LeEtta could help put a sparkle in their eyes. Moving away from all you ever knew had to be difficult.

LeEtta watched Anna Jay pat both little kapps affectionately. From where she stood, she couldn't see anything ailing the younger woman, but she had watched her father stare long at something and not even blink enough to know that all illnesses weren't on the surface.

As she left the home, LeEtta made a mental note to add the family to her evening prayers and pointed Posey toward town. Eunice had told her all about the fish fry this evening. It was interesting to watch men work the nets across the ponds, catching fish, and then see them poured into a truck. It wasn't every day you got to see that, and how often was LeEtta going to get a chance for folks to try her tartar sauce? When one had an overabundance of relish, she had to think of fresh ways to use it up.

On Saturdays, the bakery was always packed with customers. Many *Englisch* preferred to do their shopping on the weekend, but today—thankfully—there were only a half-dozen customers browsing aisles and inhaling the fresh, sweet aromas. LeEtta moved inside and quickly found a place in line.

"I'll take a dozen of those sugar-frosted cookies too," a woman said, adjusting her glasses. LeEtta stood behind her, waiting her turn, as Ivy Troyer rushed to fill her order. Three maedels ran busily up and down the wide aisle, but only one cash register could ring up a sale. LeEtta didn't miss the Saturday rush one bit. An overcrowded room always made her a tad anxious.

"I made them fresh this morning," Ivy told the woman while collecting a box to put them in.

When the doorbell jingled behind her, LeEtta looked over one shoulder and frowned. *Mike Lengacher.*

If ever there was a reason for her to think herself unworthy of a husband, it was because of him.

It had been five years since she agreed to play the silly game, and she still couldn't look at Mike Lengacher's face without wanting to run in the opposite direction. It was a stupid game, one that Eunice should have never insisted they play at all.

Still in the throes of her own rumspringa, LeEtta had agreed. Most of the youngies had already headed home, and the Lengacher parents (who were chaperoning) had slipped upstairs, trusting no one would bend any rules.

That's when Eunice had finished drinking her ginger soda and said, "We can play spin the bottle." LeEtta flushed at the memory. Eunice had given Jerry Hostetler a bashful grin. She had set her sights on him that night and talked about nothing more than getting her first kiss.

"Sure," Jerry said, equally eager to spin a bottle and kiss whomever it landed on. Who wanted to kiss someone based on that? Apparently not Mike Lengacher, as he publicly declined kissing LeEtta when his spin landed on her. He had labeled her unkissable without any explanation, and he made certain to tell all his friends.

Everyone knew. LeEtta was heartbroken. Not because she wanted to kiss Mike. She was mighty happy she hadn't, in fact. But since that first rejection, no one so much as blinked her way, and Eunice insisted she might be unkissable because of her mousy features and smarts. Just because she hadn't blossomed as quickly as other girls or known the pulls of attraction didn't mean anything. Just because she had no mamm to teach her how to bat her eyelashes didn't mean she would never marry.

A flush became a warm sensation. Someone did find her worthy once. Ben not only asked to walk her home, he also didn't mind kissing her at all. Her shoulders straightened. What a terrible thing she did simply to test waters her friends thought she was too immature to wade into. Worse, she had put Ben in a bad spot. He would probably forget all about her and that kiss and go back to Ohio to court someone more worthy of kissing.

"LeEtta Miller?" Mike stepped up the counter to her left, and she winced before turning to face him.

"Hi. You've"—his pale eyes traveled the length of her as if she were a *hund* that he was trying to decide the breed of—"grown up."

He didn't even try masking his surprise, which only fueled her wish to turn around and leave. If she weren't more concerned about showing up to a fish fry empty-handed, she would. Then again, she was stuck between the woman in front of her, who now wanted a dozen raisin cookies, and two more customers behind her. LeEtta couldn't even pretend she hadn't heard him when he angled his body to face her.

Mike looked the same as he did five years ago. Short and stubby. Jah, she was glad she didn't have to kiss him. It was wrong to harbor sour thoughts about a person. LeEtta tried to look at the positive. She'd not have to worry about marrying Mike Lengacher.

"You going to the fish fry?" Mike asked. His voice had drawn deeper.

"I don't know yet." A lie as sure as she stood there with her chin pointed abnormally high. Confidence was key, or so Mammi Iola had always insisted it was. *Even when you feel like a fish floundering on the bank, keep your chin up.*

"Hiya, LeEtta and...Mike." Ivy looked from LeEtta to Mike and quickly settled back on LeEtta. "Sweet rolls for you two?" Ivy asked.

"Jah, same order please, but we are not here...together," LeEtta said in a low tone.

"That will be $7.40, and I didn't think you were," Ivy replied once she filled the order. "Hazel thinks he's harder to match than mei schwester Hannah was." Ivy smiled and quickly quieted when Mike stepped next to her.

"I was wondering—"

"What for ya, Mike?" Ivy quickly interrupted. LeEtta tossed her a grateful look, dropped her last ten-dollar bill on the counter, and quickly hurried off. She didn't have to hold a grudge, but Mike Lengacher didn't deserve to know what she was doing today.

Harvesting catfish were two words Ben had never thought to be put together. He'd been part of many a harvest. Corn, soybeans, hay, tobacco, and even that summer he earned a pocketful of cash on a cabbage farm. Standing along the shallow end of a well-manicured pond, Ben found the Martins' operation certainly unique.

"Matthias has the youngies fishing the pond ahead." Leo approached. "He likes letting them have their fun too, but we're gonna seine this one. It's easier with just a few folks. Safer too." Leo sat on the dirt and began removing his boots.

Ben mimicked his movements, his gaze taking in everything. He could see the sense of it. A crowded seine line might be more mismanaged with too many helping hands, but would they have the muscle to drag it clear to the far end?

Eight large ponds, with a levee of dirt and grass separating them, had taken up more than fifteen acres of good farmland—or clay, he recalled, thinking back to the conversation he and LeEtta had. He worked off the second boot as he thought of her and how her eyes sparkled when she spoke of this place.

Angus cattle grazed nearby behind wooden plank fencing. Looking up, Ben took in the slow rhythm of one of the two large windmills settled on the farm. Both helped aerate the ponds. Fishing was an unusual trade for an Amish man, but he imagined a dozen men would happily give up toiling in soil under a hot sun or putting on a new roof to fish their days away.

Three more buggies pulled up the curvy drive, adding to at least twenty others already parked behind the Martins' house. "If he only wants a few hands, why are folks coming out of the woodwork?" People were gathering along one of the high banks, while others were under a shelter-house roof. Leo had said there would be a fish fry afterward. A gathering of sorts. It seemed many were looking forward to the meal.

Jerry laughed. "They've kumm to see who pulls out the biggest catfish."

"Or who falls headfirst," Leo added playfully.

"The largest catfish, huh?" That piqued Ben's interest. Nothing like a healthy competition to make up for the embarrassment of rolling up your trouser legs just below the knee and wading barefoot in a partially drained pond.

"Just stay a few feet from me," Leo told him before moving into the water. Ben followed, his toes immediately sinking into the sandy clay while warm water rose up his trouser legs. The stench grew stronger now.

"Even your bishop has kumm to watch us fall on our faces." Ben noted the familiar face. With him was a woman in the family way. She smiled and placed a hand on a silvery hund at her side. Ben immediately missed Shelly, the Great Pyrenees that he'd spent more on than most did a new Sunday suit. Shelly had been a faithful companion, but that morning when he packed his bag and climbed into the blue van to leave home, she hadn't so much as budged to see him off. Ben pushed aside the thought. Nothing lasted, not even a dog's dedication.

"That fella next to him is Bishop Schwartz from Miller's Creek. Our communities recently split, so they've been sharing the load until a new bishop is chosen for us over here."

"Worried you'll draw the lot?" Ben said with a grin.

"Why would I be? I'm neither married nor have kinner."

Ben cocked his head and looked to the miserable start of a beard.

"Once we join the church, some start early." Leo chuckled and gave his beard a pull. Proof again that not all communities were alike.

A couple more men slipped into the water and introduced themselves. "Jacob Lemmon," one man said. "Will Lapp," said another. The men both seemed about Ben's age, neither sporting a whisker.

"Danke, everyone, for coming to help." A voice drew all chatter to a halt, and all eyes focused on the man standing high on the levee. "I usually don't harvest until the first of October, but you know. . ." Matthias grinned from high on the bank.

"Good money in catfish!" someone shouted, spurring a round of laughter.

"Jah, Dawdi, there is," Matthias replied. "I called a few friends, so I hope you will all stay afterward for fellowship and some fried fish and chips." He waved someone over, and Ben felt his heart thunder. He had hoped to see her again but had been perplexed by how quickly she dismissed him days ago. Perhaps she regretted her rash decision and was too ashamed to face him. He shouldn't be this excited to see her. He knew he couldn't get attached to anyone here. LeEtta sprinted across the levee, whispered something in Matthias' ear, and sprinted away just as quickly.

"We even have dessert!" Folks seemed eager for that.

"Looks like Hazel Fisher has come to spoil us." Leo chuckled.

"Or spy on us," Jacob added.

"Hazel's the local matchmaker. If you ain't married, it's because she ain't met ya yet." Leo gripped the top of the seine in one hand while men worked to stretch it across the water's edge. "My advice is if you like the single life, don't visit the bakery."

Ben made a mental note to steer clear of any bakeries. A man without land didn't consider starting a family. A man without anyone to trust didn't either.

"Just like last time, the largest catfish is yours, and lunch will be ready when we're done." A large white truck pulled onto the levee, its rounded belly an indicator that this was the fish truck. The *Englischer* got out and shook hands with Matthias.

"Best we get started." With that, four men on each side of the pond began pulling on the thick rim of the seine. Ben's job was to keep the netting above water and flowing forward while the weights attached to the bottom kept fish from escaping underneath. They had only moved twenty yards or so when the water began to ripple just ahead of him. Even the fish knew they were about to be netted up, but all went with the flow of following the lead fish to the shallow end of the pond. *Dumb fish.*

Shouts erupted in the distance where three more ponds sat waiting to be seined next. "I reckon them boys hooked them a good one," Jacob said.

"I say it's one of them Graber boys. They always catch the biggest," someone else added.

Ben focused on the chore at hand. Corralling a few hundred fish was no simple task. Water splashed, and more than a handful of times Ben felt the weight of resistance against him. He held firm, just as he did with everything in life. He would not fall, and he would not fail.

CHAPTER SEVEN

Guilt had a way of making one ill, but as another page on the calendar flipped to a new season, LeEtta decided to put the whole matter of kissing Benuel Ropp—the treachery of her own body acting on impulse as opposed to perfect control—behind her. She'd chosen not to let illness keep her from such a splendid day.

Hot oil and spices blended with the heat of the late September sun. LeEtta wrinkled her nose as the strong stench of the fishy ponds wafted uphill to where everyone gathered, waiting.

"Fish isn't done until it's floated a full seven minutes." Hazel continued to hover over Otto Shetler, causing him to grumble. The local matchmaker had a tendency for bossiness, but LeEtta knew it stemmed from years of raising a family and employing so many young maedels.

LeEtta stifled a laugh as Otto and Hazel continued to argue cooking methods and set out two jars of her homemade tartar sauce. Hopefully, everyone liked it.

"Mammi sent over donuts, and I picked up more chips." Eunice added to one table. "I see the newcomer came out to help too." Eunice glanced toward a group of men standing in the full sun and laughing. LeEtta noted Ben among them.

"Ach, has he?" She tried to sound as if she didn't care, but inside, she was a mix of worry and wonderment.

"I thought he was only here for a visit?"

"Me too." LeEtta let out a breath. Now she would have to face him yet again, and Eunice would suspect something for sure. Nee, it was best she simply ignore Ben Ropp the best she could.

Once the food was spread out and the silent prayer was prayed, folks began lining up, eager for a plate. Otto couldn't fry fast enough, which only gave Hazel more reason to hound his manning of the hot oil fryer.

"Hiya, Letty." Jonas was now calling her by her nickname, something only her daed and mammi did.

"Jonas," LeEtta offered him a spoonful of coleslaw on his plate. A fly swarmed, and she swatted at it with her free hand.

"It's good to see you. You look—"

"Jonas," Hazel interrupted, coming to LeEtta's side. "You best keep moving or the food will get *kault* for everyone else." Her sharp eyes scolded. Jonas ducked his head and moved off.

"Danke," LeEtta whispered.

"Ach, he's but a bu with stars in his eyes, but Gott frowns on those who take up other people's time." Hazel spooned out what remained of a foil pan of baked beans into a new one. "Never met a Hostetler who did anything normal." Hazel leaned closer. "It's why I have yet to find a match for them." She crumbled up the foil pan and aimed for Otto again. Poor Otto.

"Perhaps Hazel could find Jonas a match." Eunice giggled.

Once every plate was filled, LeEtta and Eunice took the opportunity to fill one for themselves. "Let's sit over there."

Before LeEtta could stop her, Eunice was already walking toward Jerry, Leo, and Ben.

"Whoever made this. . ." Leo used a finger to rake off the creamy condiment.

"That was LeEtta," Eunice said, giving Leo a dark look.

"Sorry, LeEtta. I'm not a fan of any sauce." Leo shrugged sorrowfully.

LeEtta offered him a tender smile as she took a seat next to Eunice.

Ben sat next to Leo, his focus on his plate. He was still barefoot, his broadfalls rolled up his leg and a smile glinting unmistakably in his eyes. It warmed her to see that he was among friends. A shiver ran over her, and she quickly focused on her plate.

"How long will you be visiting, Ben?" Eunice asked. "I'm sure some would like to know." She gave LeEtta a not-so-private glance.

LeEtta swallowed hard, her skin warming to an unnatural heat of embarrassment. Thankfully, no bone presented itself in that bite or she would have to have simply died right there.

"Not long." Ben looked at LeEtta, one side of his lips hiked slightly. "I'm here to help out Shepard Eversole on his farm, and then I will be heading back to Ohio."

So he would be staying a spell longer. That should give her more time to clear the air between them and perhaps be friends after all. *How do you make friends with someone you shared a kiss with?* She'd have to think on that.

"How long will that be?" Leave it to Eunice to get answers to questions LeEtta wouldn't dare ask in public.

"I'm here to earn enough for a down payment on my own farm. I figure there's no harm in learning a new trade while I'm at it." Ben's eyes rested on hers but dulled at the mention of working for Shepard Eversole.

"Like when to speak and when to eat," Jerry muttered to his girlfriend. "Eber said your family owns a big farm up north. Whatcha all farm?"

"We—I mean, *they*—raise corn and beans, but my younger brother is soon to take over. Who knows what will have become of it when I return?" His jaw tightened, and she could see it was a sore spot.

"That's rough," Leo stated.

"Jah, I'm the eldest. I've worked that land my whole life." He turned to look at her. "My bruder doesn't even like to get dirty."

He was torn. LeEtta could see that, but life didn't always work the same for everyone. She had learned early on to find what she didn't have or know. At least he was working toward something. She measured and respected him for being driven to achieve what he wanted.

"How many siblings do you have?" Eunice asked next. LeEtta wished her friends wouldn't put him on the spot but would let him simply enjoy Otto's fried fish.

"Three. Samuel, Mary, and Lisa."

"I don't have any," LeEtta slipped and said.

"Having them can bring a few hardships, in case you're wondering," Ben said.

"Ain't that the truth." Leo chuckled.

LeEtta had her friends, neighbors, and a community that served as family in their own way. It was a terrible thing to be an only child. The loneliness pressed upon you, but she'd not complain. From Ben's account, having them wasn't any easier, but she had longed for siblings until it was apparent Daed would never consider marrying again.

Talk shifted to new construction jobs and how the Troyers had a bumper crop this year in apples. LeEtta remained quiet, a hard task when she had so much to say too, but she'd not give Eunice a reason to further embarrass her.

It was growing late, and LeEtta knew she needed to get home. Daed would be needing his supper. "I best be going." LeEtta stood, collecting her paper plate and cup from the ground.

"Me too," Ben said, coming to his feet as well. "Thanks for the invite today." He looked to Leo, who was finishing off his third plate and eyeing an uneaten donut on Jerry's.

"Don't forget your shoes." Leo pointed toward the ponds.

"This has been an interesting day." Ben walked beside her as they tossed everything in the trash.

"Can I give you a ride home?"

"I have my buggy, but I do want to apologize." She looked about in case anyone was watching. Sure enough, Hazel Fisher was. From under the shelter, she was squinting their way, a half-eaten fish sandwich in her hands.

"You have nothing to apologize about, LeEtta. We both were wrong. I know the pressures of freinden," he said with absolute certainty. "Eunice seems like one who likes adding pressure." He smirked, making her immediately relaxed. His observation of Eunice was spot-on, yet he was not troubled by her nosy questions. "All is forgotten."

LeEtta ducked her head. She could never forget those lips, but of course he regretted it. She probably didn't even do it right.

"Walk with me to fetch my shoes?"

Her gaze shot up at the request. His smile brought about one of her own. "I'd be happy to." LeEtta walked slowly, in case he was tenderfooted; but surprisingly, he wasn't. They walked along the farther pond banks, and Ben collected his socks and shoes.

"You looked to have enjoyed today," she said as they started walking back toward the buggies.

"I like fishing, but I admit, it's easier with a net."

"I saw you started painting your grandparents' house." Eunice insisted men liked to do all the talking. Thankfully, Mammi said a man who didn't want to hear you talk didn't need to take up your time. "I drive by there often and noticed the changes."

"I hope to tackle the porch next, but Shep has piglets due, and I'm learning how dangerous a chore that can be."

Both of them waved as Eunice and Jerry drove by. "Your friends care about you," Ben said.

"Or pity me. I haven't decided yet." LeEtta chuckled.

"Nee, they care for you. Can I ask you a question?"

"Jah." LeEtta was happy to answer any of his questions. Just being near him made her happy.

"Why did you kiss me?"

LeEtta faltered in her steps. Well, not that question, as she had yet to come up with a reasonable answer.

They reached her buggy, and Ben kindly helped her up into the seat. Like the first time, her hand tingled at his touch. She took a deep breath before her reply came. "Have you ever been the last one picked?"

His eyes, meeting hers—or rather, looking through her—were stone-set. No way could he understand what it was like to be her. Ben was strong, handsome, and capable.

"I have," he said. "Have a safe drive home LeEtta Miller." Ben turned and walked away. Was it possible he did know?

CHAPTER EIGHT

Arlen Miller didn't believe in gossip. In fact, he rather found it left a bad taste in a man's mouth to even be within earshot of it. That's why when Marcus Hostetler showed up at his door to talk, Arlen should have closed his ears and walked away.

"Did you know they have been spending time together? Jonas said they were at the Martins' together, and Joanie said Hazel Fisher thinks them to be courting."

Arlen had met the young man just last Sunday. Eber Ropp's kin. He'd always respected Eber and knew he ran his house as he did his conversations, simple and to the point. He hadn't a clue the fella was sneaking around his house, though. Courting was private, but somehow he felt hurt to know LeEtta had been talking with someone and not sharing it with him.

Arlen had been dreading the day his dochter would start courting. Of course, he knew it would come sooner than later, considering she was plenty old enough. In part, if he was being honest, he had hoped for it too. Despite liking how things were, a man without sohns did hope to gain one at some point. He struggled to keep the farm going, and now his infirmity was making even the simplest chore impossible. Arlen had spared LeEtta the news. His arm would never regain its full strength. He was tired. Bone-tired.

It was a wonder why it had taken so long for LeEtta to find someone worthy of her. *Because you didn't teach her much about feelings and such.* He'd failed in many ways—ways a mother wouldn't have. His dochter had grown into a beautiful woman, just like her mamm. She might have his red hair, but it was Laura's eyes, her sharp little chin, and her soft features that were sure to catch someone's eye.

Arlen trusted her. He knew his dochter, even if she thought he did not. Marcus was spouting gossip and wasting his time. LeEtta would never spend time getting to know a man unless she saw something worth building on. Jah, LeEtta might just find love. Not the kind she found in those books she thought he didn't know about, but real love. The kind of love that lasted, even in death.

Perhaps Marcus, being a father of so many rowdy sohns, was simply being cautious. Arlen watched the younger man fidget as he continued to give an account of what Jonas witnessed. Arlen closed his eyes and felt anger build in his gut. No father wanted to hear such things.

"I came as soon as he told me. If that were my dochter..." Marcus shook his head. "Jonas said he couldn't keep quiet, knowing LeEtta had been taken advantage of like that, and he didn't just tell me. You should know. He was angry, seeing what he had, and only meant well, hoping the bishop would insist Eber send his grandson back to Ohio."

Arlen narrowed a glare at his friend. "He went to the bishop?"

Marcus nodded.

"I really wish Jonas had come to me with this first." *That one* was always making his way over to their farm. Delivering feed when Arlen was perfectly capable of fetching it for himself. Arlen thought it had been out of kindness, seeing as he did struggle a bit, but now he wasn't so sure. "I best go on over to talk to the bishop before this gets out of hand."

An hour later, Arlen arrived at the bishop's. He felt his stomach sink when he noticed an extra buggy near the barn. One-handed, he made the awkward step down when the men emerged from the barn.

"I was expecting you," Bishop Simon Graber said. Today of all days, why did the neighboring bishop have to be here?

Arlen let his shoulders sink. He was the one to blame for all of it. LeEtta had been taken advantage of. No way did she have any blame in this. He'd do whatever he had to to remedy this before further damage was done. "Bishop Schwartz." Arlen nodded a greeting and then moved inside. "I was hoping to talk to you in private, Simon, about a matter." Arlen gave his longtime friend a penetrating look.

"What is concealed in the dark always comes to light," Joshua Schwartz said. He reached into his pocket, produced a piece of hard candy, and began unwrapping the plastic wrapper as if sweets might get them all through what came next.

"Unfortunately, I was here when the boy came. We had just returned from the Martins' and he was at the door." Sympathy spread over his gaze. Bishop Schwartz lumbered to a corner and gathered up three buckets. Setting them on their heads for quick and ready seats, he sat down on one.

"You look tired, Arlen," Bishop Graber said as he sat on the one closest to the neighboring bishop. The man had an eye for paying attention. He noticed much, though he seldom addressed his observations. Arlen knew him to always be a good man, a fair bishop, and a dear friend.

"I am."

"You have had a hard way of it, for sure. It wonders me if you should think about hiring help this year, see your corn harvested and cattle looked after."

"I don't have the means of affording such." Arlen took a seat but had no intention of speaking of his shrinking finances. In fact, if he held fast, they may just see through the winter. "I'll make do as we always have."

"We must humble ourselves in times like this," Bishop Schwartz added. "No man can carry a yoke that is fit for mules. You have a large farm and no sohns to help you."

"I know what burden you carry, Arlen. I too had days when I wanted to put blame on myself after losing Lizzy and the kinner. I have long hoped you would remarry and have more kinner, yet I am wise enough to know we all do not grieve the same."

Jah, the bishop saw everything—even a man still picking at wounds he should have let heal naturally. Twenty-two years was a long time to grieve, but no one could force him to stop. His love for Laura was as sound as his faith. Arlen had put to rest any foolish ideas that he would choose a second wife. Laura may have only been by his side for three short years, but it was an eternity to a man who knew love as deep as hers.

"It has been a hard row to hoe without Laura."

"For both of you." Bishop Graber lifted a knowing brow. "Yet you managed to see her healthy and strong."

"Might not have done as well as I'd hoped," he admitted. "I failed to teach her some things." Arlen straightened and cleared his throat. "Marcus Hostetler paid me a visit." Straight to the matter at hand. "I have yet to speak to LeEtta on the rumors being spread, but I know my dochter. She is not one who strays from the rules. If any wrong was committed, it was not on her part."

"We all make mistakes, do we not? LeEtta is a fine woman, and I have never worried over her choices before, but we cannot judge Benuel Ropp by rumors either," the bishop insisted.

"Yet you will my LeEtta?" Arlen stood.

"Nee, it's not my place to judge anyone, but I'll not sweep it under a rug either."

Arlen stared at both men. "Have you visited the Ropps yet? I hear he has a habit of getting into fixes. LeEtta does not!"

"We will be paying the young man a visit on this day. Please sit and don't let your temper best you. We can sort this out. Bishop Schwartz has thoughts on the matter he'd like to share too."

Arlen glanced at the other bishop, who sat quietly listening with arms crossed over his chest.

"You know if she were to marry, you would gain a sohn." The neighboring bishop sat leisurely, elbows on both knees, a hint of a grin on his lips.

"I'll not have her marry a man who clearly does not care what may come of her reputation."

"Jah, but it is clear your dochter has feelings for this newcomer, does she not? They have been seen together more than last Sunday. In fact, they were seen walking together just today. My cousin Hazel says your dochter has not shown an interest in anyone before now. Many find them a gut match. He comes from a farming family who has done well for themselves."

Both Arlen and Bishop Graber stared at the older bishop. Joshua Schwartz was a man who had a penchant for candy, smiled at odd times, and played matchmaker as much as the local baker did. In fact, the glint in his eye was making Arlen a little nervous to hear his next words.

"We are getting old." Bishop Schwartz stretched out his legs and rubbed his chin. "I say let the young be young and give us *grosskinner* to play with in our old age. Have I ever told you about my nephew Daniel and his fraa, Hannah?"

LeEtta steered Posey over the hill, home just in the distance, as clouds overhead grew darker. She quickly worked her horse out of the harness and into a stall, then spread the vinyl blanket covering over the open buggy as thunder rolled in the distance.

LeEtta had barely stepped into the house when the heavens opened. A giggle leaked out of her as she closed the door. A squeak from the sitting room caught her attention, but before she reached the doorway, there her father stood, hair disheveled and a frown cemented in place. Behind him, Mammi Iola was smiling wider than usual. It was the kind of smile she often wore when speaking of her newest beau.

Had they been waiting on her? Was Daed ill? A shiver raced up her spine and latched onto her throat. "Are you all right?" LeEtta asked. He looked in pain. Why did he keep overusing that arm?

"I've been to the bishop's today, but not before our neighbor got there."

LeEtta let out a breath. *Jonas.* Jonas' threat had borne fruit, and this was the result. Worse, Jonas had told her bishop! Her chest pounded so hard that she was sure they could hear it. "Daed—" LeEtta said hoping her words came out less shaky than her inside felt.

"LeEtta. Did you naet find yourself alone with another?"

She couldn't deny it. It would bring about more penance to pay for her sin. *Ach dear Lord, please don't give him a heart attack.* She prayed silently as her father drew closer. Lowering her head shamefully, she told him the truth. "I did, but—"

"The bishop will be here in the morning to speak to you."

Everyone knew Bishop Graber loved finding lost sheep and that he was a very understanding man to foolish maedels who made stupid mistakes. Surely if she explained it properly, all would be right.

"However, you will tell me how you met this man that you have been spending time with."

"I met him at the last gathering before the communities split. He walked me home." Her father stopped pacing and stared at her.

"And you were alone with him?"

"I—I—" LeEtta said. "He's a friend. I was only showing him the pond. He likes to fish."

"Fish, huh? Don't figure there's much left up there now. I want the truth from you, even if it is hard for me to hear. You have always been a gut dochter, but you know we do not believe in certain acts between a man and a woman before marriage. Did Benuel Ropp take advantage of you?"

LeEtta felt her head spin. Shame on Jonas Hostetler for embellishing a kiss into more. "It wasn't his fault. It was mine." Did she dare tell him she was tired of being the last at everything? That Benuel Ropp was so handsome, and when he thought her beautiful, it was like someone else had made the rash decision she had made?

"So it is true. You were alone with him, acting as man and wife?"

His dark gaze drilled through her. "Your reputation will be marked by all who hear of this. No man will want you if they think—"

"I kissed him," she admitted while shame beat her hotly. "It will never happen again."

"You permitted a man you barely know to touch you." His face grew an alarming shade of red. "If you want to act as if you are married, then so be it."

"What?" LeEtta looked to her grandmother for help but found only further opposition there as she nodded her head up and down, her smile still intact. Fresh new tears stung her eyes as his tone grew harsher than she had ever known. What punishment would he press on her? She hadn't a clue.

"You will marry this Ben Ropp before your reputation and our family name are ruined."

"I can't marry a man I do not know!"

"But you know him well enough, jah?" He lifted a sharp brow. "It is the choices we make that not only affect us but also those around us. You will make this right. You chose him over what you know to be right. You made the choice, and that is the end of it."

LeEtta watched in horror as her father marched out of the room. The slamming of the back door jolted through her, shaking her already taut nerves.

"Kumm now. Let's have some tea," Mammi Iola urged her into the kitchen.

"I must go after him. I have to try to talk sense into him. I know I made a terrible mistake, but he's not hearing the whole of it. I had a reason." *Albeit not a good one.*

"Is he not?" Mammi Iola said as she set a pot on the stove, and after the turn of a knob and three clicks, a blue fire burst to life. "Best you trust Arlen to know what is best for you. He has never made a decision before that I found worth questioning."

"But Mammi, he just said I had to marry." Was she not listening?

"I have always hoped you'd marry first." Mammi Iola looked over her shoulder and floated LeEtta a wink.

"Mammi, you were already married. . .to my dawdi."

"That was years ago, my dear." Mammi waved a hand and sought out two cups. "I loved being married to your dawdi. Always having someone there with you on the hard days and sharing the best ones with you. Having a husband will be good for you. It will be good for more than just you as well."

How was marrying a man she was just getting to know good for anyone? "It was a mistake," she repeated. Though it didn't feel like the worst mistake a person could make—at least, not enough to force her into an unwanted marriage. Oh, how she was going to be the laughing stock of all Cherry Grove once more. "Daed really wouldn't make me marry someone I don't even know, would he?"

"He isn't forcing you. He's helping you make the right decision. All will kumm out right." Mammi added two spoons of sugar to her cup and sat down next to her.

LeEtta dropped her head on the table and began to cry.

"Now, now, Letty. We must put our trust in Gott, in all things. I'd marry him for ya, but he might not like plain ol' green beans and ham." She winked again.

"You are happy about this when you should be angry at me for what I did."

"I'm happy to know my *grosskind* will marry."

LeEtta dropped her head in her hands. "This is all one big misunderstanding. Jonas is just angry. He doesn't know what he's doing."

"Or perhaps he did, but it didn't work out as he planned either. Choices, Letty. We must all make them and stand by them. Every person we meet, we touch their life," she said as if reciting something profound from a book, dramatic as always, before turning back to look at her once more. "But we are not responsible for how they react. Jonas will face his own consequences."

"Is there no way to convince Daed otherwise?"

"There's always hope. Gott takes what is dead and gives it life.

Now"—Mammi stood—"I expect you to pick me up early in the morning for shopping. We have much to prepare for. We need to visit Frannie's shop and pick out some material. Green, I think." She gave LeEtta an intent look, as if deciding how tall she was in centimeters.

"I don't want to go shopping at a time like this, Mammi." There had to be some way she could convince her daed what a terrible idea this was, and she needed to warn Ben. Ach, what trouble she had gotten him into.

"Now where are the notebook and pencil? We need to make a list."

"Mammi." Her grandmother was ignoring her, just as her father had, as she riffled through drawers until she found what she was after.

"Once the bishop announces you, there will be little time to plan. A light green would have been better with your hair, but who knows if we have enough time for that."

"So the bishop would make me marry too?"

"Jah, it has already been decided, dear." Mammi continued to write down words on her list while LeEtta feared she might just be having a heart attack.

"I thought you said there was still hope."

"There is. Hope that you and Ben Ropp have a full life together."

CHAPTER NINE

"I took my eyes off of you for a day!" Eber Ropp shook his head as he paced the long L-shaped porch. Bewilderment stained his usual stone expression. Inside, LeEtta's daed, a bishop, and two ministers, who had been introduced to Ben upon his arrival as Minister Fender and Minister Shetler, sat drinking Mammi's sweetened kaffi. It was all Ben could do to keep his temper calm and his mouth closed.

He'd said plenty already after suffering through a full hour of accusations and judgmental grunts. He'd tried to explain himself, but his words fell on plugged ears. It was one thing to have a fifteen-year-old spin yarns about your character. It was quite another to have a man demand you marry his dochter.

It was just one kiss. Ben had had three more before that, and no father demanded his life for it. Folks married for convenience, widows and widowers, but not young men and women who had time yet to decide who they'd start a family with.

"It was a mistake, jah, but not mine," Ben tried to remind him.

"I said make freinden." Eber shook his head again.

"I told you I was too old for—"

"For such behavior." Eber pinned him with a sharp look. "Blaming others seems to be your lot. You have not accepted responsibility for a great many things, Benuel. I had hopes when you came to stay with us that it might help you. After all the trouble you found yourself in last year, and now your anger at your own bruder." Eber let out an exhausted breath. How many times had Daed done the same? "When you joined the church, you made a commitment to Gott."

"I did not break it either! I may have played a part in what happened last year, and I admitted to it, but I never lied. I had no idea what Caleb was going to do that day. A day that is now a year behind me!"

"So you have excuses for the drinking and for not abiding by the law?"

Ben struggled to make his case. He had been that boy parents prayed their kinner never hung out with, but that was behind him now. He had changed. A full year he had dedicated to becoming a better man. Yet how could he move past his mistakes when they were so often tossed back into his face? "I was a youngie and made a bad choice, but not now. Since I have been here, I have done nothing to embarrass you."

"Have you not? I have a houseful of *menner* who say differently." Eber pointed to the inside where men lingered despite already instructing Ben to do the right thing.

"She kissed me! I was also attacked by that Jonas bu too." Did no one hear a thing Ben said all afternoon?

"A bu," Eber scoffed, flinging an arm in the air. "And I reckon you couldn't set her straight. That you are a victim in all of this. . .with a hundred-pound woman!"

Nothing was harder on a man's pride than answering such a question, but if he was going to get out of this trouble LeEtta had pulled him into, honesty was the only way. "I am."

"You were seen lying with her!"

"Watching clouds." Again, Ben felt his manhood slip under the dark shades of his grandfather's temper. The hole was getting deeper, and he knew it.

"I've known LeEtta since she was a boppli and her mamm left this earth. Her family has been struggling, and you have only made matters worse by ruining their reputation."

Ben said nothing to this. It didn't matter. No one would ever believe him over an innocent maed—who was not so innocent, he'd like to add. Did she plan this? He knew there were desperate maedels out there who'd do anything for a husband.

Ben liked to think LeEtta was as innocent as he was in all of this, but the truth was, Dawdi was right. Ben wasn't the best judge of character. Everyone he had ever cared for betrayed him in the end.

"We all must make sacrifices for others. I think Gott has—"

"A sense of humor." Ben kicked his boot against a loose board. Now he'd have to fix that. He groaned.

"He does, but laughing or naet, He will expect you to do what is right."

Ben was not marrying LeEtta. Dawdi could bend to keep the peace and stand up for him, but that was hoping for rain during a drought. "By marrying a stranger! I don't know her! I don't live here! I'm going home as soon as I earn enough for my own land."

Eber lifted a brow. "I don't reckon you're strangers now. A man cannot aim for too many directions and expect to hit only one target. Are you not willing to take responsibility for your part? Do you not realize it's not always about you, but others too?"

A cold silence sliced between them as thunder moved in the distance. His grandfather wasn't just talking about how this would affect their family once word spread. It wasn't just his reputation being scrutinized. Many would be affected by one woman's bold attempt to impress her friends. Had not his mamm already faced enough for his past deeds? His shoulders sank at the thought of bringing more heartache to his family.

"Even if I did agree to this, she won't marry me." At least Ben hoped not.

"She will, because that is what she has been instructed to do. Arlen will not see peace until it is done. LeEtta knows her place, and now you will learn yours. You will live with them and work as you have been doing. I expect you to see over the farm, as Arlen cannot tend to it as he once did. If you choose to return to Ohio once you secure a place of your own, then so be it, but you won't be going back alone." With that final demand, Eber slipped back inside the house.

Ben was drowning, yet he couldn't even stay under long enough to let out a good angry scream. He'd been tricked. His reputation once more smudged. That was the root of it. One woman in need of a husband. One man in need of free help. A slew of men ensuring both got what they wanted. He was the outsider who played right into their hands.

The wind crept out of his lungs as reality caved in on him. His knees weakened. If ever he needed mercy, it was now. Maybe it wasn't mercy he needed but a miracle.

Inside, the men continued talking, but Ben could no longer hear Arlen's commanding voice over the rain beating down hard on the tin roof. "Lord, You know I am not ready for marriage. I've tried hard to abide by Your rules. I'm not perfect, but I cannot do this thing they are asking of me. My heart is set on working for my fresh start. Please do the right thing for all of us." Letting out a trembling breath, Ben ended the prayer with, "Your will, Lord. Please help me out of this."

God seldom replied, which is why Ben seldom requested anything. Desperate times called for desperate prayers, and this time the answer came when the door opened and Bishop Graber stepped out. Ben was praying God was in a merciful mood. Perhaps it was a bishop's mercy that was going to rescue him from this silly misunderstanding. The man had been observant and quiet during most of the visit.

Ben was the last man any woman deserved to be strapped to, and he would say just that. No bishop would agree to a hurried marriage like what Arlen Miller was demanding—and what kind of father would have his daughter marry a stranger?

The bishop's dark hat was still covered in plastic to protect it from the rain that had once again found the small community. He was the same height as Ben, but the years visible on him weren't as hard as Dawdi's had been.

"Looks to be settling in for another spell." The bishop looked out through the heavy rain. "My Stella doesn't much like the rain."

Ben said nothing.

"She once survived a flood as a child. It still unsettles her." The bishop backed away from the splattering of the rain. "LeEtta reminds me a lot of her in many ways. Some women don't get to start life out as others. They face hardships few of us can understand." He turned his head and smiled.

Ben wasn't sure what hardships LeEtta faced, but even if she had, he wasn't marrying her, no matter how much the bishop talked her up.

"She has been a gift to many here, lending a hand when needed."

Ben noticed that too. It was what attracted him to her—the way she spoke well of others and kept busy as opposed to being idle. He had hoped to enjoy a few laughs getting to know her. Someone to pass the time with. Never once in his thoughts had he believed it would land him here, talking with a bishop.

Ben fisted his hands at his sides as heavy drops of rain rolled off the porch roof. No matter what he thought he knew of LeEtta, he had been wrong. That kiss was proof of her masked identity.

"You have come to spend some time with us, and yet you have found more than you planned for."

"I did," Ben finally responded. His history with such men had taught him silence earned him a better outcome.

"Gott does like to remind us during these times in our lives that our paths are not our own." Why he smiled, Ben hadn't a clue. It was disturbing. "Tell me how you came to be standing on this porch. Let me hear your part of it." The bishop leaned on one post.

"I told you and her father the truth already."

"Humor me," the bishop said flatly.

"We were just talking and watching clouds." *You told her she was beautiful.* She was beautiful, but pretty things often distracted men. Ben faced the bishop. "She kissed me. I don't know why, as I didn't even encourage it, but she appeared just as shocked by it as I was." Did he dare share that he welcomed the kiss? That her eyes had a way of making his heart beat faster and faster. Ben decided it was best to keep the private details to himself. "When that kid showed up and started shouting and pushing me, she ran off." That kid. Ben's temper returned. He should have squeezed him a little harder.

"Ach, Jonas." Bishop Graber shook his head in understanding. "A strong will for sure. I have suspected he's had eyes for her for some time, but youngies tend to have stars for many before they are men smart enough to know who Gott intends for them. LeEtta is a good woman, and I reckon many would be glad to be in your position."

"My position," Ben said between clenched teeth. "A man has a right to choose his own fraa."

"Jah, he does." He took a step closer. "Jonas is a bu with much to learn yet. You are naet," the bishop reminded him. "You have a good eye. She has always tended to Arlen and Iola and has never given me reason to worry over her." He scratched his jaw where his dark beard sported a few strands of gray. "This is why it's hard for me to hear you say that this is her doing. I'm sure it was just as hard for Arlen to hear of it."

Ben let his gaze fall. No father wanted to hear one of their own stepped out of line. Had not his own father suffered as much under Ben's rebelliousness?

"Arlen aims to protect her reputation from what will come of this. A father's duty is not an easy one. You will someday come to understand better. This matter has added much worry to him. He is struggling right now, and already has been struggling to keep the farm up. There is much work needed there."

"I'm sorry about all of that, but I don't see how. . ."

"He might demand you marry her, but he is also offering you much too."

Ben didn't want a farm in Kentucky. He wanted the one he had been keeping his eye on back home. He didn't want an inheritance that came at such a great cost to his dream.

"A man could make a fresh start, earn his way, and start a family, even if he had different plans. Life can be a blessing and come to us easily, unless we make it hard."

"It isn't easy to have plans and be forced to abandon them either."
Like having a father who gave your inheritance to another. Was all of
this his punishment for a few boyhood antics? Ben wasn't marrying
for land's sake.

"Let me let you in on a secret." He leaned closer again, the glint
in his eye too playful for Ben's liking. "Gott does not care what our
plans are. Only His. I know you have made a few bad choices, as we
all have." The bishop shifted uneasily. "What's come of those who
were with you last year?"

Ach, the bishop knew about Caleb and Landis. "Nothing like this,"
Ben said, lifting his chin. Life wasn't fair. It earned you punishment
when you did nothing. It stole your future, simply for being in the
wrong place at the wrong time. "They had to face a judge and insisted
that I had urged them to shoot targets in that spot. They took my gun
and made us pay some fines, but that was the end of it. It wasn't even
my idea, and I had to pay for it."

Something flickered in the bishop's dark gaze. Ben wished it was
sympathy, but he knew it for what it was. Disappointment.

"And now you are here...again. There's nothing wrong with a fresh
sunset and a purpose. You are angry for what you feel others did to you."

"I apparently have a habit of trusting the wrong people." Ben *was*
angry. He was angry at his friends for blaming him for their wrong-
doing. He was angry at his father, who stripped him of his future. He
was angry at LeEtta for being the very reason he was standing here
disputing his future with a bishop. If she had just not looked at him
with doe eyes, and if she just hadn't let the moment sweep her away...

"Anger makes a man tired before his time. It robs him of sleep and
peace. We must put our trust in Gott. Words and deeds have ripples,
and if you ever want those waters to calm, you must try to not disturb
them so often. I see you are not alone in this, but good fruit does not
grow on a bad tree."

Ben didn't care about his metaphors. He wasn't in a boat nor did
he own a fruit tree. He had been used, and now he was being asked to

pay half the cost. "I won't marry a stranger."

The bishop considered the rain once more as it slowed to a steady trickle. "I cannot force you, although Arlen hopes I will. But I won't. Nor will I write to your bishop about the matter. I suspect word will reach him no matter what, but I do believe there are some things a man has to decide for himself and not be forced into."

Ben let out a thankful breath. His future had been given back to him, and this could soon all be behind him.

"But I do wonder what will come of LeEtta if she is with child."

"A child? It was a kiss!" Ben stepped back defensively, bumping into a chair and nearly knocking him on his backside. He quickly righted himself. This gossip game had gone over the fence and hit the road at a gallop.

"I was told differently."

"The boy is lying like a rug."

"Well, now," the bishop turned. "You ask me to believe you, yet not another."

Ben did not admire the bishop's duty one bit. From his view, it was two sides to the same story, and Ben was the outsider.

"I was given his word too, a firsthand account from one who was there, and I spoke with LeEtta."

"Then, surely, she told you that she kissed me."

"She admitted to her part but didn't deny that a sin outside of marriage was made."

"That's not right." So she had trapped him. Ben tossed his arms in the air and groaned.

Sorrow filled the older man's expression. "There will be a wedding kumm Thursday at the Miller home." He winked cunningly. "It's up to you if you show up or naet."

Naet! Ben turned.

"I'm sure folks will. . .understand, and her shame will hopefully be forgotten. . .in time. I know my Stella lived with feeling ashamed for twenty-five years. I do tend to look on the bright side of things. My

Stella always tells me to do so. So I reckon if you walk away, perhaps a better man might see LeEtta's worth. Don't you think?"

A better man? The bishop was trying to make Ben feel guilty or mess with his head. Well, it wouldn't work. Ben didn't kiss her. He most certainly didn't take advantage of her. His throat became sandpaper. What would folks think of him if he turned tail and ran? What would his folks think once word traveled north? Was there a better man out there worthy of her? Ben's mind maneuvered over a hundred peaks and valleys all of a sudden.

"A man with a faithful fraa, a farm to work, and Gott in his heart is a man with much."

Ben agreed. He'd always held the same thought.

"LeEtta will weather it. . .as she has always done." The bishop stepped to the top step. "I must get going. Stella doesn't like being alone on these days, and that's when, as a man, I know Gott wants me to be nearest to her."

CHAPTER TEN

LeEtta splashed her face with cool water and lifted her head to stare into the tiny oval mirror. "You are getting married," she told herself, as if needing instructions on which direction to move her feet next. She didn't dare mention to her friends that this wasn't the best day of her life. As far as they knew, she was in love. Instant and fast-moving, not based on her stupid attempt to be just like them and not herself. She had been a fool, ruining not only her life but Ben's too. She was going to be sick.

"Kumm on, LeEtta. We must see you ready now," Mammi called from the next room. LeEtta could hear the sounds of the crowd downstairs. Friends and family readying all for her special day. On tiptoe, she quietly moved down the hall and into her room. Outside, her rooster crowed. He was better than a dog announcing more buggies arriving.

"Benuel Ropp will see you in this green dress and know just how blessed Gott has made him this day," Mammi Iola ensured. LeEtta did like this shade of green and appreciated her grandmother helping her sew it so quickly, but she was certain Ben wasn't feeling very blessed right now. In fact, his future had been kidnapped. He could have any woman he wanted, yet, because of Jonas and her own selfishness, his future was set. Unless he did what she hoped he would do. Run.

"What if my feet won't let me move and I forget what to say?"

"Ach, nerves can be powerful things. Love has the power to right all wrongs and see us through all kinds of indigestion. Just focus on the bright side of this," Mammi said, pinning her wedding apron into place. "He's here, waiting just outside for you both to start a life together. That says much about the kind of man he is."

LeEtta flinched. He was there. Well, he could still change his mind, she measured, but she had to admit that it did speak well of the man. She'd not expected Ben to arrive last evening for the wedding frolic. *But he did.*

While friends and family had helped set up tables and benches, he avoided her, jah, but she had avoided him too. Ben had seen to clearing the yard, spreading fresh gravel, and setting up the large canopy tent the Hiltys let them rent at a fair price. While women focused on desserts and salads, she and Eunice stamped out paper cards with guest names and filled glass vases with tiny stones, water, and a floating flower petal candle. A few friends had seen to arranging fall flowers, while Daed and a few of the men set up cookstoves along the center for the wedding meal. Mammi Iola took the role of head cook, instructing women what to prepare and who would act as servers. LeEtta was blessed for her help, as making any decision for her one special day eluded her. She had no idea how best to apologize for what she had pulled Ben into.

It was best if she focused on the bright side, as Mammi suggested. Ben had to feel something for her to be here. A marriage could bloom from that, could it not? He had many fine qualities to consider, even if she barely knew him. He was handsome, though looks shouldn't matter, but a woman could get lost in those eyes of his. He was also strong—plenty strong to help Daed with the harvest. Her shoulders lifted at the thought. How many nights had she fretted over her father's health? She couldn't count.

Ben wanted a farm and land of his own. Had he not told her of his lost inheritance? Perhaps Ben would be so content with what he was being given, he might not mind being strapped to her after all. Ben didn't mind her rambling, and she wouldn't take lightly the sacrifice that he was making today to preserve her reputation. Maybe they wouldn't start out in the traditional way, but love could be found. . .in time. Could it not? Hope bloomed in her heart and brought a tender warmth to her chest.

LeEtta thought of the kiss once more. Whatever had gotten ahold of her had clearly spread over Ben too, for he hadn't stopped her. No, he had pulled her closer and deepened their connection. A hot blush warmed over her at the memory. She was not the kind of woman who kissed others. In fact, she was the last person she knew who would waste a first kiss on someone who had no intention of sticking around. Ben had made it clear he had no interest in courting her, but he had offered his friendship. Yet he was here. Mammi said so.

"I'm the one getting married." LeEtta forged a smile and tilted her head to her grandmother as Mammi Iola swiped a tear from her cheek.

"Jah, and I wish Laura were here, helping you get ready for it."

"I'm happy *you* are here. I can't imagine getting through this without you." LeEtta embraced her grandmother. Mammi Iola had taught her everything she knew, as well as some things LeEtta didn't need, and she was there when LeEtta needed her the most.

Mammi brushed the quilt on the bed and sat down, darting LeEtta a somber expression. "I know Arlen has not spoken of such things with you, but the relationship between a husband and wife is very different than that of a man and a woman."

LeEtta glanced toward the bed. She had read enough books and listened to Eunice plenty to know courting and marriage were two very different things. At that thought, her heart panicked, and it began another unsure race with no ending. Ben was still a stranger to her. When Mammi spoke of going after what you wanted in life, not simply waiting for Gott to deliver it to you, LeEtta wished she had shared this part with her then.

"Kumm, sit. I should share with you what I once shared with your mother. A fraa's duty has many parts, but I'm certain you will discover some are easier than others, and some. . ." Mammi smiled. "Some create bonds that can never be broken. Bonds so strong that life springs forth out of them."

LeEtta eased down onto the edge of the bed and listened as Mammi Iola gave a horrifying detail of a true marriage. Fear shivered over her as she clutched her middle. She would have certainly not thought to kiss Ben, or any man, if she'd known the trappings of such boldness.

LeEtta remembered, as a girl, once asking her father about the birds and the bees. His reply was that bees sting and birds lay eggs. Of course, she had been but eleven at the time and was curious as to why when she heard Mandy Schwartz talking up birds and bees and kissing during recess. This was nothing like that.

"I don't know if I can—" LeEtta sucked in a breath. "Why would he ever consider marrying me? I don't know anything!"

"You know all there is to know, my dear. Don't you fret. You make a fine match. Even Hazel and the bishop think so. Your positive look on life suits his headstrong nature. You can plant good seeds together. Tend to them, watch them grow, and cultivate them when weeds start to take over. Jah, you will reap your own harvest." Mammi's brow rose, and giddiness bloomed on her face as she stood. "Well, let's not waste the day. Best you hurry on downstairs. Your husband will be waiting for ya."

As Mammi slipped out of the room, LeEtta stared at the bed with a fresh panic. Being a fraa was more than cooking and cleaning. It was caring for someone more than yourself. It was giving more than receiving. She had no qualms with that. She would do anything to help Ben through this, seeing as he was giving up so much for her, but how much she would have to give scared her to pieces.

The right thing wasn't always right at all. Weddings were held at the bride's house, and they were usually happy occasions. This was not his community, yet as the strong wafts of chicken infused the air, he was glad he wasn't completely alone.

His parents had taken the news surprisingly well when Ben had called them on Sunday. Daed wasn't even grumpy after the long drive coming here, though he had mentioned more than a handful of times that winter weddings were the best. Ben agreed with his farmer-father's idea of convenience, but some things couldn't be planned for. Ben gritted his teeth and straightened his vest. This marriage needed no more trouble starting off.

He hadn't been inside yet, and he gave the small two-story home that was now to be his home a judgmental scrutiny before slipping in the back door, hoping to avoid as many people as possible. He'd entered a washroom, if the gas-powered wringer washer and shelves of laundry soaps, Sevin dust, and Miracle-Gro were any indication. The floor was cemented and painted with at least a half-dozen coats of light brown, oil-based paint—the color of mud.

The kitchen was to his right, and there was no other way inside without walking through the bustle of women preparing salads, adding icing on cookies, and keeping little ones from tipping small cups of water over a freshly polished linoleum floor that resembled wood.

Two small windows over the sink and another at his right filled the room with enough light that it was hard to remain in the shadows. They held pots of violets, herbs, and what looked like a dying geranium being nursed back to health.

It was homey, with golden cabinets constructed along one wall and under the rich gray stone countertops currently holding pans of potatoes and all the other wedding notions. In the far corner were canisters of flour, sugar, and chocolate chips. He smiled a little.

Mamm looked over her shoulder, sensing him near. She always liked being part of something. He didn't see what she was cooking, but he knew she'd be browning butter soon to add to her noodles. One thing he looked forward to today.

"I am surprised, but I am very happy to meet my new daughter-in-law," she had told him this morning over breakfast. Mamm had cried, but she often did anytime couples married or bopplin were born.

Ben floated his mamm a tender grin before moving stealthily along the wall and passing a homemade rack overflowing with spices before continuing into the next room. The living room was a tight fit with all the men gathered inside.

Ben nodded to Arlen, who looked up from a battered recliner that Ben suspected was older than he was. Another recliner, small and dainty and the color of a rusty nail, sat across from him and was currently filled with a large man whose beard lay across his protruding middle, aiming straight at Bishop Graber across the room. A propane lamp hung overhead, while another was housed and protruding over a magazine rack.

The couch was draped in an old quilt. There, his family sat. Three generations of Ropps. Sam looked up and gave an encouraging smile. Ben quickly turned away, wordless on what to say to any of them. He certainly wasn't sharing out loud his wish not to be here. Daed didn't need yet another reason to be disappointed in him.

Ben was tempted to turn around and stalk back outside. Instead, he moved to the bottom of the stairs, tucked between two walls separating the kitchen and sitting room.

Casting a brow heavenward, he wondered what part of God's plan this was. *A stolen kiss. A forced marriage. A home he didn't want to live in.* Did God see the good in a man or just his mistakes? He was here, doing the right thing for everyone, yet no mercy was spared for him.

No matter. Wasn't the first time Ben had to face a day out of his control. He'd follow through, but he'd not give his heart to a woman who had deceived him, just as he couldn't conjure up a single sentence for the brother who had taken from him.

Since that kiss, his life has spiraled into a bad dream, but now that he had all his senses, Ben knew he needed to establish a few rules for his future. He needed to speak to LeEtta. Set things straight before everything started. He had thought to do so yesterday during the cleaning frolic, but no sooner would he see her dart one way than she'd see him and dart another. Guilt tended to make one scurry off.

Slipping up the narrow staircase quickly, Ben aimed to seek out the one responsible for this whole mess. The stairs groaned beneath his weight, and as he reached the top, he couldn't ignore that one step was dangerously in need of repair.

Which room was hers? He studied four doors. "LeEtta," Ben whispered. He heard small footsteps from behind the nearest door and stepped up to it. The knob turned slowly, revealing the top of a crisp white kapp.

"You came," she muttered, surprised that he had. Did she not think her plan had worked in her favor?

Ben pushed his way inside, closing the door behind him.

"You shouldn't be in here." She turned her troubled eyes his way and clutched her hands to her stomach. She didn't look like a woman who had tricked him but one as nervous as he was.

"Haven't you heard?" he said. "I don't care much about following the rules." She looked beautiful. A splinter of a sunbeam landed on her perfectly. The green suited her pale red hair and eyes the color of pale skies before a storm. His heart did a trick, kicking a little harder in his chest, but he managed to look beyond her, lest he be fooled again.

"Ben, I'm so sorry. I tried to explain—"

Ben held up a hand. "I don't want to hear your excuses. We are too late for that, are we naet?"

She lowered her head as if a woman accused.

"I'm here because I have to do the right thing, but you should know before you walk down those stairs that our marriage will not be a traditional marriage. I will not share with you what you've already given away."

"What I have given away?" Her forehead formed a frail line, and then it must have hit her what he was implying. "I didn't want to marry either. Well, not like this anyhow. I can't believe you would think me capable of such. Think me the kind of woman who would—" She brought a hand to her mouth and smothered a startled gasp.

"I don't know what to think." He didn't. "It's too late for all that now. We are in this as partners, no more."

She nodded, understanding, accepting his conditions.

He expected more from her but was glad she knew where they both stood in all of this. "Also, my family arrived this morning. Well, my immediate family." He cleared his throat and strolled to the window. Despite Mamm's eagerness to call all their cousins, aunts, and uncles, Ben had managed to persuade her that he wanted a quiet, no-fuss occasion, because his bride-to-be was...shy. *What a thought*, he rolled his eyes.

"Their names are John and Miriam. Mamm is excited to meet you. You are her first daughter-in-law." A fact that he had only now considered. "You should know they will be staying the night here before heading back home tomorrow morning." Quiet lingered behind him. Did she realize what he was saying, that they would have to share a room to spare his family the truth?

She inhaled a breath and let it out slowly. He was none too happy about it either. The last thing Ben wanted to do was share a bed with a woman who'd trapped him into a life he didn't want and tasted like sunshine.

CHAPTER ELEVEN

It was finished.

The only good thing about this wedding was that it was finally over. What was done was done. LeEtta had pulled him into this mess, but the way Ben saw it, now it was *their* mess.

Throughout the day, Ben stole a few glances at his new bride. She didn't look at all like a woman capable of deceiving others. In fact, she looked pale and alone and like a victim of the same cruel fate as he had found himself in. However, had he not learned that he was not a good judge of character? Caleb, Landis, and his own family were proof of that. Looks could be terribly deceiving.

She had quietly obeyed instructions to kneel while the bishop prayed over them. Ben wondered if she heard a word of the prayer. He didn't want to dismiss who she was, but he never liked seeing others ill, and LeEtta certainly looked ill.

Most women talked up their wedding day. His sisters were always chatting about colors and silly things for the day when they would wed. Mary even had a secret collection of magazines hidden in her room for future ideas. Ben wondered if LeEtta had imagined this day: best friends at her side, the scent of rosemary chicken filling the house. . . . Was she disappointed it was him she had chosen?

Once the vows were exchanged, Ben suffered through the noonday meal and smiled gently as they opened a few gifts. The community had been wonderfully generous. When asked how long they had been courting by an older woman LeEtta introduced as Mary Alice Yoder, Ben quickly responded, "Long enough to know her heart." LeEtta stared at him sorrowfully, knowing the truth behind the comment.

"I knew you had an eye for her, but you don't waste no time, do ya?" Leo Hostetler remarked.

"Life can be short," Ben replied.

Once the final supper was served and folks began making their way home, Leo winked and told him, "Don't do anything I wouldn't do," before leaving too. Despite the tremor in his chest, Ben had tossed him a smile. His first night as a married man would be nothing like he had always hoped for it to be.

While the women worked to tidy up the kitchen, Ben set aside those unsettling thoughts as he and his father began carrying Ben's belongings upstairs.

"Where do we stow these?" John asked, carrying a suitcase filled with Ben's clothing.

"That second room there." Ben motioned with his head. At least that was the room LeEtta had been in this morning when he informed her their marriage would never be a traditional one. Ben struggled with two boxes he suspected consisted of his work shoes, farmer magazines, and possibly his ball and glove from long-missed boyhood days. Its oblong shape stretched his arms.

"LeEtta fixed up the room next door for you and Mamm. I hope you are both comfortable there." The Millers' house wasn't large compared to the houses nearby. Two stories with slanted ceilings and narrow stairs. There were only three bedrooms compared to the six Ben had grown up in.

But who built more rooms for a house that would never be filled? Ben couldn't imagine how the two dealt with the loss of LeEtta's mother so early on. Arlen had never remarried, leaving LeEtta an only child. The thought barbed him, knowing that his father-in-law at least had one child. One he clearly would move mountains for. Ben, on the other hand, would never know the joys of fatherhood.

Ben would have taken the spare room, but if his parents knew of the deception, their relationship would be even more bent than it was. At least now Daed could speak to him without frowning. Arlen in the nearby room and his schwester downstairs, sleeping on the couch, left a man no place to lay his head without someone noticing. He had considered slipping out into the barn. It had to be more comfortable out there than in a house that suddenly felt like a prison, but he'd find a place to scratch out for himself once his family returned to Ohio. Surely he could manage one night without letting LeEtta's beauty tempt him further.

"It's for a night, and better than sleeping in a van, for sure." Dad set down the suitcase and gave the room a scrutiny. "Not *verra* big, but small houses tend to grow quickly when love resides within them." Ben flinched at the comment.

"Your mamm and I are happy to see you settled, but. . ."

"But?" Here it came. Ben readied himself for his father's common negativity.

"Waiting would have given you longer to know one another. You have not known this woman verra long. We are confused by the urgency of this wedding."

"No more than I was," Ben muttered, scooting the boxes against a far wall and placing his suitcase on top.

"We did not expect you to kumm here for more than putting distance between us. I know you are sore, but. . ."

"Sam never cared about the farm as I did, but it does not matter now. A man must make a start somewhere." Ben hated the gravity in his tone. Sam had thought it best to spend the night with their grandparents. Proof that Sam, like Daed, didn't think Ben was capable of making good choices.

If they only knew what I was giving up, for her and for them. He was saving everyone from embarrassment. Was that not worth something?

"Change comes to us all, Sohn. Sam is not like us. His heart isn't set on farming the way we have for generations, yet he has a good head on his shoulders. He never"—Daed scanned the room once more—"got himself into fixes either. I worry this decision to marry so quickly is you making another bad choice without thinking it through."

Once more he would be scolded for something out of his control. Ben felt his blood run hot. "It's not. LeEtta is not a woman to make a bad decision. She chose me." *Unlike you.* "I've learned plenty to not be so trusting of others." Ben didn't like butting heads with his father. . . again. It left a sour taste in his mouth, but his father seemed to always want confrontation over quiet.

"Jah, but if you trust in the Lord, all will kumm right." Did he dare tell his father he had tried trusting Gott with his life, but look where it had gotten him? "There is much I never told you about being a father or a husband."

"I'll figure it out, as I always do." Ben waved him off. He would not take advice from his father. He would not follow his example that only left one son empty-handed and another heavy with praise. "But I do hope you will welcome LeEtta as part of the family." When he'd bid his mother good night, it had not passed his notice when Mamm embraced her new daughter-in-law too. At least Mamm wasn't suspicious of this union.

"Your mamm already has. You're the first to wed, and she's already mooning over when to expect her first grosskind."

That won't happen, he refused to say. No way would he allow his heart to ever be fooled again.

LeEtta had never been jumpy in her own house before, but now that everyone was settled for the night, her nerves were racing to the edge of cliffs.

Running a dishcloth over the table once more, she hoped the clock would chime another passing hour soon. She was in no hurry to go to bed, despite how weary she was, but there was nothing left to tidy unless she wanted to begin washing tablecloths and get an early start. "Nee, you'll wake everyone," she chided herself. She was going to have to face what was to come sooner or later. Her breath shuddered as she lifted a lamp and glanced up the gloomy, dark stairs.

All was quiet, with the exception of one of Ben's sisters snoring in the next room. Ben's brother had left with Eber and Mary. Sam had been wonderfully polite, but LeEtta couldn't ignore the awkward tension between the brothers. Hopefully, the rift between them would settle soon.

A strangled snore cut through the air once more. Sam might have simply chosen a good night's sleep, which he would not find sleeping under the same roof as such noise as that.

Ben and his father had moved all his things up there. . .into her room. *It's our room now.* Her imagination ran wild with all the things she thought she knew about husbands and wives and what went on between them in the shadows of night. Mammi Iola had been very forthcoming about that. LeEtta wished that she hadn't done so. Her own imagination had been so much easier to stomach than Mammi Iola's romantic notions.

The door was closed, and she slowly turned the knob. At the sound of movement in the next room, she quickly slipped inside. Her eyes looked directly toward the bed. The blue and white quilt lay perfectly flattened over the top, just as it had this morning. She felt safe enough to let out a pent-up breath.

Ben must have taken to the barn. Wherever he decided to sleep was fine by her. It had been a long day of facing friends and family full of uneasy questions about her rush to marry, knowing a lie sat just beneath the forged smile on her face.

She set the lamp on her dresser and slipped off her shoes and socks. Then she relieved herself of her apron, carefully folding and setting it aside. She'd properly wash and stow it away come morning, along with her wedding dress.

Her arms felt like noodles as she removed her kapp and began removing the pins from her hair. She was bone-tired. Stress and worry had made her muscles stiff and uncooperative, but if God chose her to be Ben's fraa, she'd step into it with all the best intentions.

She made a few swipes with a brush through her hair and considered how she could build this life between them. They had been instantly drawn to one another, had they not? Eventually she could grow more comfortable with him, and he with her.

It would have come naturally, she liked to think, if Jonas hadn't seen to running to the bishop. Thankfully, he hadn't come today, and for that she was grateful. LeEtta didn't harbor ill feelings, but it was too early yet for her heart to bestow forgiveness.

The floor creaked behind her, and she froze, trying to determine exactly where the sound was located. Sucking in a breath, LeEtta turned slowly to the shadowy corner. The harvest moon had filled much of the house with needed light, but at this end of the house, it barely reached the corners.

"Ben?" Her eyes squinted, barely making out the long shape stretched out on the floor.

"Jah, it's me."

"I thought—" She clamped her lips tight. He need not know how she hoped to crawl into bed and fall fast asleep without a care to his needs.

"I told you I would not honor this marriage that way, but I will not have my mudder think differently. Go to bed, LeEtta. It's late."

Guilt stabbed her knowing he had to lie to his own mother. What a terrible person she was. She'd disrupted his sweet family. He rolled over, his makeshift bed on the floor looking as uncomfortable as she felt. Still in her wedding dress, LeEtta quickly slipped under the quilt.

Sleep would be hard sought for this night. With insides riddled with guilt for disrupting Ben's life so fully, and knowing he was sleeping at arm's length, LeEtta pushed aside her weariness and decided to stay vigilant. She pulled the book hidden between the mattress and boxspring and did what she often did on nights when her thoughts were troubled with something

Life was complicated. It was a whole lot easier focusing on someone else's life, and she did have a new mystery to solve. Her newest heroine had left the Amish to become a police officer, and LeEtta suspected the killer, who had taken his life years ago, wasn't so dead after all. It was always best to read about someone else's story when your own had too many torn-out pages.

CHAPTER TWELVE

The sun was still sleeping as LeEtta slipped out of her room and quickly changed from her wedding dress to her everyday chore dress and matching apron. Despite a sleepless night, she wanted to make an impression on Ben's family. Eunice was always trying to impress Joanie Hostetler, and Ben clearly held a close connection with his own mamm that LeEtta admired. She would do whatever she could to not disappoint him. Perhaps she and Miriam would become fast freinden too.

Yesterday was gone. The wedding she numbly followed through with and its expectations were gone with it. It was time to welcome a fresh new day, even if it would be riddled with uncertainty and plenty of obstacles.

When she turned on the propane lamp and began preparing breakfast just as she did every morning, LeEtta felt no different being married, but she wouldn't let herself succumb to ungratefulness. God had provided for her all the years of her life, and surely He would see her through the uncertainty in the days to come.

Within a short time, LeEtta had put together the perfect breakfast: scrambled eggs with cheese and fluffy biscuits nicely golden on top. She had opened the last two jars of canned sausage patties, eager to see Ben's family enjoy the special blend of seasonings she had created.

Even the gravy turned out just as it should, peppered lightly and not too thin.

The blueberry muffins were Daed's favorite. That's why LeEtta made them with an extra crumbly top, since she knew that after years of living with just the two of them, he too appeared to be a little uneasy this morning. He chewed every bite so slowly that it must have become liquid in his mouth as he talked. Unfortunately, Ben's family talked about everything from tobacco prices to favorite wedding desserts instead of filling their mouths. Clearly, they didn't find breakfast very appealing. So many years of quiet had skidded away under endless chatter and a few left-handed compliments.

LeEtta forced herself to smile as she began clearing the table. Lisa, Ben's youngest schwester, found nothing worth tasting on her plate. LeEtta normally didn't add so much pepper to her eggs, and adding more salt did them little help, but the blueberry muffins were as moist as Hazel Fisher's. The local baker had taken LeEtta under her apron, teaching her many skills a mother normally would, and that had earned LeEtta not a crumb left from the whole batch of muffins.

"It's a shame we must return today," Miriam said, moving beside her, no stranger to the next duty, and she began filling the sink with warm water and soap. Miriam was wonderfully kind, but LeEtta knew she had questions about the urgency of their marriage. Thankfully, she didn't ask and only welcomed her new daughter-in-law with loving arms. She wished Miriam knew how much that simple embrace meant to her.

"I would have enjoyed more time getting to know you," Miriam continued.

LeEtta warmed from knowing Ben's mother was as kind and loving as she had hoped she would be. For the first time, LeEtta had something beyond the love between a father and a daughter. She had a family.

"We had about as much time as Ben did." The muttered insult came from Mary. She was seventeen, with looks that were similar to

Ben—including the frown that made LeEtta uneasy from the moment she introduced herself. LeEtta didn't bruise easily, and she let the comment go. According to Eunice, you didn't have to agree with family, you simply had to love each of them. LeEtta would love them, even Mary.

"I pray you have a safe trip home and return quickly. I'm sure Ben would enjoy having you all with him longer too." LeEtta began scraping John's plate clean. At least Ben's daed had eaten her eggs, but he clearly didn't find her homemade sausage to his liking.

"Or you could both come to Ohio for a visit," Miriam added. "I know you will need time to settle. Two people have much to learn in those first weeks, but winter will be here before we know it, and I don't want to wait until spring."

"Neither do I," LeEtta said with complete honesty, though she didn't want to think about all the things she needed to learn. How many years had LeEtta prayed for a family? Though it was not exactly the prayer she had cast up, God had answered it.

"If Ben even comes." Lisa took up her plate and moved to the sink. "You know he won't return now that Sam has the farm. Cannot blame him for it." Lisa was not the sister LeEtta had conjured up in her vivid imagination, but one didn't always get to separate the wheat from the chaff. Sometimes, you had to simply take what was given and be thankful for it.

"That will be enough talk of things best forgotten. You are a visitor in your bruder's home. Mind your tongue and help tidy up." John spoke sharply.

LeEtta glanced at her daed. Was he troubled with the comment? It was his home, was it not? She could see tension in his shoulders as he considered the newcomers at his table. Ben had mentioned his sisters had wanted their part of the farm as well, but in the end, John and Miram saw fit to leave it in Sam's hands. Daed often said a father knows best, and though LeEtta had her own thoughts about that, she did feel the Ropp siblings weren't realizing just what they did have.

They had a home, a family, and people who loved them. Wasn't that plenty? Hopefully, she could help melt some of the ice built around these hearts before they severed.

The front door opened, and Sam appeared in the kitchen doorway. He clearly had not slept either, given the dark circles under his eyes. He had the same dark hair and eyes as his older brother, but unlike the rest of the Ropp siblings, LeEtta sensed a gentle spirit within him that she could appreciate.

"He smelled food and found his way." Lisa giggled.

"Gut *mariye*, Sohn," John greeted.

"Let me fetch you a plate," LeEtta quickly said as the sun burst through two east-facing windows.

Sam held up a hand, stopping her. "Danke, but Mammi stuffed me to my ears before I said my so longs. Where's Ben?" His question aimed to the full room.

"I suspect he's waiting for us to leave," Mary put in. She had finally worn out pushing food around her plate and brought it to the sink. "He'll never kumm down as long as Sam's here," she whispered.

"While you wait for your driver, how about I show you men the farm?" Daed scooted back his chair and fetched his straw hat, eager to escape. Even he had tired of the outspoken sisters. John and Sam, despite being veterans at hearing the sisters go on and on, happily followed.

"It wonders me why you married our bruder. He's terribly stubborn, and you have known each other for only a short time," Mary said boldly the moment the men left the house. Three sets of eyes landed on her, waiting for her answer.

"I care for Ben," LeEtta replied quickly. "He's very kind. . .and easy to talk to."

"If you know my bruder so well," Mary continued her plight, "then you know he only came here because he needed money for land."

LeEtta closed her eyes and let out a slow breath. She didn't like that Mary was trying to make trouble between them. They had only been married a day! "Jah, I do," LeEtta said, facing her. Ben had been honest with her from the start.

"I reckon he doesn't have to work so hard now, does he?"

"Mary," Miriam tried shushing her.

"I know my husband, and all men work hard lest they not be worthy of what Gott has given them." Hopefully, in time, LeEtta could smolder out these fires that Mary was continually starting. If LeEtta had been blessed with a bruder, she would never shine a bad light on him as Mary was.

"Then you know he had to work elsewhere because Sam has all our money now to spend on cows. But since he married you, I reckon he has more land than he lost."

With that, LeEtta felt her muscles turn rigid and her skin turn cold. It was custom that once children reached an age to work outside of the home, they gifted at least half their wages to their parents. The Amish family was as one, its survival dependent on all its stretched-out parts. Had not she and her father learned how little one could live on after two years of poor crops? Devotion and sacrifice were at the center of who they were.

"God has His plan, and that is why Ben is here." LeEtta lifted her chin. "I knew the minute we met that he would be someone special in my life, and my life is sweeter now because of him. What he carries in his pocket means little to me."

As if knowing he was being summoned to defend himself, Ben lumbered into the room. His dark locks were disheveled and his eyes sunken from a long, restless night of sleeping on a hardwood floor. He had tossed and turned plenty while she quietly turned pages with soft fingertips. Sleep found them both strangers sharing such a small intimate space.

"It's a terrible thing being born a dochter and not a sohn," Lisa said seconds before turning to see her brother standing there. "Ben!"

"Being a sohn can be a terrible thing too, but not so bad as being a bruder to you two," he muttered before moving farther into the kitchen while Miriam pulled out a chair for him at the head of the table.

LeEtta knew nothing of being a part of a large family, though she did have some ideas considering Eunice was always going on about hers. She understood that siblings quarreled, but they weren't bent on making each other miserable.

Ben scanned the room, recognizing conflict in the air. His jaw clenched, but his eyes landed on her protectively. Jah, this marriage might stand a chance if he kept looking at her like that.

Mammi insisted love would come. That friendship blossomed into protectiveness and familiarity. She insisted LeEtta work to help Ben plant seeds that helped them both grow, and in turn, he would find her a dutiful fraa, worthy of his affections.

Beyond kissing, there was more. Suddenly, as she looked at her husband taking a seat at the table, she hoped the blossoming didn't take long.

CHAPTER THIRTEEN

Ben took one look at his new fraa and could see she was beside herself. Her left hand clutched her dress as tight as her lips held together. Ben could only imagine the morning she had endured without him. He glanced at his youngest sister as she pretended to dry a plate and wrinkled her nose at the chore. He knew right away Mary and Lisa were to blame. Those two had a habit of stirring up hornets' nests.

Why had he woken up so late? He knew why, because he'd never shared a room with anyone before. He liked his space and solitude when it could be found. His livelihood suited him, much better than dealing with hundreds of squealing hogs all day.

Images of last night barreled through him like a bull on the run. It had been one thing to turn and see LeEtta's long, soft hair hanging beyond her hips. In lamplight, it was enough to keep a man up all night. It was another surprise to learn he'd married a book enthusiast. He nearly smiled at the latter because thinking of those yards of her soft, pretty hair would drive him insane. It was near sunup before she finished the book. He appreciated a person who finished what they started, but how did she look so ready for the day after a night such as they had?

"Gut mariye, LeEtta." He took the seat his mother offered up, putting the images away. "Sure smells gut in here."

"Danke," LeEtta returned, a sparkle lighting up those pale blue eyes of hers. She reached into the oven, pulling out a plate she had saved for him. Perhaps marriage wasn't such a terrible thing after all. As long as he kept his heart intact, he could enjoy the rest.

"There were muffins, but. . ."

"We ate them," Mary smirked. "Had to eat something," she muttered under her breath.

"Of course you did," Ben replied.

A few hours later, Ben walked with his family to the van that had only weeks ago delivered him here. He gave his mother a long embrace. He hated being such a disappointment to her. She slipped something in his hand, smiled like mamms did when they knew things, and climbed into the blue van. He shook his father's hand and told his sisters to stay out of trouble, but when Sam remained standing there at the front passenger door, Ben knew his little brother was hoping he'd give in and tell him he was no longer sore.

Ben couldn't do that. No matter how miserable Sam looked, Ben couldn't tell him all was forgotten. How could his own brother take so easily what he knew to be Ben's?

"Blessings to you bruder, and LeEtta too," Sam said before closing the passenger side door. Ben watched the van drive away, a pinch of guilt souring his stomach, or perhaps it was that odd combination of flavors from breakfast. Either way, forgiveness was taught from the cradle, but Ben couldn't muster up even a smidgen of it right now. When the van disappeared around the bend, the tension between his shoulder blades eased. It was best to face his dismal future without his family watching him stumble through it.

Reaching into his pocket, Ben pulled out the paper. In perfect penmanship were his *aenti* Oneida's name and phone number. Ben smiled. Mamm surely only meant to remind him to call and let her know of his recent marriage. She had always been his favorite as far as aentis were concerned.

Ben would call her, even if it earned him a lecture for marrying before she was there to witness it. Then the thought hit him. Aenti

Oneida might be an answer to all his troubles. If Ben was going to work full-time and see over Arlen's farm, all while keeping a distance from his new fraa, he'd need help. Aenti Oneida was a fusser. She'd be so busy doting over LeEtta that Ben could figure out just how this nontraditional marriage was going to work.

He strolled along the drive leading to the barn and took in the place. On his right, cattle grazed along with horses. On his left, corn as far as the eye could see, vast stretching stalks the color of Mamm's supper plates, rustled in the breeze and dry air.

At least out here, he knew how to navigate. Here, he didn't stumble. He noted the northern pastures, with grass in desperate need of cutting. He'd start there. His new father-in-law clearly couldn't tackle the chore. The barn door was lopsided, with one corner buried in dirt. He added that to the list in his head and went to get familiar with his surroundings.

Inside the barn, he shot up a prayer for guidance while he tidied the large area. Hot, late summer air and cattle left an unsavory mix. He sought out a shovel once all the livestock was set out to pasture and went straight to work, mucking out the holding pens first. His boots sank. How long had it been since these floors saw daylight? He groaned under his breath. Disease could easily breed here. Then again, Arlen wasn't able, he reminded himself. Thankfully, bones healed. Soon enough, LeEtta's father would be able to lend a hand.

Ben shoveled and tossed all the manure onto the spreader wagon just outside the door. It felt good, the work, releasing a surplus of energy that had been building up in him since the bishop arrived at his door. He paused only to notice all the farm machinery lined up along this side of the barn, and a new ember ignited as he looked at the equipment so perfectly kept that it looked brand-new. Scents that he'd been missing for the last two months suddenly wrapped around him, seeping into his pores. Equipment he knew by movement and purpose, ingrained into the very fabric that made him.

Jah, at least Gott had seen fit to let him continue what he loved to do most.

Once the holding lot was cleared, he worked on the horse stalls. A faithful southern wind had already cleared out the smells, but flies swarmed relentlessly. Sweat trickled from his forehead. He removed his hat, swiping the moisture clear before replacing the shovel with a wide-surface broom and finishing off the rest.

Ben was a stickler for order. It was one thing he and Sam quarreled over plenty. Along the far wall, hay was stacked high to the ceiling. He'd climb the pile and drop down a few more bales this afternoon. Cattle didn't need much, not with grass still thick, but he knew enough about the four-legged beasts to slowly introduce them to the coming change.

Work benches sat cluttered. He'd see to putting tools up next, at least where he believed them to go. His new father-in-law surely wouldn't make a fuss as long as everything was within better reach.

At a narrow doorway with a bridle hanging just below a horseshoe, he found a small room tucked in one corner. Inside were old leather, worn-out spurs and paint cans covered in thick layers of dust and dirt. It was just the right amount of space for a man to lay his head. With enough blankets, his back would thank him, and he'd find no further temptations of strawberry-blond hair and pale blue eyes under lamplight. He didn't see LeEtta objecting, not with the frightened look of hers still burned in his mind from when she discovered him in the shadows last night. If he was careful, not even Arlen would have a clue.

He ran his hands over the stiff, chaffed leather hanging along one wall. It had been some time since everything had had a good oiling. Once he sought out oil and a few rags, Ben carried everything out to the workbench with better lighting.

Time went on as it always did. Ben had tendencies of losing track of the hour when deep in a chore, but he guessed it was nearly noon by the way his stomach was asking him to head to the house, hoping to quiet its grumbling. However, he'd never left a chore unfinished, and he ignored the plea as he worked oil over the leather in long, steady strokes. Many folks had shifted to the newer Biothane harness with its shiny gloss and durability, but Ben preferred leather in his hands.

It was raw and real and nothing like the life pushed on him.

But you agreed to it, he silently grumbled, working in more oil with a fresh vigor. He should probably search out a kettle, fill it with oil under a good fire, and give everything in here a healthy soak. How many times had his own dawdi sworn by the method?

"A chore that has long been forgotten."

Ben jerked his head toward the barn opening. Arlen stood, an ear of corn in his good hand, half-shucked. Bits of sunlight caught the mingle of gray in his beard. He wasn't old—the same age as his father, if Ben was to guess—but farming alone all these years wasn't as easy on him as it had been for his own father.

"Those have been needing attention for some time." Arlen stepped closer, taking note of the freshly cleaned barn. "I hear you plan on returning to work tomorrow."

"Can't earn a living if I don't," Ben replied.

"I hear you young folks like to take honeymoons," he said almost mockingly before scraping his boot over the concrete, his jaw tight.

"Shep offered to give me a few days off, but I don't need them." Many newly married couples did travel to Tennessee in hopes of spotting bears and riding chairlifts. His cousin Joshua had taken his new fraa to Florida. Ben wondered if LeEtta had hoped for such, but then he quickly squashed the care.

"Gut. Letty ain't got any need for seeing hills or water when we got plenty right here." Arlen moved to the long table, inspecting Ben's work as if he hadn't been doing such chores since he was school age.

"So it does," Ben replied, holding his gaze. Clearly, the idea of LeEtta going far didn't sit well with her father. Ben couldn't figure the fella out. He sheltered LeEtta, yet married her off.

"Don't be shy on oil." Arlen's command drew Ben back to the present. It had been more than two handfuls of years since someone watched over his shoulder to see a job finished. Ben held his tongue and added more oil.

"Your daed says you know plenty about running a farm."

"I know enough," Ben replied. The massaging mixed with the scent of the oil eased him back into a familiar rhythm.

"You're family now, and you can see I have more than one man my age can keep up. I'm far from old." Arlen shrugged. "But I know time will cure that soon enough. LeEtta doesn't know, but...the arm ain't gonna heal right." He lifted the blue cast upward, revealing a little dirt and the wear of dangling threads. "Dok says the elbow ain't no good, and what funds I had are already spent."

Ben lifted a brow. "You own more land than most. Surely there will be funds for a new elbow, or at least something to help you get along better, after the harvest." Even if Ben had sore feelings toward Arlen, he still didn't want to think Arlen might never be his full self again.

"There would be, if I didn't have a few hands waiting on it already," Arlen said without a care in his tone.

"LeEtta doesn't know that either?" His elder nodded, and Ben collected the severity of the situation. They were broke, and Arlen needed the harvest to pay his debts. As if his life couldn't get more complicated.

Ben internally stiffened. If he hadn't invested all his wages on his family's farm, he could have helped with this one. What little he had was a roll of hundreds that he hoped to add to his future farm. There was no sense in revisiting that sore, picking it fresh to fester. It was what it was. Ben was a farmer, and farmers had to account for many struggles. Weather, unexpected costs, livestock dying, and equipment breaking down. There was always a way out if one had the will to survive and the determination to hold on. Ben just wasn't sure surviving Arlen Miller would be as easy.

This was his struggle now too. He was married to a stranger and penniless. He'd have to figure it out. At least with the farm. The woman still was a confusion he'd not waste time on. "There are other ways."

"I won't lean on the church, but for her sake." Arlen pointed a thumb toward the house. "A man has to depend on himself." His chin lifted stubbornly.

Ben understood that. Though pride was a sin, it was embedded in some men's cores so deeply that it was mighty hard to hide. Perhaps they shared that trait.

Ben considered his options. There were always options. "Fall wheat, and we can cut a fourth cutting on that hay. It needs to be done soon though."

"The cattle need to graze it," Arlen said as if Ben suggested a dumb thought. Did he not know how much he had to bargain with?

"Not if you don't have any cattle to feed." That got the older man's attention. "Hay is high right now. With winter coming soon, folks are stocking up for their livestock. Sell off the cattle, and sell the hay except for what is needed for the horses. I make enough to keep us from starving, and there should be plenty for spring crops if we're careful."

Arlen stared at him blankly, running a hand over his cast. If he was considering Ben's thoughts, he was grinding them slowly. Was there any other option?

"I reckon the market is still holding, but we'd have to sell quickly before it goes down." Cattle always sold cheapest in winter. No one wanted to feed daily unless you were in the business of buying.

"I'll call a driver I know with a trailer and see to it right away, but. . ." Arlen paused and looked at the house again. "Don't think I didn't consider that already. It's just. . .LeEtta has had her heart set on a milker for some time."

Ben watched his frown die a slow death at the mention of his only child. Ben had never been the only child to worry over, but he understood Arlen Miller would bend rivers for his and for his livelihood. A milker wasn't such a bad idea. It would see them through this rough patch. Hopefully, LeEtta knew how to milk one. She had mentioned that Arlen was determined to keep her from laboring over the farm, though Ben sensed she wanted to.

His roll of cash would be lighter, but Ben agreed with his father-in-law. "I'll see to buying one and keep helping Shep for my wages. Both should hold us over. Do you have a full team for the harvest?"

"Jah. Moses and Mike are fine Belgians. Bishop Schwartz raised them from colts, and they're capable of keeping those three dumb animals I let myself get talked into in line." Arlen rested his good arm over his cast. "You will wear down by getting in the harvest and working full-time."

"Jah, but I'm not alone," Ben said, and he was a little taken back at his own comment. But he was married now, thanks to the man before him.

"I'll not have her working a team!" Arlen glared at him and stiffened.

Ben's own mother had helped set tobacco and pick corn. He wasn't asking more of one woman than he had of another, and he suspected this was one decision LeEtta would be happy with. Jah, he was sure of it. She wanted to do more, and more was needed. Arlen was in no position to argue that fact.

"The two shall become one. If she needed help, I'd do that for her. Your dochter is stronger than you think and is willing to do what must be done. My wife will help me."

Arlen stared at him angrily as the sound of a truck pulled in. Ben stifled a grin as he fell in line with Arlen to see who was there. The white truck was loaded down with lumber and metal.

"Someone must have taken a wrong turn."

"Nee." Arlen cocked a grin over his shoulder. "It's mine. Tomorrow a few friends will be along to help."

"You just said you were light on funds. What are you building?"

"My house," Arlen said flatly. "I can't live under your roof for long, and I suspect you'd sleep better under your own," he cocked a brow. "I ain't got blinders on, Sohn, and those old floors make a mighty racket when a man sleeps on them." With that, Arlen went to greet the delivery driver, leaving Ben to let that sink in.

Once the lumber was unloaded and stacked, Ben readied the two Belgians and began cutting hay. The weather was agreeable, according to the truck driver, and waiting was not in him.

The sounds of blades and gears were a common comfort. The

sweet-smelling scents of timothy, alfalfa, and fescue were a solidifying thing. They would be all right, he told himself. His father might not think him capable of scratching something out of nothing, but Gott certainly thought he was capable. Why else would God want him here?

Turning a wide corner, ensuring grass lay evenly to dry, movement caught his eye. Ben brought the large Belgian to a halt as he watched LeEtta stroll into the small white chicken coop and emerge clutching her apron. Pausing, she closed her eyes, took a deep breath, and lifted her face to the sun. She stood like that for a time, so he waited. Was she praying? He wasn't sure, but even at this distance, he didn't miss the smile blooming on her face as she walked back to the house. What a fix this tiny slip of a woman had put him in.

CHAPTER FOURTEEN

Her first day as a married woman, and nothing was going right. It was a good thing Ben's family wasn't here to witness the limitations of her abilities as a fraa.

LeEtta saw to cleaning the floors down to the grain after so many footsteps had left scuffs and dirt behind. She spent three whole hours scrubbing vigorously, Mary's harsh words propelling her forward. It was best to let such things fade into a dark corner to live, where all other menacing things dwelled, but she didn't like to think Ben had only married her for land or simply to not live under the same roof as a snorer and complainer like Mary Ropp.

The house smelled of lemony oil and fresh bread, and she hurried through the washing while considering how agreeable the wind outside was, but one stubborn stain was adding to her turbulent morning. She scrubbed harder, determined to see it vanish. Mammi had never schooled her on laundry, and Daed's knowledge had been limited to soap, plenty of softener, and a good breeze. LeEtta seldom tackled such a stubborn stain. The rich blue bled and embedded itself deeply, proof that Ben favored icing more than *kuche*.

She added a heap of baking soda. Had she not overheard Nancy Lengacher mention she often resorted to such? As a caregiver over an aging Englisch couple, Nancy knew plenty about stains and laundry. Still, as LeEtta worked it vigorously into the fabric, it refused to disappear. Hot water would certainly help, which she considered next. Unfortunately, it didn't.

Oh blunder. Ben would not be pleased that she couldn't even remove a stubborn stain. Setting the chore aside, she quickly put together a meat loaf. Ben hadn't even come inside at noon. There had been so many leftovers to choose from. Then she decided he may not like leftovers at all. No matter. Cutting hay all day earned her new husband a full supper.

While that was cooking in the oven, LeEtta tried tackling the stain again. She massaged in a little bleach. When that didn't help, she added a bit of dish soap. After a few more frustrating minutes, LeEtta gave up, dropping the shirt into a pan of hot water. "It just needs time to soak," she told herself with confidence.

Outside, she began pulling pins from the laundry that she had hung earlier. She pushed the laundry cart, a gift Mammi had given her two years earlier, along the line hanging from the house to a post planted firmly in the ground. Reaching the end, it suddenly dawned on her that her green dress was no longer there. Clearly, she had let herself get out of sorts. Nothing had gone well all day.

Sifting through the laundry cart, she hoped she had just overlooked it, but the dress wasn't tucked within the rest of the clothes and linens.

"Now where could a dress up and go?" Her eyes traveled to two apple trees nearby. If the wind had picked up while she was inside, perhaps one of the limbs had stolen it, but neither produced her dress. Around the house she searched, perplexed not to find it anywhere.

"It's gone!" What a thought. If the wind hadn't suddenly picked up enough to rip it from the line, someone had to have taken it. That made about as much sense as apples growing on cherry bushes. Unless. . .

A strong scent wafted out the windows and into the yard. *Burnt meat loaf.* Of all the stuff. Furthermore, she hadn't even thought about collecting eggs or feeding her hens. Her first day as a fraa and she had forgotten her everyday duties. This day was all upside down. Taking two shaky breaths, LeEtta quickly wiped away an overwhelming tear, collected the basket, and hurried back inside before she ruined supper next.

With supper safely tended to, LeEtta hurried out to the coop to deliver a most sincere apology to her white-feathered friends. "It has been a busy day, so danke for being patient with me." She gently placed egg after egg into her apron, closed the chicken coop door, and took a moment to collect herself.

Her green dress was missing, Ben's shirt was clearly not fit for church, and she only had a tiny slice of cheese left in the icehouse to melt over Daed's supper. Arlen Miller never ate a meal without cheese in it.

LeEtta closed her eyes as warm sunshine kissed her face, and she shot up a prayer. "I can't do this alone. I could use a little help if I'm going to make it work." Warmth spread all around her. The Lord would see her through. Opening her eyes, it was with fresh hope that she and Gott had reached a mutual understanding and that no matter what the rest of the day had in store, she would not tackle it alone.

LeEtta had been certain nothing could go wrong with meat loaf. After all, it was one of Daed's favorites, but as she glanced across the table at Ben eating his third slice of bread, she regretted not inquiring what his favorites were. *Mighty hard to do when he avoids me altogether,* she silently muttered as she took another bite of her own. Miriam had not mentioned he was such a picky eater.

"Another fine meal, Dochter," Daed offered. She never recalled a meal he hadn't thanked her for, but he had gone out of his way recently after informing her of the new dawdi haus that would be built.

"I best go see to washing off this day. I have a bit of reading to catch up on." His plate was nearly clean, with only a few potatoes remaining. The grease she feared she had overindulged on mingled with the cheese sauce she had stirred into the canned peas. Her lips curled into a smile as she watched him lumber out of the kitchen, but they fell quickly when she turned to Ben.

"The bread was gut," Ben said. The unexpected compliment soured quickly when he grinned. He'd not touched anything except for the bread. All her hard work was rejected. LeEtta had made two pans of meat loaf, just in case one wasn't enough. It was Mike Lengacher all over again.

"I should have made two loaves of bread instead, I see," she responded while carrying dishes to the sink. Did she dare ask him about her dress? Part of her wondered if Ben hadn't taken it himself. Clearly, he was no happier with this pretend marriage than she was, that or he knew she had ruined his shirt.

Behind her, Ben rose from the table. A ripple of nerves ran through her when he moved next to her at the sink. He set down the plate, still full of food, but made no attempt to move on. Thoughts of dresses and ruined white shirts vanished in his nearness.

"I've never tasted meat loaf made that way." He didn't even try masking his disappointment. "I'm sure I'll get used to new flavors eventually."

LeEtta turned swiftly, her shoulder bumping into his. The still-wet glass in her hand was clutched tightly to her chest, as if that alone could protect her feelings. He didn't back away, his resentful gaze boring into her. He could see her blunders, her vulnerabilities.

She'd blame a hot kitchen for the heat on her skin, not the man before her. She had hoped for a summer kitchen long ago, but farmers always had to settle for what Gott allotted them and prepare for harder days yet. She was a farmer's daughter and learned early on that if something didn't work, you simply fixed it.

"Or. . .I can learn to cook what you are accustomed to," she replied with equal pluck. She would not let one bad day determine the next one. She did, though, make a mental note to write Miriam as soon as possible. The man had to eat.

Ben continued to stare down at her as if debating which favorites to share with her. He smelled of his day's labor. Summer and livestock, grass and oil, and earth and nature had collected on him.

"I'm not picky. I'm just not used to drinking three glasses of milk to swallow one bite of meat loaf." That cocky brow tilted higher yet.

"Ach, the jalapeno!" How had she not considered that he might not like warmer flavors? "I didn't have a regular pepper and replaced it." It was her lot in life, always trying to find the best substitute for what she lacked in recipes. That's why any time she had a little money saved up, she tried to invest in extra spices that never spoiled.

"You keep baking, and you'll not hear me complain," he said.

Would he care if she used plain ol' sugar and not brown sugar in *kichlin*, she wondered? Since they were being honest, it was best to come clean. It was mighty hard to keep secrets to herself with him looking at her as he was.

LeEtta swallowed and lowered her gaze. "I ruined your shirt while trying to get the frosting stain out. I'm sorry." An eerie silence filled the room, with the exception of the propane lamp hissing nearby. She didn't dare glance up. Seeing further disappointment on his face would be the last straw of her vexing day.

"Shouldn't matter, as I'll only marry once," he finally said. "I've got a few more things to see to in the barn. Don't wait up."

Moving away, Ben collected his hat and walked out the kitchen door. She jerked when the door clicked shut behind him. She was married to the most handsome man she had ever met, but his heart was as dead as the crispy potatoes pushed to the side of his plate. How could she manage a meal if all he ate was bread?

Unless. . .

LeEtta never stumbled while baking. At least not when she had plenty of the right ingredients. Setting down the freshly washed glass and ignoring her damp dress front, LeEtta hurried to the icebox, a room attached to the side of the house filled with melting ice blocks, and fetched a whole frozen chicken from the last culling. Chicken potpie was the perfect match for a man who liked baked goods but needed substance to stay strong. If food was the way to a man's heart, LeEtta was going to give it her best shot.

———————— ⚓ ————————

Ben swept the tack room floor and dusted the cobwebby corners. He had confiscated two quilts and his suitcase of clothes and slowly rutted out a place to rest his head. As he tried to get comfortable, his stomach groaned. From somewhere in the barn, a horse blew out a breath. He had married a woman who read books but clearly not recipes. Who couldn't wash a shirt, and who put jalapenos in meat loaf? Arlen Miller clearly had the digestive system of a goat and no concern for his Sunday best, or he would have seen LeEtta schooled by now.

Breakfast would come soon enough, he thought as he tried to calm his appetite. Hopefully, muffins would be involved. If it was more of those watery, cheesy eggs, he'd have to grab something on his way to Shep's.

A smile curled his lips while frogs lulled the warm night air into a lullaby. She had been disappointed that he didn't like her meat loaf, but she had not let it hold her hostage long before her optimistic heart sought out new ways to please him.

Ben was certain he was going to forget how she got him in this mess in the first place when those pale eyes aimed to please as she did and when a tender wisp of red hair lay on her cheek and tempted him to brush it away. *Nee*, he shook his head. He need not let her into his heart. He'd not be betrayed ever again.

CHAPTER FIFTEEN

October bloomed with the sound of mourning doves conversing in the side yard. Under a shade of boxwoods, they dug into the rich mulch for breakfast, and a house finch inserted himself quietly among them. A few more tackled the woodpile debris nearby, all happily cooing with the bounty.

LeEtta had packed Ben's lunch. He hadn't touched the chicken potpie and did not find the chicken casserole with salsa favorable, but he did scarf down cinnamon bread, biscuits, and muffins as if he couldn't get enough. Her husband had a sweet tooth, she thought with a smile. That's why she stayed up last night making brownies and fresh bread. Ben never made a sour expression over her bread.

LeEtta also hoped he would return from the barn, as for the last few nights she had waited for him to do so. It never took Daed so long to see to the livestock at night, but each night when the clock chimed, revealing the late hour, she knew once more that he would not return. Her husband would rather sleep in the barn than in the same house with her. Surely the couch would be more comfortable than a dirty barn. Though she did hope to win Ben's heart—a true marriage she was not in a hurry for—she did feel safer with him at hand. Since her dress had gone missing and no wind was so clever to have tucked it away from sight, she knew she'd sleep better with him in the house.

Tossing one last handful of corn toward the collecting birds, she aimed for the coop. She greeted her remaining flock of fourteen hens with a cheery hello. "Gut mariye, ladies. What do you have for me today?"

Standing on her tiptoes, LeEtta peeked into the upper nesting boxes. "Empty," she said, scrunching her nose. "Well, you are all sure slacking," she added. A scan of the rest of the nesting boxes revealed the same. Something had to have happened to keep them from laying, as they were as predictable as the clock on the kitchen wall.

Outside, LeEtta did a full inspection of the coop's run. All the wire was intact. No holes were dug under the wooden frame resting on the ground. There wasn't a trace of an egg thief anywhere. Perhaps a wild animal, a coon or fox, was visiting but failed to break in. That would explain why the hens weren't laying. Now she felt guilty for scolding them, and just for conscience's sake, LeEtta returned to the coop to gift them an extra handful of grain for calling them *faul*.

The sound of hammers broke through the morning silence. LeEtta stared at the men on ladders and the slanted rooftop and frowned. Daed surprised her, choosing to make his own place and leaving the house to her, despite there being plenty of room for the three of them to live together.

A shiver ran over her. Soon Daed would move into his own place. Ben clearly was content sleeping in a dirty barn. She'd be alone. If she thought she had been lonely before, she'd soon be lonelier still.

Three buggies sat in front of the house. It was kind of the men to come out and lend a hand, seeing as Daed couldn't do more than measure and cut. Ervin Graber surely had jobs contracted already, but he, his eldest son, Matt, and John Shetler set aside these last couple of days to see the little dawdi haus put up. When a fourth buggy appeared, LeEtta felt her spirits lift immediately at the sight of Eunice and Ellen.

"I know you have only been wed a few days, but we missed you and thought we'd have a Sisters' Day." Eunice jumped from the buggy with Ellen right behind her.

"You have no idea how happy I am to see you!" LeEtta motioned them both inside as giddiness filled her heart. Sisters' Day was one gathering LeEtta had never been invited to, as she had no sisters or mamm. Only Eunice would have guessed how badly LeEtta had wanted one. On most Sisters' Days, everyone gathered at one house to tend to cleaning, sewing, canning, or whatever else that person needed. It was more often than not on a Thursday. Thankfully, Eunice didn't look at calendars or follow every tradition perfectly.

"What are they building?" Ellen asked as she set down two small buckets LeEtta was certain were filled with blackberries. A late spring and lingering summer had stretched the season.

"A dawdi haus." LeEtta blew out a frustrated breath. "I'm set against it, but Daed is determined."

"But you and Ben are married now. You'll be wanting to start a family, will you not?" Eunice said grinning. "Unless you only married because you didn't want to be the last to wed." Eunice added playfully.

"Of all the stuff," Ellen scoffed. "I ain't even courting. We all know I have little time for it. I'll most certainly be the last one." Sweet Ellen. LeEtta hated not telling her friends the truth behind her and Ben's marriage, but if Eunice knew, she'd never let LeEtta forget what a horrible person she was.

"LeEtta clearly loves him, and he clearly loves her, or they wouldn't have married," Ellen continued, her words like a tight grip on LeEtta's throat.

"Well, I never thought she'd marry first is all I'm saying." Neither did LeEtta. "So how is it? Spending time *alone* with your husband?" Eunice prodded.

LeEtta's cheeks would have warmed at the thought of a true marriage, but she managed to erect a proper response. "It's a lot more work trying to please another, that's for sure and certain."

"Of course it is. You've never had to see to a large family like we did," Eunice teased. LeEtta knew her friend didn't mean anything by her left-handed comments, but they stung nonetheless.

"It will take time. You barely know each other," Ellen inserted, always the voice of quiet encouragement. "Since we lost our mamm, I know how hard it can be seeing over so much alone."

That was the whole of it, LeEtta considered. She struggled with the simplest task, whereas Eunice would have no trouble at all, because Eunice had a mamm, two grossmammis, and schwesters. She always had someone to help her, to teach her.

"I can't wait until Jerry and I wed. Of course, we will have a larger gathering than you did. You sprang that on us all too quickly, LeEtta," Eunice continued. "But I can clearly see that Ben has stars for you. He is blessed to have you."

Blessed. She had ruined his shirt, and her husband just might starve if she didn't find a way to remedy his appetite. "More like unfortunate," LeEtta blurted out. "I'm the worst fraa ever!" Dropping into a nearby chair, LeEtta let out the sobs she had been holding onto so tightly. "I can't cook anything he likes. I ruined his wedding shirt, and now the hens won't lay, and I can't make meat loaf." More tears followed the previous ones in cascades of overlapping failures.

Ellen hurried to her side, placing a supporting hand on her shoulders. "Ach, LeEtta. You ain't been married before. My sister says it takes time. Both of you have to learn each other's habits and discover one another as a partner."

"Ellen is right, and you can make meat loaf just fine. I gave you my own recipe," Eunice encouraged.

"He doesn't like it." The truth soured Eunice's expression.

"Then something is wrong with his taste buds," Eunice said snubbingly.

"I bet he'll like jam," Ellen prompted. LeEtta lifted her head and stared at her sweet friend. "Blackberry jam. I brought everything we need, and you know Arlen loves blackberry jam."

"Danke, Ellen. Daed would sure love that, though I cannot know if Ben will. The way this marriage is starting off, it wouldn't surprise me if he's allergic."

"Stuff and nonsense. You overthink too much." Eunice was right.

LeEtta tended to try so hard that she sometimes overdid everything.

"Ben is likely learning too. I mean, he came here for a visit and found a fraa. You two didn't leave much for courting. Perhaps he's missing his family. You could write his bruder. Perhaps he could kumm visit, help him feel more at home here."

"Ellen wants you to do that because she likes the looks of him." Eunice scoffed.

"Nee, I don't," Ellen replied.

LeEtta stifled a grin, watching the banter between friends. These two never left a day to dull without something to make you giggle. "Sam won't kumm, at least not unless Ben asks him to." LeEtta shared about the rift between the brothers and the strain it had taken on his family. As much as she looked forward to more time with Miram, she knew Ben felt differently. His cold farewell when they left was proof he was not ready to deal with the troubles between them.

"Well, if he is upset that his bruder got the farm, he should be happy to have married you. Your family has one of the largest farms around." Ellen sought out a strainer and began washing berries. "I say having his bruder visit is still a good idea."

"You would," Eunice darted her a look. "I only hope Ben Ropp didn't marry you just for this farm," Eunice added as she sought out a pot deep enough for both containers of berries. "Please tell me you have plenty of sugar."

"Jah, I have plenty of that at least." LeEtta wiped her face and stood. It was best to stay busy. So busy she'd not fall into crying jags and embarrass herself.

"I'll go fetch the container." As she moved to gather up the sugar bin in the pantry, Eunice's words ran through her thoughts a second time. It was true. Ben no longer needed to work to buy a farm of his own. Had not Mary said as much? Trust, she reminded herself. Ben said he agreed to their marriage to save both their reputations and that of their families. He'd not married her for a farm. She collected the sugar container and decided to put the false concern behind her. She would believe it in her heart until it stuck.

By early afternoon, LeEtta felt like her old self again and had twelve fresh jars of blackberry jam to add to the pantry. Eunice scribbled down three new recipes that might put an end to Ben's appetite drought. Yumasetta was a recipe no Amish fraa failed to make. Though LeEtta had no garlic, she'd simply add extra onion. The recipe called for one cup of sour cream, but cottage cheese and milk were just as equal a substitute.

Outside, the sounds of hammers and men filled the air. LeEtta set down the recipe and got straight to work. While the yumasetta baked, LeEtta decided it was time to replace Ben's shirt. She had plenty of white fabric, and despite his thoughts on brushing the mishap aside, LeEtta was determined to right the wrong, closing further tension between them.

At the kitchen table, she stretched out one of Ben's other shirts over the material spread out along the table. Carefully, she folded each sleeve to the chest before tracing the outline. She had done a dress just this way and managed fine. How difficult could it be?

She was just working the scissors through the fabric when the side kitchen door opened. She had been in such deep thought that Mammi Iola's unexpected arrival startled her enough to push forward just enough to cut into the line of the pattern.

"Ach no!"

"I'm so sorry, dear. I didn't mean to startle you." Mammi came to her side and quickly surveyed the scene. "Well, it has not reached beyond the excess. Once you sew these two halves together, the stitch will hide everything," Mammi said with absolution.

LeEtta nodded, though her gaze couldn't leave the cut in the fabric. Was there not one thing she could do right?

"I see already that married life suits ya." Mammi Iola removed her black bonnet and presented LeEtta with a bag filled with materials. "I thought you could use these for a quilt."

"I can't even cut a shirt out. I don't dare attempt quilting."

"Now why would you think so? If ever a maed was more determined to see a task done well, it is you." Mammi Iola gave the kitchen a full scrutiny. Even the poor violas LeEtta had repotted and set in the windowsill looked defeated.

"I say that we have a cup of tea, then see about a new shirt." Mammi winked and went straight to heating water and sifting through the tea canister filled with a mingle of tea flavors. She settled on two and dropped each one in brown, heavy-based cups. "We are all made different. It's Gott's plan, so we don't confuse one husband for the next."

LeEtta couldn't help but laugh. Mammi Iola had a way with words that made absolutely no sense, but her confidence was a force to not be ignored.

Mammi Iola poured two cups and set one in front of LeEtta. "What you do not know, you make up for in other ways."

"I don't know enough to fill a teacup. Ben will suffer forever if my mistakes keep piling up. Eunice and Ellen came by."

"Friends are good to have."

"We made fresh jam, but I'm doubtful he will even taste it. He has decided to live on bread alone."

"I see, and yet the Lord says he cannot." Mammi Iola sat and took a tentative sip of her warm cup. "I'm certain you will find Ben's tastes soon enough. You just have to keep trying. It took me time too. Your dawdi said he knew I was the one when he tried my taco soup and burned his tongue so badly he couldn't even ask to take me home until the swelling went down." Her smile came easily at the memory that time had sustained. "You have a house but have yet to build a home."

It was the truth of it, and LeEtta had dreamed nearly all of her life of the latter. "How do I build something I never had before?" It was an honest question. LeEtta knew how other families did it, but not the same applied to her and her father.

"A home is built on a strong foundation. Like a gut jam kuche. If one skips out on an ingredient, the friendship—the first part of any loving home—falls away like seeds upon stones."

"Are you saying I need to make a jam kuche or try planting more seeds next?" LeEtta knew the proverb and that seeds could never root among stones, so clearly Mammi was telling her to keep baking. "No matter what I try, I keep messing up."

"Ach, I'm sure you are doing fine, my dear, and jam kuche is always worth the extra effort." Mammi took another sip.

"What would Mamm say to do?" LeEtta asked once more. It was terrible of her to keep putting her grandmother on the spot, but LeEtta had felt this absence since her first breath.

"She would say, 'Start with a cornerstone and keep building.'" Mammi Iola patted her hand.

"What if I run out of stones?" LeEtta continued to unravel the riddled advice.

"You won't." Her grandmother assured her. "Gott offers plenty of what we need, but if you are still doubtful... I have plenty in my garden that you can collect." Mammi laughed and rose from the table.

"I best be going. I thought it good to come by and see how they were coming along with the new haus. You'll soon have no troubles getting to know your husband once Arlen is settled."

"But. . ." LeEtta jumped to her feet. "You haven't even told me about how Dawdi fell in love with your cooking yet. Did taco soup really make him love you?"

Her grandmother fetched her bonnet and turned to her. "That is for another day. Thursday when we do the shopping, jah?" Mammi wrinkled her nose and glanced behind her. "I don't want to be late. I have a date."

LeEtta needed answers. Her life was dangling over rough waters, and her grandmother was going on a date.

"What's that smell?"

LeEtta smelled it too. Something scalded and something charred. "Ach! My yumasetta!" LeEtta hurried to the stove. She quickly took up a nearby towel and pulled the large dish from the oven. Smoke rolled out, escaping its confines, and she coughed from inhaling a little. The bubbling mess had run over the sides of the glass dish, and now the oven would need a good cleaning.

"After working all day with Shep, I thought Ben might finally work up enough appetite to eat something besides bread." LeEtta closed the stove door and turned off the propane. She ran a spoon through the bubbly concoction. It stuck tight to the high angles but looked rather good, if not for the fact that it had the consistency of soup.

"Well, that should go over well with bread now. Don't underestimate your talents, dear. I have never let a dish best me yet. Now I should go before the heat outside ruins my jam kuche."

"So jam kuche might work?" Again, LeEtta begged for wisdom.

"Hasn't failed me yet, but white raisins are the key," she pointed. "I'll leave you with this. . ."

LeEtta was all ears.

"Stop trying so hard and court him. Don't fret over being perfect, for none are, but take time to know the man you married, and don't forget to be yourself and show him who you are. Love will find its way."

"What if it doesn't?" LeEtta stood and wrangled her lip. Would she forever live with a stranger who made her confidence as well as her knees wobbly?

"I would suggest a kiss, since you know it works for you," Mammi Iola said as she hurried off to her date. It wasn't wind or imagination but laughter LeEtta was certain she heard, but that could be sounds from the stove still popping and cracking.

It was a kiss that had gotten her into this mess. LeEtta was doubtful another kiss would suddenly improve her cooking skills.

CHAPTER SIXTEEN

Autumn painted Cherry Grove into a vast landscape of brilliance. Pastoral grasses had been cut short recently, no longer speckled with cattle head down and grazing but sold for a profit. LeEtta smiled as she took in the view of mirrored hillsides, careful not to let milk from the pail in her hands splash as she pivoted around to view the full spectrum.

Two nights ago, and to her complete surprise, Ben told her that something was awaiting her in the barn. They hadn't exchanged wedding gifts, but she liked to think Rosey was a gift instead of a necessity for each of them. She liked to think Ben had extended an olive branch in their marriage.

The young milker had the longest eyelashes of any Jersey LeEtta had ever seen. She was young yet, but it didn't take long before she settled into a routine that suited them both.

For too long, life here felt more like a place to live than a home. Ben had brought life into the land again. He worked each day at Shep's, and evenings he added final touches to the dawdi house. If only there was more she could do to show him how grateful she was. Jam kuche did nothing to help bring them closer.

His mercies are new every morning, her heart whispered. A soft breeze of cooler air, damp from overnight rains, caressed her cheek. She welcomed the touch to tend her wounded heart. In her pocket was a letter from Miriam. Now she knew at least one thing her husband enjoyed. Miriam had been kind enough to share her beef noodle recipe, but between lines and ingredients, LeEtta sensed the mother's heart was missing her firstborn.

Inside the overly warm kitchen, she strained and poured the milk into the milk containers. A fly swarmed, no doubt seeking warmth inside. She wouldn't ponder the why. Ben clearly didn't like cows, and Daed had long ago said the upkeep wasn't within budget. LeEtta was simply thankful.

Once the milk was strained and stored, she hurried up a quick breakfast of hot toast, crispy bacon, oatmeal, and gravy. Gravy was a science, she concluded. It either turned out lumpy and thick or thin as water. LeEtta had been so concerned with crisping the bacon perfectly that she let the flour, grease, and milk boil over, creating a mess she would have to tend to later. The pesky fly swarmed again. She'd not let something as small as a fly ruin her perfectly wonderful morning. She was just setting breakfast on the table as both men strolled into the kitchen.

"No eggs today either?" Daed asked as he sat down at the table, not seeing his signature morning dish. He would soon not live under the same roof, but LeEtta had persisted just enough that he agreed to take his meals with her. Between the two of them, she had always been better in the kitchen, and the last thing she wanted on her conscience was him starving too.

"Nee, it's like they've stopped altogether." Though days were shortening, LeEtta had hoped they would lay longer yet.

"Perhaps they're old," Ben said, spreading jam over his toast. She placed a glass of fresh milk in front of him and tried not to smile as he dipped the spoon a second time into the jam jar. He was clearly not allergic. Surely she had a cobbler recipe somewhere.

"They aren't but a year yet. Jonas gifted them to me just this spring. Could be that a fox or coon is stirring. I heard something rustling out of my window a few nights ago." Ben bit into his toast angrily. She shouldn't have mentioned that Jonas had gifted them to her.

"Well, we have plenty of coons, that's for sure," Daed said. "Chickens know when they are being threatened. I'll check the wire for holes."

"I already did," she assured her father and caught Ben's gaze. He chewed slowly, his piercing gaze stalking her as she sampled a slice of bacon dipped in gravy.

"Then we have a smart racoon indeed. I bet you will find them wherever your dress is," Daed patted her hand.

"What dress?" Ben suddenly stopped chewing and deepened his gaze.

LeEtta looked at her father. She hadn't wanted to share that with Ben, in case he had a hand in its whereabouts.

"Letty washed her dress soon after your wedding, and it went missing. We've yet to find it."

"You didn't tell me that." Ben sounded hurt that she shared something with her father she had not considered sharing with him.

"You didn't tell me you liked beef and noodles. There is much yet for both of us to learn. You should call Miriam if you find the time today. Your mamm misses talking to you." Ben's frown deepened. Was he troubled to know she and Miriam had exchanged letters?

Ben blinked, opened his mouth, then closed it again before rising from the table. "Danke for breakfast." He walked out, and her father soon followed, neither eating another bite, which left her alone to eat breakfast in a hot kitchen stained with gravy and concern, a pesky fly, and another sink full of dishes.

Ben double-checked the chicken fencing, looking for weak spots. Inside the coop, he discovered no gaps between walls or ceiling that a critter could squeeze through. Shutting the door, he stared blankly at the white hens pecking dirt as if they weren't fat enough to fill two stew pots already. He didn't know much about chickens, but enough to know this breed was for butchering, not egg-laying.

"A kind word shouldn't taste like vinegar." Arlen stepped to his side.

"Nee, it shouldn't," Ben agreed. His "danke" hadn't been delivered as it should have, but knowing LeEtta had been communicating with his mamm about him didn't sit well. "I don't see where anything could get in."

"Animals know when trouble is lurking. They're scared." Arlen spoke with wisdom and displeasure, narrowing Ben a look. "When something is afraid, it never functions as it should. Fear and doubt are the devil's best tools." With that, he strolled toward the cornfield.

Ben followed, a shadow on the heel of the man who had changed his course. Ben didn't want to agree with his elder, but Arlen was right. Fear and doubt bred uncertainty. Ben feared a life without love. A life where no family would spawn from all his efforts. Unlike his daed, Ben would work hard to give all his kinner a good start.

He doubted LeEtta feared the same but had to admit the woman he met on a worn-out trail was confident, chatty, and strong-willed. The one he married was not. She had thanked him four times for the purchase of Rosey. She would have thanked him four more times if she knew how much a young milker cost, but he'd not burden her with such matters. Not when her eyes twinkled the moment she ventured into the barn and was introduced to the young Jersey.

Ben had thanked her in return for sewing him two new shirts, though he suspected Iola's lingering of late had a hand in that as well. No matter, he hadn't spoken the gratitude she deserved. It was as if both of them were going through the steps, duty bound and forever yoked. Neither actually letting nature take its course. Marriage wasn't supposed to be that way. Fear was strangling them both.

"I can set a trap. I saw one in the barn." LeEtta liked her chickens, though he reckoned she'd like chicks to raise just as much. He'd spend whatever the cost to replace them, butchering them himself so she didn't even have to watch.

"Gut idea." Arlen reached for an ear of corn and gave it a tight inspection. "I reckon we shouldn't put it off much longer. Rain will be here soon."

"I agree. It's a good crop." Ben had checked how the crop was going a handful of times already. The earth in Cherry Grove needed little nutrients, as it was as rich as Ben had ever seen.

"The Hostetlers supply the gravity wagons. Best we head on over and fetch them. We'll start on Monday and work around your schedule."

"I thought you wanted to move furniture into the dawdi haus today," Ben queried. He'd have to hurry through his work for Shep and harvest in the evenings.

"I'm in no hurry," Arlen spoke firmly. "Mei dochter has never slept in that house alone yet."

Ben had been careful to leave long after Arlen turned in for the night, but clearly not careful enough. He didn't like knowing he had disappointed LeEtta's daed, yet until he could accept LeEtta into his heart, Ben simply wasn't ready to share more with her than a few passing words. He'd provide for her and keep her safe, but he couldn't trust her. Too many mistakes were good teachers for a man who dared not let his heart be broken into.

A half hour later, Ben veered the one-seater down the graveled lane and pulled to a hard stop as the eager horses were ready to work. Arlen hopped out, walked awkwardly with a stiff arm weighing him a little heavier on the right and disappeared inside the hardware shop, leaving Ben with quick instructions to hitch onto the gravity wagons he'd find around the side of the store.

A strong wind from the west pushed over the landscape, casting a sour scent of livestock from somewhere nearby. Ben was beginning to look forward to Saturdays the most, a day free from the stench of working a hog farm.

"How's the married life?" Leo approached in his common leisurely way, a large sandwich in his hand. His newly trimmed beard had Ben absentmindedly scratching his own new growth.

"Not *that* good yet," Ben jested motioning to the half-eaten sandwich stuffed with ham, lettuce, cheese, and two thick slices of tomato. Four weeks of marriage had slipped by, and his overindulgence in sweets was beginning to show. Sweet pastries and kuches had added to his waist, but he did hope noodles sat on the supper table again tonight.

"Wait until you got a houseful of your own," Leo replied. "I'm the eldest and remember well when mamm burnt suppers, and stew pots boiled over. Now she's the best cook in five counties." He took a healthy bite, and a loud crunch and falling crumbs had Ben salivating. *Potato chips.*

"LeEtta had no one to teach her. And Arlen," Leo frowned. "I don't suspect he did much more than keep her shackled to his side anytime they left the farm."

LeEtta had done well for herself, Ben measured. If his father hadn't taken him to task, teaching when soil was rich or in need of nutrients, if he hadn't learned the best days for planting, weeding, or harvesting, the Ropp farm would not have been as successful with only Daed at the helm. Nee, it took many hands and heads and years of know-how to do well. Jah, Arlen Miller might just be the most stubborn man Ben knew.

"She'll figure it all out. That's LeEtta. She figures it out. Give it time," Leo advised.

It wasn't time Ben thought LeEtta required, even if her potpies needed to be eaten with a spoon and her penchant for cheese wrestled his digestive system into tight knots. She needed to stop trying so hard. Guilt budded a new branch in his conscience, knowing her fierce tenacity for pleasing him was his own doing. Perhaps he could try harder too.

"Arlen's inside. We've come to fetch the gravity wagons. We start the harvest first thing Monday." Ben quickly changed the subject.

"Well, Daed's working the store today," Leo chuckled. "They might be all day. Let me help you get hooked up. I'll run your buggy back this evening if that's all right." He shrugged. "Gives me a chance to ride home without Mamm fussing."

Ben laughed. All young men ached to ride like cowboys instead of taking up reins. In two bites, the rest of the sandwich disappeared, and both men worked to hitch the empty gravity wagons to Mike and Moses. Ben's eyes trailed movement to his left. On the hillside, he spotted the younger Hostetler twins tending to the chickens. *White*, he groaned, and his gaze zoomed in on Jonas. Did Leo know what a troublemaker his sibling was?

"That's a lot of chickens," Ben commented when Leo followed his gaze.

"Jah, those two wanted to start their own business." Leo chuckled. "Jonas has big ideas but, thankfully, a head for numbers. Unless it's fried to a crisp on a plate, I don't care much for them. I met your bruder, Sam, at the wedding meal. Seems like one with a head for numbers too."

Ben had to agree. Sam had always excelled in school. It was in the fields that Sam lacked. Sam couldn't predict bad weather, and Ben was always reminding him when it was best to cultivate and fertilize. He would do well with a barn full of milkers. Though it took up a man's mornings and evenings and left little time in between, Sam was a man of routine and predictability.

He looked at Jonas again. LeEtta should have set him straight, but she was too kindhearted. She fretted over chickens and cows, and. . .

"You ever have any problems with folks sneaking around your place?"

Leo lifted a brow. "Nee, you're our nearest neighbors. We sometimes get a few customers after hours, but not many travel back this far for fun. Are you having troubles?" Leo's brow lifted in concern.

"It could be nothing, but. . ." Ben wasn't sure he should even mention it. LeEtta probably misplaced the dress. Then again, how did one misplace such an important thing? "LeEtta did some washing, but when she went to take it up, a dress was missing."

Leo scratched his ear. "Wind could have carried it off."

"Jah, maybe so. Now she says all her hens have stopped laying." Ben visually measured the distance between parcels. The neighboring farms were stretched about if one traveled the roadways, but if one cut through pasture, it was no distance at all.

"Varmints."

"Could be, but I'm not finding any proof of that," Ben replied. Sensing eyes on him, Jonas stopped midchore to turn and lock gazes with Ben. Even at this distance, Ben could see the narrowed eyes and the upturn of a grin.

"I'm sure all will kumm out right. You know, tomorrow's visiting Sunday. Why don't you and LeEtta kumm for *break*?" Break was just as it sounded: a break from a chore or a long week. A gathering of sorts, with fewer faces to learn, and easy talk. Ben had hoped for a few hours of fishing and maybe calling his mamm as LeEtta mentioned. Just because he and his daed were at odds didn't mean he should let her worry.

"Some of us will be hanging out downstairs. Jerry will have Eunice here, and you know by now that those two are gut freinden. The women can gossip about us, and I can beat you at Ping-Pong."

A laugh sprang out of Ben. LeEtta would appreciate time out of the house, and Ben had never been beaten at Ping-Pong before. "We'll be there."

Back at the farm, Ben unhitched the gravity wagons while Arlen put Moses and Mike out to pasture.

"Still plenty of daylight if you think to put up some of that hay."

Ben looked into the sun and drank in the scents of familiarity. "Jah," he said, looking toward the house. "But first, I'm starved." He turned and aimed for the house. He'd eat whatever she cooked, try to be more appreciative of her efforts.

Laundry snapped in the autumn breeze as squeals of delight erupted from the side of the house.

"Reckon she's got a yard full." Arlen chuckled.

"A yard full?"

"You know little of your fraa," Arlen scoffed. Ben swallowed his reply. Arlen knew little of his dochter.

"I'm surprised folks gave her any time at all, as good as she is with the kinner. That sounds like Mark and Sadie's little ones." He laughed again. "She will surely have her hands full today."

Ben rounded the house, and sure enough, there LeEtta was, a boppli on her hip, chasing two kinner around the yard, laughing under straw hats and darting under clothes hanging on the line. She wore the sensible black kerchief, but it did little to conceal the soft colors in her hair.

"You're it," LeEtta called out before darting behind a pair of stretched-out broadfall trousers. The child in her arms squealed happily, a tiny white kapp not hiding tufts of downy dark hair. A second child, barefoot and barely reaching LeEtta's slim waist, giggled as he hid in the flow of her faded gray chore dress.

The eldest child spotted him and Arlen first. He didn't flinch in surprise at a stranger but ran over quickly, slapping Ben on the side of his leg.

"You're it!" He was off again.

"Nee, Henry. Ben doesn't want to play." LeEtta offered him an apologetic look.

She looked content with a boppli on her hip, surrounded by kinner. His chest squeezed, filling his head with visions of possibilities he had squashed early on. Arlen turned to leave, a grin on his lips. Ben wasn't an ogre, and he never liked disappointing kinner.

"Afraid that I can catch you?" He replied cockily. LeEtta's gaze rounded at the remark. There was the woman filled with childish enthusiasm and confidence he'd first met. His breath caught in his throat, and his brain turned to mush.

"I'm not afraid at all." She lifted her chin, smiled invitingly, and took off. He should turn around and follow Arlen in the opposite direction. This wasn't safe. Challenging eyes and a flash of gray fabric disappeared around the house, but sometimes a man had no choice, and his feet propelled him after her. Laughter filled his lungs as he took up the chase.

CHAPTER SEVENTEEN

What the Hostetler farm lacked in acres, it gained in beauty. LeEtta had long admired the large, three-story home, though she had never envied Joanie Hostetler for keeping it tidy and well cared for. The long drive had freshly spray-painted white fences on its edges, a tree of perfect symmetry every thirty feet or so with golden leaves sprinkling the gravel drive.

On the porch, ferns hung from each section with rockers and benches, clearly from Schwartz Lawn Furniture. Zeb had recently handed over the business to his nephew Ethan, and now those poly rockers were sitting on nearly every porch and storefront in the county.

LeEtta had made a cherry pie despite knowing there would be plenty of snacks and sodas for everyone. She had a rule: never enter a house empty-handed.

"I know those bruders are up to something." Eunice crossed her arms over her chest as Ruben Smoker and Barbara Yoder walked into the basement. They quickly found a seat next to Ruben's bruder Ernest. The two shared more than a deep affection for each other. They had been courting for three long years and were born on the same day.

"Happy Birthday to you. . ." Voices lifted as the couple both looked at each other in surprise. Birthdays were recognized during church gatherings, but here where youngies collected, it was more embarrassing, as the birthday person had to stand and be revered or the song would never end. LeEtta recalled the time they sang to Leo Hostetler. A stubborn one he was, as they sang for a whole twenty minutes before Jerm and Jerry forced him to his feet, bringing it all to a long end.

"Happy birthday to you," the group continued, but as LeEtta too joined in the chorus, she could see a group of young men move toward the couple, mischief spread over their faces. Oh, she hoped they didn't make poor Barbara's face any redder than it was.

"Happy birthday, dear Rhu-barb. Happy birthday to you." Chuckles and laughter filled the house.

"I told Jerry it was foolish, but he said if Ruben and Barb planned on being born on the same day and soon marrying, it was easier folks called them Rhubarb Smokers."

LeEtta stifled a giggle. It was truly clever, she thought, as Eunice talked her into a game of checkers.

LeEtta plopped the last crumb of a cookie in her mouth, waiting on Eunice's next move. Checkers was a simple game, yet her friend struggled for every king. If she paid more attention to the game than Jerry, they would be done with it already. Did she dare warn her friend that marriage was harder than they both imagined it to be?

On that thought, LeEtta peered into the corner of the basement, where Ben and Jerry stood at opposite ends of a Ping-Pong table. Her husband never mentioned he'd played the game before, but clearly he had, considering he'd defeated Jeremiah Hostetler, Jason Eicher, and Timothy Glick.

Mandy Schwartz whispered something in Leo's ear, a smile between them, then walked toward LeEtta's table. LeEtta had been curious about the two for some time. Perhaps the Hostetlers would have a dochter verra soon.

"Don't let my bruder beat you," Leo said in his booming voice that only those without ears could miss. "He can't even dribble a ball." If Leo had hoped the distraction would cause Jerry to flinch and disturb the perfect rhythm of the game, it worked.

LeEtta sat straighter when Ben scored and turned to Leo. "I won't, and you're next." He pointed a paddle in Leo's direction. The men were equal in height, but Ben clearly had the advantage if those long arms were any indicator. LeEtta watched as the two goaded one another and started a fresh game. A smile bloomed on her lips. Ben went at everything he did as if he had something to prove.

"I just stole your king," Eunice said, jerking LeEtta back to her own game.

"Ach." She should have been paying closer attention.

"You two gonna hog that board all night?" Malinda Lengacher asked. LeEtta blew out a breath, sliding down the bench to make room for them.

"I'd give you my turn if you think you stand a chance," Eunice offered up to Mandy. "I did knock her down a king, if that helps."

While Malinda studied the board deciding, the basement door opened and all eyes aimed toward Jonas walking in. LeEtta wondered where he had been keeping himself, though she did hope it was upstairs in his room all night so she and Ben could enjoy the evening.

It wasn't their way to hold anger in their hearts, she reminded herself. Gott said forgiveness was essential. Jonas' fondness for her had led him to make a terrible decision. That was all. Didn't everyone make mistakes? She certainly had. Would Malinda be sitting this close to her now if she knew LeEtta had been so bold? Would they think LeEtta was so desperate for a husband that they would decide not to speak to her again?

When his eyes found her in the crowded room, LeEtta offered him a half-hearted smile. She'd not carry the burden of anger, for her duties weighed enough already. Jonas returned her smile, and then he made his way straight to the Ping-Pong table.

At the sight of Jonas, Ben gave Leo the upper hand and strolled to the dessert table. He'd not acknowledge the boy. "Excuse me. I think Ben is about ready to call it a night," she told her friends and went to him. "That's your third slice of pie," LeEtta whispered to her husband.

"It's good pie," he said, smiling back. He hadn't even touched her cherry pie. LeEtta knew because she had paid particular attention. Maybe she should ask Chrissy Keim for the recipe, then scoffed at the thought. Chrissy had tendencies to let simple requests swell her head and cause her eyelashes to spank her cheeks like a raving lunatic.

"We should head out. I'd like to get into the field as soon as the sun rises."

LeEtta nodded. She didn't want to play checkers or talk about married life with her freinden any longer. Tomorrow they would start harvesting the fields, and a late night was not going to do either of them any good.

"While you fetch your boots and hitch the buggy, I'll see to helping tidy up," she told him, knowing full well that he was still bothered that he had stepped too far to the left of Posey, resulting in dirty shoes.

"If I knew you were so bossy, I'd run for Ohio as fast as I could." He winked before walking out the basement door.

LeEtta watched him leave, a blush warming her cheeks. Like yesterday as they played hide-and-seek with the kinner, his smile had a way of making her weak-kneed. Love was blossoming in her heart. Whatever spurred his good mood, she wished she could bottle it and sprinkle it on his next meal.

Grabbing three bottles of soda, LeEtta made her way up the narrow stairs to the kitchen. She had just reached the threshold when Jerry burst through the front door and raced two steps at a time to the top floor, as if he were truly on fire.

"What's gotten into you, Jerry Hostetler?" Eunice called after him. Her dark brows narrowed in motherly fashion.

"That bu is always *dummle*," Joanie remarked as she washed glasses in a nearby sink. "One twin rushes about, and the other is too slow."

LeEtta giggled. Jerm was prone to slow moving and slow speaking. A moment later, Jerry came racing back down the stairs with a pair of black shoes in his clutch. He came to an abrupt halt when he locked eyes with Eunice standing with arms crossed.

"Your mamm might not mind so many unruly buwe, but. . ."

"Ben's shoes are missing. He cannot verra well go home barefoot!" Jerry defended.

"What?" LeEtta set the sodas down quickly. "His shoes are. . . missing?"

"Jah, he left them at the back door when you arrived, and now we can't find them anywhere." Jerry lowered his voice and looked at LeEtta. "He's a little. . .frustrated."

LeEtta imagined so. "Have you asked Jonas if he's seen them?"

"Why would I?" Jerry lifted a brow.

What could she say without shining a dark light on his brother? LeEtta felt half a dozen sets of eyes trained on her in the comment. "He likes pranking. You know he does. Remember when he brought your horse over to our pasture, and it took you two days to find him?"

"I wanted to thrash him for it." Jerry shook his head from side to side and grinned. "He's been helping us search. If he had taken them for a laugh, he'd have returned them by now." With that, Jerry hurried back out the door with no mind to close it behind him.

"It wonders me if he has a thought in his head some days," Eunice muttered softly and closed the door, but LeEtta could see stars in her eyes for Jerry nonetheless. Love wasn't discriminatory; it was unconditional.

Outside, LeEtta spotted Jonas standing alone on the porch. "Hiya, Jonas." He turned swiftly and ducked his head as if being scolded a second time.

"I don't care what either of you think, but I ain't stole no shoes. I have two pairs of my own." There was an angry boy beneath the young man trying to emerge.

"I'm sure they will turn up," she offered. His head lifted, his pale eyes wide in the fading daylight. "Gut *nacht*, Jonas." Maybe Jonas was innocent, but who would steal dirty shoes?

The ride home was not as LeEtta had hoped. She didn't blame Ben for the quiet. He probably wasn't very comfortable in Jerry Hostetler's shoes, but she was missing the laughs from earlier and the way his smile reached his whole face as he won at Ping-Pong. It was only a game, but he was happy—for a moment. He'd been so content that he had even flirted with her. Now he was stone-set, eyes forward, and frowning.

Moonlight and light poles from Englisch houses lit this area well enough that LeEtta could see him plenty clearly. In only a few short weeks, his scruffy beard made him even more handsome, but every time she felt them getting closer, something pulled him further away. Patting her dress pocket, she felt the new stew recipe tucked inside. Miriam insisted a meal that included meat and potatoes would end in an empty plate.

Now if she could only find a way to feed his heart.

At the barn, Ben got down from the buggy and, to her surprise, lifted her down as well. "I saw you talking to Jonas," he said as unhitched the horse.

"I told him good night," she replied over the sound of a frog song and crickets, but nature wasn't loud enough to hide his audible grunt of displeasure. LeEtta had done everything she could think of to be kind and forgiving. If only Ben tried a little, perhaps he wouldn't feel let down so often.

"I know you don't want to be here," she began before her confidence wavered, "but you are. I'm as much to blame as he is for it. We must forgive him, Ben. It is our way." She looked up at her husband and watched as he wrestled with the idea. Was he so miserable being married to her that he had no forgiveness in his heart for Jonas?

"He's got a lot of growing to do," he said looking down at her.

"Jah, but so do I." She shrugged. "I don't know why he did what he did, but I've known them all my life, and. . ."

"He has feelings for you," he said, taking a step forward, his gaze landing on her ear. Reaching out, Ben tucked a loose strand of unruly red hair under her kapp and behind her ear. "A man who cares about a woman does all kinds of foolish things."

Like marrying a stranger? She hoped those were the words fluttering around in his thoughts. Her heart drummed as they stood under the sounds and rhythms of the world around them. Before Ben Ropp, she had been content with community, but now LeEtta yearned for love. His love.

"He lied, hoping the bishop would send me back to Ohio. Now he's making a pest of himself because that didn't work out for him."

"Or you?"

"I didn't say that, LeEtta, but I won't pretend I'm happy to be somewhere I never planned to be." He took a ragged breath. "It's my own fault. I should have never—" He shook his head, but she knew he wanted to say he should have never walked her home.

"Everyone in my life takes and takes." He wrestled with the breeching lines before removing the buggy shafts. LeEtta watched, unable to help with his struggles. She did not know how to help him make peace with his family or forgive Jonas and her. LeEtta's heart went out to him.

"What if this, our marriage, was Gott's plan?" No matter the path taken, was Gott not the designer of this life? "Maybe no one betrayed you, really, but led you."

"Gott had no hand in this," he said flatly.

Jah, she should have never let her thoughts out of her head. "I pray this hurt you feel is taken away." Did she mention she'd been praying for his peace ever since they'd wed?

"You pray," he scoffed insultingly, pushing the cart away from Posey with enough force that it rolled into the side of the barn. LeEtta would not let his temper intimidate her. Ben was struggling, and he needed her. A wife's duty had many layers, but woven within those layers was to be his helpmate. Helping her husband with his internal dilemmas and dire thoughts.

"I prayed too. I prayed that the land I was born on, that I'd worked on my whole life and where all my history and roots began, would continue. Now it's Sam's, and I'm here. I prayed that my family would forgive me for foolish things I did as a youngie once

I joined the church and followed all the rules. They still remind me of my mistakes often." He pointed her a look. "Tell me, LeEtta, what have you ever gained by praying?" His dark gaze bore into her. It was a trick question because she had prayed for a great many things that she had never received. Gott didn't always give you what you wanted most, but He did give you what you needed.

"Nothing," she said honestly. She could not lie, pretending her prayers that life would be different for her too were ever answered. Yet God had never forsaken her. "But I will tell you what I lost. I lost my fear of being seen as different. I lost my confusion about never knowing my mamm or wondering why every birthday I have makes Daed's heart break over and over. I lost feeling so alone, because I know Gott is with me, even if you never are."

Tears ran unbidden as awareness warmed over her in her confession. She wasn't alone. She held no hardened heart, and every time she was in need, Gott placed someone in her life to help her at that moment. Even if her love for Ben was one-sided, she refused to give up. Ben needed peace and forgiveness in his heart before he would ever have room for her. Mammi Iola always said that Gott frowned on quitters.

"Are you crying?" He squinted and leaned in closer to investigate.

"I'm not crying," she said, swiping her face to remove the evidence of his disapproval. "I'm. . .hot."

"So. . .your. . .eyes. . .are sweating?" His odd brow hiked a little higher, mocking her.

Frustration built up like that black line on a pressure gauge that warned you before everything got too hot. Too much pressure had built up, and an explosion was coming. "That's not even a possibility, and if you'd rather eat raisin pie over cherry, you could have said so. A husband shouldn't keep such things from his fraa." She hated the sound of her voice and the jealousy woven between her cutting words.

"Nee, secrets only make for a miserable marriage." He narrowed her a look.

LeEtta turned and aimed for the house. It was late. Surely it was best that she get some rest and wake up ready to think of fresh ways to help him.

"I don't like pickled eggs," he called out, slowing her steps. "I don't even like seeing a pickled egg. The meat loaf wasn't bad, but it's just not like my mamm would make it."

She turned around at the desperation in his voice. "So you didn't . . .hate it?"

"I like your mashed potatoes," he admitted. "Mamm could never make them that good." Perhaps she wasn't a terrible cook after all. "No one in this state or the next can make a better muffin."

"I want to make you happy, Ben. I'm trying, but. . ."

"I'm not, and that's the problem."

Finally, a first step. Ben looked defeated, but how could he not see that he had everything he needed right here, in front of him?

"I'm sorry you feel hurt by so many people, but land is just dirt. Roots are where we plant them, and we cannot live in our history, but we can make our own." LeEtta craved his willingness to be her partner in whatever tomorrow held, and she paused in hopes that he found her words encouraging.

He hesitated at the invitation. "Best you get on inside now." Ben turned and walked into the dark lonely barn.

A few moments later, a light came on in Daed's tack room and the dull ache in her chest began again. LeEtta was sowing seeds that she might never see harvested, but a farmer's daughter always planted them anyway.

CHAPTER EIGHTEEN

Days had lingered since LeEtta had tried helping Ben find forgiveness in his heart for those around him. A mid-October sun peeked through all the windows, a reminder that each new day was a fresh start. She'd not give up on him. She only needed to find a better approach.

Sifting through her purse for her wallet, LeEtta quickly counted out the bills she'd been saving back. The list on the table was small: laundry soap, thread, shaving cream, and socks. She had mended Daed's socks for the last time. The pantry was becoming thin, but thankfully the food truck was delivering this morning at Milford's Machine Shop.

With so many families in the area contracted through the large food chain, the company returned much of the overstock and items reaching expiration to the local families. Families were free to come and help themselves to everything from overripe bananas and peppers to juice and crackers. No one took more than a fair share. Larger families and those struggling were blessed that Lester Milford agreed to use part of his shop to help.

All LeEtta needed was enough for a small donation to drop in a jar Lester kept on the counter. Those funds paid the driver of the truck, and hopefully, there'd be plenty of potatoes left. Ben did like potatoes, as long as they weren't smothered in cheese.

"Lose something?" Ben stepped into the kitchen. He went to the sink and poured a glass of water straight from the faucet. The harvest had begun at sunup, and even now he carried the scent of husks and dirt.

"I need to see to a few things today," LeEtta replied, pushing the bills back into her wallet and digging toward the bottom in hopes to find her red comb and missing ponytail holder she often used to hold her thick nightly braid. It was a wonder she even remembered how to pin her kapp on straight as idle as her brain had been lately.

"I offered to help pull the gravity wagons in and feed everything into the corncrib, but. . ."

"Arlen is set against it. I know." He chuckled, causing her to bristle.

"It wonders me how Daed will help you with one arm, and it's not right that you have to work the team to pick the corn, then stop to see the corncribs filled too." She might have no bearing over her father's thoughts, but Ben had to see the truth of her words.

"We'll manage today. . .while you see to your errands," he informed her as he glanced down at her list. Was her husband considering letting her help?

"Shaving cream?" He shot her a wide look.

"For you." She blushed. Did she dare mention she didn't use the stuff on her legs and ankles when conditioner always worked better for her easily irritated skin? "I thought you might want to trim your beard a little." She swallowed. She hoped he didn't take it as an insult. Scruffy or not, Ben was as handsome as the day they locked eyes on each other. In fact, more so now, she thought, as she studied him a little too closely, almost forgetting what they were discussing at all.

Ben rubbed his face. "It is getting a little out of hand, I reckon. I'll need razors too." He pulled out his wallet and offered her a few folded bills.

LeEtta hesitated accepting his money. Guilt pitted her stomach against the threshold of normality. Ben hadn't asked to be married to her or to provide for her.

"Your daed told me you were heading out. That's why I came in here. LeEtta, I am your husband. It's my place to provide for you." He remained there, hand outstretched. She suspected he would stay there as long as it took, as he had the stubbornness of Arlen Miller if she was being honest.

LeEtta accepted the money and thanked him. If she wanted this marriage to be more than two strangers sharing a life, she had to do some bending too. The bills were crisp and new, and when she gave them a look, she felt him being overly generous. Clearly, her husband didn't know how frugal his fraa was.

"Ben, this is too much. I'm only purchasing a few things. We might need this later." Though her father hadn't mentioned it, LeEtta had been suspecting for some time that funds were running short since his accident, and Ben had come to Cherry Grove for work. She wasn't what she considered poor, but she did know they were mighty close to it.

He took a slow drink, studying her. "You need enough for everything. There's a shoe shop behind Wickeys'. I'd be happy if you'd pick up my new shoes." They both looked down. LeEtta hid a grin behind one hand. Stuffing a size thirteen into a size eleven had to be terribly uncomfortable. His laugh came easy, and her smile followed.

"Your driver will be here any minute. There's enough to pay her too."

"Her? A driver?" LeEtta didn't need a driver, not when she had a buggy.

There came that laugh again, and she shuddered under the effect he had on her. LeEtta simply didn't know how to be around him. Mammi Iola insisted she be herself, but how did a guilty LeEtta and a determined one come close to complimenting her former self?

"Ruby. She dropped me here. You two will get along just fine." He smiled cunningly, finished his glass, and gave her a curt nod before slipping back out the door again.

LeEtta clutched the money to her chest. Her husband wanted her to pick up his new shoes and buy him razors. Another seed had sprouted, and she was eager to watch it grow.

The sound of a vehicle quickened her readiness. The van was blue, but the front fender was a rustic shade of red. They seldom used a driver. Only for Daed's doctor appointments since it was an hour drive, and once when a snowstorm and a fever had Daed calling Driver Dan to take her to the hospital. Thankfully, LeEtta had never scared him again after that night.

"Good morning, sweetie. I'm Ruby." The woman behind the wheel had short, cropped hair that was a mix of charcoal and light gray ash. Her glasses were terribly large for her petite face. She patted the passenger seat, and LeEtta quickly sat down beside her, clutching her purse on her lap.

"Good morning," LeEtta spoke softly. Eunice had told her so many tales of chatty drivers, all eager to ask personal questions about being Amish. LeEtta hoped Ruby wasn't a chatterbox, and she was not looking forward to answering personal questions.

"Your husband says you have a full day ahead. Where to first?"

"Do you know where the bulk store is on 57?"

"Of course I do. Now buckle up. I can't be going nowhere without a secure cab." Ruby winked, and LeEtta quickly latched her seat belt as Ruby put the van in gear. She pressed the pedal and raced down the drive.

"I thought I knew every Amish family from here to Michigan. Though I will admit, I didn't know you married Benuel until he called me this morning. You snuck up on me there." Ruby winked.

LeEtta doubted anyone knew every Amish family. She sure didn't, but she pushed the remark aside. "So you drive most of the families nearby?" Daed had always insisted they only use Driver Dan. LeEtta liked the older man. His quick wit proved entertaining. She knew there were other drivers in the area, though.

"I do, except when I'm sleeping." Ruby laughed. "Lost my husband eight years ago. The kids scattered as soon as they found wings." She glanced at LeEtta, flipped a switch to signal her next turn, and pulled out onto the next road. "Oh, they call, come home for holidays, and such, but they have lives of their own now."

LeEtta gripped her purse tightly to her chest as the car continued to gain speed. She tried to understand, but there was so much about the Englisch life she felt was a waste of time to discern. Like, how they could eat out so much, or how having a life of their own didn't include the whole family unit.

"I'm sorry to hear about your husband." She was, and she gave Ruby a sidelong look. Unlike Daed, who knew about the trappings of widowhood, Ruby seemed to have accepted her loss and the life she now lived.

"I had a great life with Walter. Won't hear me complaining one bit." She used both hands to take the next curve a little faster than LeEtta liked. "My Walter worked hard. Thirty whole years he worked on the pipeline, and he never had a cross word for me, even when I had a few for him." She smiled at the memories of pleasant days.

"You are newly married, but let me say, these are your best years. Getting to know each other. The sweet moments. The romance." Her thick brows wiggled playfully. "Don't you turn red on me. I know that Benuel looks rough on the outside, but those are the ones with the sweetest centers, like my Walter."

LeEtta smiled. Ben tried to appear rough, but she had seen his tender side—the way his eyes softened and smiled so often. It was trust and faith that he had difficulty with, and she had a long row to hoe to earn his trust. But slowly she was seeing each new day bringing her closer to that goal.

"You enjoy this time. Soon you'll have a houseful of babies and need to build a bigger table."

"I hope so," LeEtta replied as they pulled to a stop in front of Joel's Shoe Shop. Ruby had filled the whole morning with rambling gossip. LeEtta didn't like rambling or gossip but found herself immersed in the slow southern accent and kindred spirit of a woman who was happy the sun rose each morning.

"I hope you don't mind if we stop at the bakery next. I have a hankering for chocolate kuche."

"Of course not," LeEtta replied happily. Hazel made the best kuches. She considered Miriam's recent letter. Ben had a fondness for oatmeal whoopie pies. Hopefully, Hazel had some already made up. She'd only buy a couple, she told herself, not wasting too much on sweets, but if it made him think of home and brought him joy today, she'd pay the cost.

On the way home, LeEtta cradled the Miller's Bakery box on her lap, her eagerness to see the look on Ben's face when she presented him with the box making her anxious. By the time they reached the farm, LeEtta knew all of Ruby's children by name, their jobs, and how old each grandkid was. Ruby also possessed a recipe for what she called "a no-fail meat loaf" that she gifted LeEtta. She hoped to remember each ingredient. She had even spent the extra for the onion soup mix powder just for it, as Ruby insisted it was what made her meat loaf a husband-proof winner.

Retrieving her groceries out of the sliding door of the van, LeEtta spied the two large bags of apples and smiled. Applesauce was way more appetizing than oats each morning, and what about that apple kuche recipe Eunice had given her? She considered all the dishes she could make for him and came to the conclusion that learning everything about another took lots of lists.

The rhythmic clang and shift of the picker in the background drew her attention north. Ben sat upon the metal seat, with Moses, Mike, and four other workhorses working in cadence with one another. All looked to be in their element, content with the chore, and happy to be out there. She raised a hand to shield the sun from her eyes just as Ben looked toward the house and threw up an arm. LeEtta quickly waved back, as did Ruby. She wondered which of them he was waving at but decided not to dwell on anything that would keep her up all night.

"Best be working on that larger table." Ruby chuckled, taking up a few bags in her hands and helping LeEtta put everything inside. LeEtta wanted kinner. She wanted Ben's kinner, with dark eyes and raven black hair. If they ever did reach a point where love could deliver them from this place to the next, she hoped he didn't mind if red hair came instead. One thing she did know—if she wanted a family and a marriage filled with love and respect, then it was time to court her own husband.

CHAPTER NINETEEN

LeEtta hummed while mixing flour, yeast, sugar, and oil, and then spread the batter out and along the corners of the pan. Next, she added canned, shredded potatoes, followed by the crumbled-up sausage. She beat a dozen eggs and smiled that the hens were laying again despite the shortened daylight hours. The eggs were the color of the harvest moon that spilled over the house that first night she became a bride. That seemed so long ago, and yet only weeks had passed.

Life had fallen into an acceptable routine, and despite what had brought them together, it seemed she and Ben were working for the same goal. The no-fail meat loaf Ruby insisted she try had disappeared, as had the apple kuche she had made for dessert. Ben had even inquired if she would be using up her jar of chocolate chips anytime soon. This evening, she hoped to make a batch of oatmeal chocolate chip cookies, adding nuts for Daed.

Focusing on the dish at hand, she saw that next came the cheese. She usually applied cheese with a liberal hand, but Ben's reluctance to eat the cheesy dishes that her father often devoured told her to be more cautious. She cut the amount in half before sliding the breakfast casserole into a hot stove.

At the icehouse, she fetched the pitcher of grape juice. She never slacked in picking grapes, cooking them slowly, and rendering out the pure juices to be sweetened up. Over the years, they had been blessed with an abundance of grapes from only three roots.

Next, LeEtta fetched the large glass container of granola. She made the large batch last week with twelve cups of oats, flaxseed, nuts, coconut, and honey. It, too, was disappearing quickly. She readied three bowls of the cereal, wishing she had yogurt instead of milk to go with the last of the blueberries from the ice house. Perhaps she could learn to make her own. Surely it wasn't so difficult, she reasoned.

She was just pulling the breakfast casserole from the oven when she heard the front door open and boots scraping the mat placed nearby. The table looked inviting and full, and she kept her joy contained as she watched both men polish off their plates happily.

"Another fine meal, dochter," Daed complimented.

"Jah, danke," Ben offered, taking up his own plate and carrying it to the sink. She appreciated his efforts more than he knew and swelled in knowing she wasn't the worst cook ever.

"When you finish up here, will you see to bringing the gravity wagon to the bins?"

LeEtta hesitated at his words, uncertain who Ben was speaking to. When his eyes landed on her, a quiet joy sprang up inside her.

"Rain is coming in a couple days, so there isn't much time," he added.

LeEtta looked to her father, who was more focused on picking blueberries from his cereal, then back to Ben. "You'll let me help?" Her voice was low, as if she feared he'd change his mind in the next five seconds.

"You wanted to farm," he cocked her a knowing grin. "Arlen will see you know what to do," he added before fetching his straw hat and heading out the door.

LeEtta looked to her father again. His frown said he wasn't in agreement with how Ben ran the farm. LeEtta pasted on a smile immediately. "Would you like another glass of milk?" she offered.

"That boy knows nothing about how to run a house."

"Nee, that's my duty, but he does know how to get a job done," LeEtta replied. Her father stood, collected his hat, and out the door he went as well. Jah, Ben was causing ripples, and LeEtta was suddenly fond of a few wrinkles in calm waters. In a few short minutes, she'd seen to the dishes, slipped on sturdy shoes, and run eagerly outside to work alongside her husband.

Posey didn't like mules, but after LeEtta explained the importance of teamwork and offered a half of an apple to both Posey and Tiny, who wasn't tiny at all but a full sixteen hands tall, the two set their stubborn differences aside.

LeEtta's duty wasn't complicated if you had done it before, but with Daed's instruction, she made lighter work for Ben as she moved an empty grain wagon to Ben once his was full. When he brought his team to a stop, she knew it was her time once again.

"Best go fetch it," Daed told her, some of his earlier gruffness fading. LeEtta didn't hesitate to work her small team toward the empty rows and in line with the full wagon. Ben then unhooked his full gravity wagon and attached the empty one before he was off again. The timid grin in passing said he didn't find her lacking at all in helping.

Posey and Tiny struggled with the fuller wagons. Rain had been scarce recently, but the ground was soft under the heavier weight. LeEtta took things slowly, not to overwork her precious Posey or give Tiny any cause to disrupt their rhythm.

At the corn bins, Daed helped muscle the elevator into place, open the side door of the gravity wagon, and see to it that everything was transferred into the tall wire corncribs. By the time one gravity wagon emptied, Ben was bringing the team to another halt.

The whole process took muscle and teamwork.

It was wonderful.

Ben watched his fraa work the mare and mule back toward the barn. He'd already forgiven Arlen for his harsh comment about inviting LeEtta to work alongside him. The man simply thought sheltering and hiding his only child would keep her safe. Ben admired his love for his daughter, but marriage required both sets of hands, and accidents happened inside as much as out.

By now, as the sun worked its way to decline, LeEtta's father was a firsthand witness to how well LeEtta could handle a small team with expert hands. It hadn't escaped him how many times she stopped to give the animals encouragement, and whatever she had in her dress pocket sure kept them eager to keep up the hard work.

Leo had been right. There were few things LeEtta couldn't do well. She could even hold her own against his stubbornness, he mused as he turned the team into an upper row of stalks. Despite all the things in her life that could have weakened her, she looked undefeated. She was a rarity, full of confidence and determination. A man could build a life with a woman like that by his side, willing to be his equal.

Under a shady eve of the barn, Arlen stood, chin up, one arm crossed naturally, the other by the bend of his cast, his gaze directly on LeEtta. If he only trusted in his daughter. Ben knew the constraints all too well—a parent bent on seeing you incapable of something Gott clearly made you for. Daed thought him incapable of running the family farm, yet Ben was proving he was plenty capable with how he was managing this one.

What Arlen needed was a distraction. That's what Ben concluded. LeEtta would be far less concerned with pleasing everyone if Arlen's focus was elsewhere. What LeEtta needed was a woman in her life who wasn't more focused on widowers than spending time with her granddaughter.

Ben was expecting his aenti any day now. She was the perfect remedy for both, and Ben had been missing her dumplings for some time. Aenti Oneida lived with his onkel and, like LeEtta, was fervently obedient. She aimed to please, so much so that she tended to overdo it. If anyone needed time away, it was her after living under her brother's roof all these years, and if anyone needed a woman in her life, it was LeEtta.

LeEtta deserved the companionship of someone who would be happy to share some of her wisdom with her. If Oneida was there, Arlen would pay less mind to keeping LeEtta indoors. Ben could focus on the crops, the land now his responsibility, and keeping them all from going hungry this winter.

Ben wasn't a fool. He knew he was the reason they had yet to grow closer as husband and wife. Too many betrayals were lining his conscience. Every time he let his guard down and forgot what brought them together, he found he was taken with her, especially her cute antics and her eager attempts at winning his heart.

So many times, he trusted others. So many times, that trust was severed with a sharp blade. *But she is trying,* the voice in his heart spoke. Jah, Aenti Oneida visiting for a while was a good idea, or else Ben might keep forgetting his heart was his own.

The warm autumn air kicked up, collecting dust and dirt in its tailspin. Moses and Mike led the team of six Belgians over the soft ground. He recalled what LeEtta said about prayer when he tried to explain that not everything was so easily dealt with, but LeEtta was right about everything, even prayer. She lost everything that binds the soul to bitterness. He wanted to lose that too. Prayer wasn't about gaining but about losing what held us hostage.

But could he let go?

Arlen waved him in, as it was getting darker and the horses would be needing a deserving meal and rest before it all started over again in the morning. He suspected his father-in-law was a man who didn't trust easily either.

Leaving the gravity wagon not yet full in the field, he aimed for the barn at a slow, meandering pace. A crimson blush of dusk leveled the sky. The landscape was breathtaking. The same rolling hills and valleys of home, but here, no one would tell him what to plant and when to harvest. Arlen had made that clear and that he was ready for rest, perhaps to tinker with something new if the arm would allow it.

Ben hated to see his elder give up such a perfect life. Farming was the most rewarding of all the trades. It only took a blink for life to change. Elbows shattered, loved ones passed, and numbered days could never be marked on a calendar.

At the barn, he and his father-in-law saw to it that the horses were fed, watered, and bedded down for the night. Arlen looked tired, with his left shoulder dropping heavier than usual. He'd give his elder credit. Age and his current disability didn't slow down his determination to see to what needed to be done. They had cleared the cornfields toward the west, filling wagons all day long, and Arlen had instructed his own daughter through it. It had been a good plan, Ben silently boasted, the father teaching the dochter as he should have years ago.

There was little Ben could do to change the past in his own life or mend rifts between him and his own father, but he could help LeEtta and Arlen. LeEtta was no longer that little girl needing to be sheltered and coddled, but a woman capable of working alongside her husband. The sooner Arlen knew it, the sooner he might focus on his own healing.

"Letty, head in to get supper on," Arlen said, giving his shoulder and his casting a hard rub.

"I could use a hot bath and supper. We made a lot of progress today." Ben decided not to comment on whatever LeEtta put together and to be thankful for it.

"I saw a light last night," Arlen said abruptly. "By the time I managed to get my boots on and get outside, it was gone, but you should know of it."

"A light?"

"A lantern. Out by the road. I don't much like thinking that someone is sneaking around."

"Me either," Ben agreed.

"I don't much like seeing Letty out there having to work like a man either."

"But you taught her well, and she did it as well as any other. Daed has yet to convince mei schwesters to handle more than one horse at a time."

The elder blinked. He removed his hat and gave it a hard smack on his leg. Ben could see the process of his thoughts battling one another and waited to see which side he would contend with next.

"She ain't faul and has a good head on her shoulders. Did you think she couldn't?"

"Nee, I didn't know what to think, but I will say you did well raising her. There ain't much she can't do."

"Nee, that's my Letty." Arlen lifted his chin and slipped back into the barn. It took all Ben could do not to burst into laughter right then.

CHAPTER TWENTY

A lid popped, proof that the seal was set on another thirty-five quarts of applesauce. Two more bushels were finished. It was good to know the pantry was becoming more full. LeEtta happily sighed as she finished drying the large stockpot. There was afternoon milking yet to do and supper to get ready, but admiring autumn's last reign before storms blew in, undressing the trees to complete nakedness, shouldn't hurt. Work would be there no matter how long she gawked out the kitchen window.

Hearing the sound of a motor outside, she quickly dried her hands and went to see who had come. She suspected Dan Schwartz needed her to see over the kinner again, as Anna Jay had what many were calling a setback. Yet LeEtta still had yet to determine what ailed the young mother.

LeEtta recognized Ruby's van immediately. That maroon fender did stick out. Stepping out onto the porch, she watched Ruby exit the vehicle and toss up a hand before opening the sliding door. LeEtta waved and smiled. She did like the chatty Englischer. Her arm slowly lowered when an Amish woman stepped out. Ruby set two suitcases on the ground and took a few bills from the woman.

"I'd stay and chat, but I gotta get home and feed my cat before he thinks I've abandoned him," Ruby said, chuckling as she drove off.

A cool afternoon wind bit her cheeks as the small woman turned in a half circle. Her round face and bright, wide eyes framed in tinted glasses took in the barn and pastures before settling back on the house and LeEtta standing there. On her wrist were two shopping bags. She looked to be in her upper forties, with brown hair that didn't show a single thread of silver and a smile that looked happy that she had arrived. The trouble was, LeEtta feared she had been dropped off at the wrong house.

"Hello," LeEtta greeted. Hopefully, she would be able to deliver her in the buggy to where she needed to truly go before time for milking and preparing supper.

"Oh hiya, dear. I was just taking in this beautiful farm. Benuel said it was beautiful, but you know Benuel, he thinks even old women like me are worthy of a look." Her smile widened as she struggled to latch onto both suitcases.

LeEtta flinched. Ben hadn't mentioned anyone coming, and clearly she was no stranger. Panic filled LeEtta suddenly. She had a visitor.

"You must be LeEtta. Ach, how young you are," she said scrupulously.

"I'm twenty-two." Not necessarily an old maid. "Here, let me help you." LeEtta grabbed the larger suitcase. "Are you. . .family?"

The woman stopped and gave her a quizzical stare before her shoulders sank. "He didn't even tell you I was coming, did he?" Then she laughed, a loud and booming sound that rattled windows and made youngies sit straighter. LeEtta was taken aback momentarily by the fact that such an infectious sound came out of such a small slip of a woman.

"I'm Benuel's Aenti Oneida Eicher. I'm here for. . .a visit." She sounded uncertain, but LeEtta was thrilled to meet more of Ben's family. In fact, company might improve LeEtta's poor sleeping habits of late.

"Ach. Then *wilkum*. I'm so happy to meet more of Benuel's family."

"I'm now your family too." Oneida winked, and LeEtta couldn't help but smile at her inclusion—and that her house would be blessed with more noise. It would be blessed with more. . .family.

"I haven't made up a room, and I was just about to do the milking and start supper."

"Now don't you go fretting about that. I wanted to arrive sooner, but that Ruby sure likes to shop." Oneida laughed again. "Won't hear me complain," she said, lifting two bags, "as it gave me a chance to fend off my cravings. Now I ain't here to sit about and do nothing. I know my nephew enough to know it takes a special sort to keep up with him." As they reached the porch, Oneida paused to look at her. "Benuel failed to warn you of my coming. Much like John that way, but you see to your milking and I'll see to supper."

"Ach, I can't..."

"I've been craving taco salad since last Friday, and I'm determined to get it."

"Taco salad?" LeEtta wrestled the heavy suitcase into the house.

"Just point me to a kitchen, and kumm hungry."

LeEtta was about to tell her she was a guest, but her elder already predicted her next words.

"You look worn to a nub, dear. I'm not spending two whole months here and letting you wait on me hand and foot. A woman has to do something"—she let out a huff as she closed the door behind them—"or she'll wither up to nothing."

LeEtta knew not to question her elders and had to admit that her sore hands and lagging arms were grateful Gott sent someone at the perfect time. After years of being tended to gently, the labor was taking a toll on her body.

"What is..." Oneida squinted to read a label on LeEtta's overcrowded spice shelf, "Alaskan Sea Salt?"

"The store owner said it tastes better on fried chicken," LeEtta tried to explain.

"Doesn't all salt? Now you go see to your milking while I put my things away."

LeEtta carried the heavy suitcase up the narrow stairs and set it down in Daed's old room. Ben had moved the guest bed in there recently, saying it had more room. She had hoped he was considering sleeping down the hall instead of in the old barn, but now it appeared he had a plan all along. His communication skills needed help. LeEtta would have happily readied the room if he had mentioned it.

LeEtta hurried through her milking. She strained and stored the milk and watched with interest as Oneida made quick work of browning beef, adding spices and tomato juice, with just a spoonful of Therm Flo to thicken the liquid.

"While that simmers, can you chop some lettuce, onions, and tomatoes?" Oneida began pulling ingredients out of her bag. "Ach, and this pepper." She had clearly shopped at the Amish market in the nearby community before coming here. No one sold peppers as large as they did.

"Now I didn't account for dessert, so. . ." Oneida reached into a second bag, revealing a pecan pie.

"Daed will be begging you to stay longer when he sees that. It's his favorite." LeEtta laughed. Oh, how she liked having another woman about.

Oneida lifted a brow. "Well, I didn't know your father lived here. I sure hope I won't be taking up someone's room."

"Nee, he lives behind the house, though he didn't have to." LeEtta focused on dicing tomatoes. "He loves pecan pie. I'm not very good in the kitchen, except for making bread." She bit her lower lip.

"I see you can handle applesauce just fine." Oneida motioned toward the jars cooling on the counter nearby.

"Some things I can't mess up."

"Ach, I'm sure you do fine, my dear, and don't you fret. I know Benuel's favorites and will soon learn yours too. I love to cook and won't be a guest that only eats, though I do love eating." She pointed a look at LeEtta, but there was a playful smile beneath it.

Jah, she was going to enjoy spending time with Benuel's aenti.

"I can do most of the cooking. I don't mind."

"You will too," Oneida pointed out. "A woman must learn how to feed her family, but you and Benuel have just wed. I know farming requires four hands and lots of faith. That crop isn't going to harvest itself, you know." She tilted her head, revealing more of her dark brown hair.

"It's best if you two have some time working together. A couple who works together well, their life will be swell." She smiled and pushed her glasses up higher on her nose. "I hope we can enjoy our time together too. I look forward to getting to know you."

"I will like that. What will your family do while you are here with us?"

"Ach." Oneida waved a hand in the air. "I am unwed and was happy for a break from under mei bruder's roof. One tends to forget they have plenty to do when someone else is doing it."

LeEtta imagined a woman so forward got things done. She hated to think her strong will was being taken advantage of.

While the room filled with strong spices, Oneida spoke of her bruder, Clayton, and his fraa, Liz. "They grew to a place where doing for themselves was no longer worth the energy. I'm saving them from diabetes and an early grave," Oneida insisted.

The back kitchen door opened along with the sound of boots scraping along the floor mat. LeEtta looked up from setting the table as Ben and her father entered the room.

"Aenti Oneida!" Ben smiled brightly, wrapping the small woman in a hug so tight that her feet lifted from the floor. "When did you arrive?"

"I have been here for two hours, and I'm surprised it took you this long to notice," she jested as Ben let her go and she turned to LeEtta. "LeEtta was kind enough to set up my room, but I had to beg her to let me make a taco salad. You know how I am with my cravings." They both laughed out loud at the remark. It seemed Oneida had cravings often. LeEtta wondered if she ever craved dumplings. No matter how many recipes she'd tried, they never tasted quite right.

Ben gestured toward Arlen. "Aenti Oneida, this is Arlen, my father-in-law."

LeEtta watched Daed remove his hat, and his bald spot dipped slightly as he nodded and locked gazes with Oneida. In a matter of just two breaths, the two simply stared at one another as if seeing an old friend for the first time in years. First glances turned into timid smiles. Strange, she thought. Daed was always polite and tolerable, but he liked life just as it was. Perhaps moving into his own place had made him more appreciative of visitors too.

"You have a nice place here, Arlen," Oneida offered.

"Danke, and whatever you're cooking sure smells good," Daed returned, as his smile eerily remained in place.

LeEtta collected forks, sour cream, and corn chips. Oneida insisted it was the only way to eat taco salad, and the higher everything was stacked, the better. LeEtta didn't miss the soft look of appreciation her father gave Oneida when she set the pecan pie closer to him. Sitting to Ben's left, LeEtta felt a tender warmth fill her as all heads bowed. Today, her empty house was full. For that, she was thankful.

"That was a fine meal, Oneida," Arlen said. If LeEtta wasn't mistaken, Oneida blushed at the comment.

"I'll see to the kitchen, since you bought all the ingredients and did all the cooking," LeEtta insisted once the meal was eaten.

"Let me show you around, Aenti. I still need to see to a few chores anyhow." Ben escorted his aenti outside.

"How long is she staying around?" Daed asked, helping himself to a second slice of pie.

"A month or two is what she mentioned when she arrived. Ben didn't tell me she was coming, but she seems wonderfully kind."

Behind her, Daed grunted. LeEtta began washing the dishes as daylight faded and Ben and Oneida's shadows moved across the yard outside. Daylight was fading quickly these days, and the air was growing colder. It was easy to see Ben favored the woman by the way he casually strolled at her side, pointing out this and that and talking as if he had been saving up all his words for her. LeEtta loved seeing him so content.

"I think I'll go take a shower and get ready for bed," she told her father.

"Jah, I should head that way myself." Daed reached for his hat. "Ben didn't mention his aenti was coming to me either."

Her daed stared at her for a short moment, before leaving for his own bed, under a different roof, just around the corner.

The presence of family pleased him to the core. Ben had been missing the connection. His heart seized, thinking about how Mamm was probably in her sewing room, most likely sewing another quilt or a dress for one of his schwesters.

He should have shared with LeEtta that his aenti was coming. Even though the two seemed to be fast freinden already, he didn't like to think he caught her unaware. His father-in-law, on the other hand, appeared more surprised, though Ben had noted more than a handful of times over supper how he stole glances at Oneida.

Ben stifled a grin. Arlen was too set in his ways to get to know his aenti. They also had nothing in common, Ben thought as he breathed a sigh of relief. Arlen Miller was set firmly in his old ways. Oneida was a breeze over dry land. She didn't speak harshly about anyone and always found the brighter side in any situation.

"I like her," Oneida said, adjusting her kapp. "Miriam said she was a verra nice young woman. Your mamm is happy to see you settled."

"It takes little for her to be happy." It was the truth. Mamm found joy in everyday things that most brushed off naturally.

"LeEtta says you work on a hog farm." She crinkled her nose.

"We can use the money," Ben admitted. He could always be honest with his aenti. Of all his family, she never made him feel as if he had failed at doing something.

"You saw Arlen's arm. He had a bad fall before I got here." Ben explained Arlen's condition and how the farm hadn't turned a profit after last year's drought and the summer floods that ravished corn the year before. "I have but a small savings left since Daed handed the farm over to Sam, you know."

"You put more than all your hard work into that farm," she huffed and slipped her hands in her coat pockets. "But no matter the choice others make, we must do what we have to."

"I'm glad you're here, Oneida." Ben knew little of his aenti's past, only that she had never wed by choice. That never seemed to cause her any hardships, though, as she was always fussing over her many nieces and nephews.

They strolled along the fencing and around the barn. Ben introduced her to Mike, Moses, Posey, and the rest of the horses. "We got a milker inside," he said. "LeEtta likes her." It was an unnecessary comment, and when Oneida smiled at him, Ben felt his face warm.

"I'm certain she does. You mentioned on the phone that she had no family aside from her daed."

"She has Iola." Ben chuckled. "LeEtta's grandmother is…widowed." LeEtta had informed Ben about her grandmother's odd obsession. He liked Iola, with her oddness and all. Ben appreciated a person who had no agenda, no false intentions, and kept others entertained. "I'm certain you two will make fast freinden."

"I'm certain we will. It's a shame he never remarried."

"Who?" Ben looked at her perplexed.

"Arlen. He is young yet, and LeEtta would have certainly bene-fited from having a mamm." She leaned in close and giggled. "I see what you meant about that spice rack. The poor dear seems as if she is searching for the perfect blend. For what, I haven't a clue yet."

"She can test the taste buds, for sure." Ben laughed too, though he did find he liked many of the strange blends and flavors LeEtta cooked with. If only she didn't have such an obsession with cheese.

"Arlen likes to coddle her too much." He kicked a clod of dirt. "He nearly took my head off when I let her help us bring in the harvest. We don't see eye to eye on much."

Oneida nodded in understanding. "I have seen my share of such, but you have to see it from his perspective. She is his only child."

"But she is no longer a child."

"Nee, but a father's love has no end, as so we have been taught from the cradle."

CHAPTER TWENTY-ONE

LeEtta ripped October from the calendar as a cold wind picked up outside. While Oneida seasoned brown beans on the stove, LeEtta slipped out of the house and hurried toward the mailbox at the end of the lane.

With a scarf fitted tightly around her shoulders, she sifted through the mail. Her tender palms still bore the redness from helping to see the last of the harvest put up. The crop brought more than enough, Ben had said. LeEtta didn't know what more than enough was but trusted that it meant less worry lines would wrinkle her father's expressions.

Hints of a storm filled the air. Rumors of harsh weather moving across the country had been the center of recent talk, bringing with it lots of wind and rain before temperatures were going to drop even more. LeEtta never minded rain or snow, but no one liked ice unless it was in a glass.

She paused in her steps when she came to a white envelope. The return address read Samuel Ropp, 455 Baltic Rd. Though she and Miriam had already exchanged four letters, this was the first contact in nearly two months between the brothers. Sam had taken that first step.

Hopefully, time will heal this sore. She prayed it was news that her husband would be ready to hear. Carefully tucking the letter in her pocket, LeEtta raced back to the house to help get supper ready.

The moment Ben arrived, LeEtta couldn't help but notice how tired he was. Even with Oneida there, he was quieter than usual.

"Don't be skipping dessert," Oneida ordered in motherly fashion. She wasn't the only one who noticed Ben's appetite wasn't much this evening. "LeEtta made something special."

Ben's eyes lit up, giving her heart a jolt. "I fetched the mail, and you received a letter today." LeEtta slid the letter across the table. He glanced down, taking note of the address as well, and set down his spoon. Wounds etched the lines across his brow and turned his narrowed look into a distant cold one. LeEtta had hoped he would welcome news from home with less resentment.

She peered over to Oneida, who was more focused on crumbling cornbread into her beans. The chopped onions added to the flavors just as Oneida promised they would. Sensing Ben's inner turmoil, LeEtta thought it best she excuse herself and let Ben read his letter in private.

"If you don't mind," she said, collecting a plate for Daed in the dawdi haus next door, "I'll just take Daed a plate. I want to see how his doctor visit went today." She placed a towel over the plate and wrapped her shawl around her shoulders.

"The whoopie pies are in the container if you want them," she offered before slipping out of the room. Ben had become terribly fond of her whoopie pies, so LeEtta made sure he never ran out of them as long as the right ingredients were on hand. Oneida was teaching her that not all ingredients had a good substitute—and how important that was to a recipe. Marriage was a lot like that too, she considered as a cold wind snaked around her as she reached the dawdi haus door.

The dawdi haus had one bedroom. The small, simple kitchen and sitting area made up one wide room. Just this week, Daed had hired Ervin Graber to attach a small bathroom to the side nearest to the cooking stove, so hot water was readily available.

It was cozy but terribly small. Then again, Daed would have fussed if he had too much to tend to himself. LeEtta had taken care of all the painting herself. Unfortunately, Daed favored brown. Such a dreary color for walls, but other than collecting his laundry and seeing his pantry filled with simple necessities, she didn't have to live here. If he was happy, then she would pretend to be.

Knocking softly, she laughed at herself for knocking at all, and she crept inside quietly in case he was napping. She stepped lightly over pale gray cement floors. She hoped that over the winter months, she'd have time to add a second coat of paint, but Daed insisted that one was plenty. Did he not take into account kicked-off boots and the scrapes of living in such a tight space?

LeEtta immediately spotted her father in the old recliner that had once been the center of the sitting room of their home. On his lap lay a copy of the *Connection*, with its glossy pages shining in the light of the propane lamp on the nearby table. His bald spot was shining too, she noticed and grinned. He preferred to read the farming magazine and was a faithful subscriber to its small-scale farming articles. He'd spend hours scanning the pages of the *Busy Beaver*, even though he never planned to buy any of the farming equipment sold there. However, there were times, scant ones, when he drew quiet and resorted to reading the *Connection*. It contained articles on farming, cooking, health, and spiritual reflection. The latter she always felt helped draw him out of his solemnity.

Did grief really last as long as his had? She had often wondered. There were many in the community who had lost a spouse, but after a time, most remarried. Not her father. He spoke nothing of the woman who took up residence in his heart so strongly that he fell into bits of melancholy. LeEtta let out a quiet sigh. Her mother must have been the most wonderful fraa.

Not wanting to wake him, LeEtta set his supper plate on the nearby table. Quietly, she slipped out of the house and into a sea of blackness that had quickly taken over, with the exception of a few flashes of the coming storm off in the distance. Even nature drew quiet, knowing something lurked there in the distance. As she turned the corner leading to the washroom door, a flicker of light caught her eye.

Not a flash, but something lower to the ground. She couldn't make out a single shadow or tree, not as dark as it was, but knew instantly it was a flashlight as it moved ahead of its own brightness, maneuvering back and forth as if to ensure its handler didn't stumble through the short forest of oak, dying ash, and maple.

Knowing someone was there caused a sudden chill to run up her spine. She had heard the strange noises, passing them off as a wild varmint. She had a missing dress, and there was still no explanation why her hens had stopped laying for a time. Fear wrapped her chest and squeezed. "And Ben's boots," she muttered into the darkness.

With that in mind, LeEtta rushed into the house, closing the door behind her and turning the lock. She had never locked the doors before. Folks didn't have a reason to, but now her suspicions were confirmed. Someone had been stealing their things. It had to be someone close by, someone who had been at the Hostetlers that evening when Ben's shoes disappeared. Jonas was her first suspect, but she had seen the look in his eyes and the anger there—that she'd even considered him capable of stealing Ben's shoes. It had made sense, yet LeEtta believed him. Jonas was just a boy, incapable of causing fear in others, and right now, LeEtta was afraid.

"Ben," LeEtta said, rushing into the kitchen to let him know. Surely he would investigate and see who was traveling the woods line, but the kitchen was empty. Her husband, gone. Had the light she'd seen been him wandering about through the night? If ever she wished their marriage was a more solid union, it was now. Instead of trembling as she was, she would be wrapped in Ben's arms and cradled firmly through whatever would come next.

Around her, the house grew suddenly colder, darker, and quieter than it had ever been in all her years. A thought to wake her father hit her, but how could she show him she was no longer a child if she ran to him over every hiccup and storm she found in her path?

"You look a fright, dear." Oneida emerged from the shadowy

staircase. "Is your father ill?" She stepped into the light, revealing a worried look.

"Nee, I just thought. . ." Did she dare scare Aenti Oneida? Did she want Oneida to think she was fearful of every little thing? "It has been a long day, and I should go on to bed."

"Jah, that is a gut idea for both of us. I just wanted to see that you returned all right. LeEtta, if something is troubling you, you know you can talk to me, jah?"

"I do, danke. I'm glad you're here, Oneida. I don't know how I would manage all this alone." With that, LeEtta hurried upstairs. She didn't run, as that might scare her elder, but the moment LeEtta entered her bedroom, she locked the door behind her.

Ben made sure all the animals were settled, giving Moses and Mike each half of one whoopie pie. He shouldn't have favorites, but both were clearly worthy of more than grain and fresh water.

With flashlight in hand, he went to the tack room and the corner he had cleverly staked out for himself. Lifting the lid from the old crate, he fetched the bedding safely tucked inside. He wasn't looking forward to another miserable night sleeping in the barn, but distance and space were best for a man who had made a promise to himself.

LeEtta was a hard woman to avoid, but he couldn't trust his own heart anymore. He had trusted his daed, and look where that got him. He rolled out the blankets and then fetched the pillow. He had trusted his friends, and they turned their backs on him. He had trusted the fast friendship he and LeEtta made, and here he was.

Gott was surely teasing him by putting a woman who easily complemented him at his side. A farmer's daughter. Ben felt the smile emerge as her image filled his thoughts. He liked hearing her hum while milking when she thought no one was around, or how kinner seemed to gravitate toward her. The way her head cocked to one side when she listened intently to what he had to say.

Ben shook away his daydreaming. He couldn't even trust his own thoughts to stay on course. He had a farm. One that would make most men envious. Why couldn't he simply be content with that?

Because you're sleeping in a barn when you have a beautiful fraa not far away. He lowered his head and stared at the dirty bedroll. He was lonely, tired of sleeping in a barn, and tired of dreaming about LeEtta's lips. LeEtta's sore hands. The way LeEtta smiled at chickens!

He had been drawn to her the moment he caught a glimpse of her red hair. When she smiled while talking about creeks and orchards, he knew he was in trouble. She had no qualms about working hard, and it barbed him to see her nursing her blisters in silence. Mary and Lisa would have cried for days, fearing permanent scarring. Not his wife. He blushed at the thought of how many times he stole glances at her womanly shape when she wasn't looking. How her brows lifted curiously as she waited for his approval for whatever dish she served up.

Ben had also noticed the subtle changes. She no longer rambled while talking. Ben missed the rambling. The twinkle in her eye changed to her worrying her bottom lip. He clenched his fist at the thought. If another had made her look so broken and so overwhelmed, he would have had something to say to him about it, but it was him. He had no one to blame but his own steadfast determination that his heart could not be given away. His pride sat at the center of their marriage. Daed had always accused him of being prideful.

Marriage had not been kind to her. He had not been kind to her. His duty was to honor and love her, and yet he wasn't doing either. He couldn't even stay angry for her part in any of this. It was not LeEtta's fault he was here. In truth, Bishop Graber never told him he had to marry her. Ben made that choice. He had a choice. He had made it, and so had she. He could have gone home and begged Daed to change his mind, but that too was a choice, and now he was finding that everything about his wife was worthy of his love.

Love.

Nee, he didn't love her. He couldn't.

Warmth crept over his flesh as cool night air seeped through cracks he had yet to see filled. Shoving both hands into his pockets, he found the letter. He knew LeEtta hoped he'd read it and that something inside might help soften his resentment. Maybe it would, he thought as he tore the envelope open.

Ben,

I know you don't want to talk to me, so writing seemed like the only way to speak to you without seeing your disappointment. I miss you, brother. I had to get that out first. You are the one person I could always go to when I needed advice.

Daed's decision was a surprise to me too. He came to me the night before, but I refused. At first. I cannot know his reasons. The rift between you two is wider than the one between us now, but when you left and later married, I felt you made your choice. This farm has been in our family for many years, and I did not want to give that up.

Ben squeezed his fist as anger heated his veins. Words he didn't want to read stared at him with a pointed finger. Ben had left. He had married. His decisions left Sam to make a choice. The same choice he would have made if he were in Sam's shoes. Of course, Sam had to accept Daed's offer or the farm that had been part of their very roots for generations would have been cut into pieces over time. A few acres here for Mary, a few there for Lisa, and a few for him and Sam. It would not be the farm of their childhood any longer.

Reality stung sharpest when it was your own mistakes staring back at you. Ben continued reading his brother's words.

As you knew I would, I have started a dairy. I already purchased fifty good milkers and am waiting on milking supplies to be delivered as I write this. I wish you were here to help set things up.

Ben felt a tug of emotion. He wished he were too. Sam had a knack for numbers but not for starting new ventures. Then again, Daed would see to it that he did not fail, Ben thought with regret. How many times had his father tried to instruct him, only for Ben to choose a different path? It was hard to admit, but the better son had been chosen.

You always had a better head for that. Mamm misses you, and last week she made your favorite kuche. Mary and Lisa are just happy to have separate rooms. Your fraa mentioned you have already made friends and have already made a home there. I'm happy for you, but I hope you will visit soon. Don't keep away from us or from me. Especially if I ask Mary Eicher to marry me. Should I? I wish I knew your thoughts. You chose well. I want to do the same.

If his brother only knew Ben hadn't chosen at all. *"But she did choose me,"* his heart spoke as a tear leaked from his left eye.

I have to go now. Milking supplies are here. Put the check in the bank, brother. You worked hard for the future you wanted, and so did I. May God bless you and keep you.

Your only brother,
Samuel

Ben reached back into the envelope and produced the thin paper check. Through watery eyes, he made out the number and felt his knees weaken. It was an answer to all their prayers. It was a fresh start and a saving grace.

Ben closed his eyes. "Danke, Lord. I don't deserve this, but You have given us exactly what we need. I'm not sure I'm deserving of it, but knowing Sam sent this has shown me what a fool I have been." At the amen that followed, Ben felt fresh air climb into his lungs. He had done everything wrong, yet the Lord had seen fit to continue to bless him.

Opening his eyes, Ben caught a glimpse of a light from a dusty old window toward the far end of the farm. It was faint, glowing, and most certainly out of place in the wooded area. Arlen had said he was concerned someone was sneaking about, and it seemed the older man was right.

Ben gripped the flashlight in his hand and went to investigate. Working the light back and forth, he searched for signs but found none. Once he reached the end of the fence, where grass took over the dirt, Ben spent nearly an hour checking out disturbed ground and broken limbs.

Another gust of wind kicked up, ripping his straw hat from his head. Ben quickly retrieved it. It was best to wait until daylight, but as he turned to head back to the barn, Ben couldn't help but have an unsettled feeling that Jonas Hostetler was still sore at both of them.

CHAPTER TWENTY-TWO

"You could have a gut start if you're of the mind to," Shep encouraged Ben as he waved the last newly weaned piglets into holding pens.

"I appreciate the work, as it has fed us well, but I have never been one for raising livestock."

"You sure?" Shep cocked his head. His dark beard hung wide across his chest, a silver streak secluded to one side. "For someone who doesn't like livestock, you're sure a fast learner."

"Didn't say I couldn't," Ben replied. It wasn't hard raising pigs, not with the 3-3-3 rule of pig farming that kept a man busy. Shep kept his own breeding stock in one hog barn, and from conception to birth, it took three months, three weeks, and three days for new piglets to emerge. Now the weaned ones were getting settled in the finishing barn, where they would be fed and cared for until they reached two hundred fifty pounds for the wholesaler. Then the whole process would start all over again.

Farming, now that was work. One could not predict the outcome, no matter how much labor and care you put into it. Ben had his hand in many trades over the years, but a job that challenged you, he was well-suited for.

"Have you always raised livestock?"

"I worked for one of the construction crews when I was younger. I reckon my heart would have stayed there if I hadn't fallen off a ladder."

Ben had noticed that after a long day, Shep tended to favor his left foot but passed it off as the perils of age and man butting heads.

"Busted the ankle up and cracked my skull." He leaned closer and chuckled. "Don't tell those kinner of mine. They already think me soft in the head." Shep winked.

"Your secret is safe," Ben said.

Ben had put in a long day at Shep's, the scent of his clothes saying as much. Sam's check was burning a hole in his pocket each time a sow decided to take another nip at him. Taking the young from their mothers was not a chore for the fainthearted. They filled the organic grain bins, helped two seasoned sows into birthing pens so piglets were less likely to be trampled on, and readied for market a hundred pigs from the third barn that had reached the ideal weight the supplier requested.

Now his own work waited for him. The cold November wind reminded him he had wood to chop, a barn to clean, and fresh straw needing to be put down. He pulled into the drive. *His drive.* Why was considering this his home still a foreign thought? *Because you have not left your past behind.*

It was hard to admit to being wrong, and Ben had been terribly wrong. Still, fear of letting himself trust another seemed close. He hated to admit how much like LeEtta's father he was becoming, holding on to the past as he was.

It was the chickens racing in a mix of directions over the yard that he first saw as he pulled up to the barn. Instinctually, he looked to the sky. Hawks and owls were fearful predators. Not a wing flapped against a backdrop of pale blue.

LeEtta would be watching Dan Schwartz's kinner today. Ben smiled, recalling just how happy she was when the young father stopped by yesterday, hoping she could see over the youngest of his household. His smile widened, thinking how much she chatted about the girls, especially little Laverna, who had taken up residence in LeEtta's heart.

A chicken squawked, gathering his attention, and he quickly climbed out of the buggy, tethering the horse to a nearby gate. LeEtta had a thing for these critters and would be heartbroken to lose even one.

As he neared the coop, his fraa emerged from behind the house with a hen tucked tightly under her arm. He hadn't even looked to see if Posey was in the pasture. LeEtta had clearly returned home earlier than he expected today.

"Ach, Ben," she said in surprise, but no less concerned by his presence than keeping the fat hen content in her arms as she hurried to the open coop. "The door must have blown open, although I'm sure I latched it this morning before I left. I haven't even started the milking yet." She blew out a breath. A thick strand of hair escaped the dark blue scarf around her head.

Ben watched as she tossed the first runaway into the coop and closed the door. She turned to the remaining escapees and considered her next move. The wind worked her dress along with a few strands of her red hair. God had blessed him with a beautiful wife and an expert chicken wrangler, he thought with a laugh.

"I'll see to your supper in a bit," she assured him, "but I can't let them think it's safe out here. Not with so many coons and all."

"Let me help you," he offered. After all, did he not tell Arlen they were a team? "I can do the milking after we're done." A smile bloomed over her face, and he couldn't help but smile back.

Chasing chickens and catching chickens were totally different things. LeEtta caught chickens, while Ben seemed to only be chasing them. She spoke softly, inching up behind a hen that was happily focused on wild feed, before reaching out and taking it into her hands.

Ben, on the other hand, had never been soft-spoken, and when you were six feet and an inch with big feet and smelled like a hog farm, the element of surprise didn't work in your favor.

"That's nine!" LeEtta floated him a wide grin, as if catching chickens were a game he should consider mastering. Normally, he would have taken the bait and played her foolish game, but Ben had only wrangled one hen into submission so far. A man knew when he stood a chance and when it was best to surrender.

He laid eyes on his next victim, who was scratching and displacing mulch under a boxwood. Reaching out, he was surprised at how quickly he caught her.

"Two!" *As if it compared.*

They made a team effort to catch two more, with Ben scaring them into a corner and LeEtta laying hold of them. It was the last hen, white as the fourteen before her, but LeEtta named her Callie, who was on to both of them and not ready to give up a day of free ranging.

"Go around her," Ben instructed. Putting up hay under a hot August sun would've seemed less daunting. They both sprang toward the hen at the same time. Ben went to his knees, skidding on the ground. LeEtta must have caught a shoe on her dress or second-guessed her current direction and stumbled toward the base of a maple tree.

Ben quickly reached out, one large hand cupping her head to protect it from hitting the maple's trunk. With the other, he pulled her to him to soften her fall. If he hadn't been so taken aback by her surprised eyes and the soft grunt that escaped her, he might have let her go. Instead, Ben held on as if she were still in danger and he had to protect her from what lurked. He breathed her in, relishing the closeness of her small frame tangled with his.

"You smell like donuts," he said in a low tone. He liked donuts. He also liked holding her. He expected her to jump quickly to her feet to continue her chase of. . .Callie, was it? When her eyes blinked at him warmly, he couldn't recall his own name, much less a chicken's.

They remained there, enamored with one another, until the sound of a door closing from somewhere on the other side of the house ended the moment. LeEtta pushed off of him and got to her feet.

"You smell like a hog farm." She got up, quickly straightened her dress, and smiled playfully before she resumed the chase.

"Did you catch them all?" Oneida yelled from somewhere in the distance.

Ben gave Oneida a sheepish look before seeing to the afternoon milking. Rosey didn't mind his rougher touch, and Ben tried to put aside thoughts of LeEtta in his arms while milk continued to fill the stainless steel pail. Was it wrong to admit that he liked holding her so close? Would God provide him with a second chance to do so soon? Keeping his heart locked up safely was becoming a chore. It was also holding him hostage.

Once finished, Ben entered the cozy little haus feeling strangely fresh. For the first time in over a year, he had a reason to anticipate tomorrow.

The Schwartz kinner had been full of too much sugar. LeEtta only wanted to see those precious smiles and didn't hesitate to make donuts for them when they claimed they had never had them. The way they devoured them, LeEtta was certain she had been tricked. Despite how tired she was, she was happy to see that they had come out of their quiet, timid shells, leaving behind whatever sadness had loomed over them from their first encounter.

But once she pulled into the yard, LeEtta had set aside her weariness at the sight of a loose hen. She had set the latch as she always did. Of that she felt certain. Was it possible someone set them free for predators to devour? There were too many odd events surrounding her. Since spying the light in the woods, she decided it was best to remain vigilant.

Despite the troubling thought that someone was bent on making life miserable for her, LeEtta was thankful Ben arrived when he did to help her see them all secured back in the coop. Watching a grown man catch a chicken brought a second smile to her face.

She finished putting away the last of the dishes as the clock chimed eight times. She was too weary for even a glass of warm milk. All she wanted was a soft pillow under her head and a warm blanket to hide under, where she could dream about Ben holding her. She knew he had only meant to keep her from falling into the tree and scraping her arms, or worse, hitting her head, but once he had rescued her from her clumsy attempt to catch Callie, he hadn't let go.

It was evidence that Ben did care for her, but how could she help him heal his betrayed heart and open up to her if he was determined to stay stuck in his past hurts? She felt perfectly safe there in his arms. A blush warmed her face as she turned off the mineral spirit lamp over the table and went about seeing the house secured for the night.

With a flashlight in hand, LeEtta checked all the windows. Each was still locked as they had been since the day she'd seen the light in the woods. With quiet steps, she moved to secure the side kitchen door and the back door and was just about to check the locks on the front door when a tapestry of familiar scents found her.

Roses. A citrusy scent was also present. *Lilies.* Lighter tones of mint were there too. Cautiously and curiously, LeEtta opened the door. Sure enough, there on the rocker next to the door lay the culprit that had rattled her senses. Wrapped in old newspapers, the flowers looked starved for water. Her heart galloped in her chest. What fraa didn't swoon over such a beautiful, sweet-smelling gift?

Taking up the flowers, her smile stretched, thinking about how he had held her and the way he stared at her through supper, talking about his day and asking her about her own. He laughed when she shared how many donuts Laverna and Bethie consumed. It was only after Laverna's third that LeEtta convinced them to save some for Anna Mary once she returned from school.

Familiarity was being gained, and all she could hope for, as she buried her nose within rose petals. Movement caused her to still in the dark doorway. Clutching her flashlight in a shaky hand, LeEtta turned the light toward the direction of the noise.

"What are you doing outside at this hour?"

LeEtta swiveled the light until it landed on Ben, standing in the shadows.

"I found—" The words dropped as she noticed him shirtless and walking her way purposefully.

"What is this?"

"Flowers. I could smell them, and when I opened the door, they were lying right here."

His scowl deepened. "Do you want to tell me who left them there?" His tone had become gravelly, and her heart sank under its accusing cadence.

"I don't know who left them there. I thought. . ." She bit her lower lip and looked at him. Worse than knowing Ben hadn't left her flowers was that she hadn't found a way into his closed heart.

"I did not put them there." His frown deepened. "Gut nacht, LeEtta Miller."

She watched him slip back into the shadows and felt another chin bump in her way. "Ropp," she whispered. She was his wife. *In name only.* How quickly had he forgotten the moment that had passed between them just hours ago? They were back to starting all over again.

Her stomach twisted in nauseating knots with all the effort she had put in to win Ben's heart, swinging her determination between making him as miserable as she was and being a devout fraa as Gott instructed. She wanted to call him back and demand he listen to her, but instead, she set the flowers back on the rocker and went back inside. Despite her inner turmoil, LeEtta knew Ben still struggled with trust. Someone was deepening the crevasse she was working so hard to bridge over. She'd choose grace.

CHAPTER TWENTY-THREE

Oneida sprinkled brown sugar and cinnamon over the spread-out dough. "This used to be Ben's favorite thing to do, helping me make cinnamon rolls."

"I didn't know he liked helping in the kitchen," LeEtta said as she handed Oneida dental floss. This was not a time for worrying over your teeth, LeEtta thought, but no sooner had she opened her mouth to offer to finish the cinnamon rolls did Oneida speak.

"Ach, this was his favorite part. I know a knife works just as well." Oneida slowly rolled the dough. "But my cousin Irene owns a bakery and insists this is the best way to cut your dough."

LeEtta watched with piqued fascination as Oneida took over two and a half feet of the dental floss and wrapped the ends around her first fingers. She slid the floss under the dough, crossed the ends over each other, and pulled as if tying a shoelace. A perfectly sliced piece fell gently on the floured surface.

"Here, now you finish the rest."

LeEtta happily did, and one by one, each slice looked as even as the last. "What kind of glaze do you like to put on top?" LeEtta asked as she placed the slices in the greased pan, leaving just a hint of space between them.

"We can make plain icing, but I have been hankering for...peanut butter." Oneida had many cravings, and LeEtta loved them all. How often had Eunice teased her for her creative ways? LeEtta was discovering she wasn't the only one who liked trying new flavors.

"Peanut butter icing sounds *wunderbaar!*" LeEtta went to the pantry and found the jar of creamy peanut butter. "I hope Ben likes it." She faltered in her steps. "Should we make half with regular icing and the other half with peanut butter icing?"

"Nee, Ben will eat anything," Oneida laughed. "He's not one to be picky. Miriam was always picky when she was growing up. I think that's why she never liked trying new dishes as often."

While the rolls were rising in a pan on the counter, LeEtta began to assemble the icing.

"My friend Eunice thinks one should stick to what is common, but she shares many recipes with me." LeEtta refrained from sharing how often she failed making them.

"She is courting Jerry, jah?" Oneida had been trying hard to remember everyone's name in the community. She found the best way to do that was to say their names over and over when she spoke with someone. Being a newcomer, she believed the process helped put names to memory easier.

"Jah, and Leo is courting Mandy, though they both think no one knows," LeEtta chuckled.

"Mandy makes pottery, and Leo is the one you see riding in a saddle all the time?"

"You already know Mammi, and Shep's fraa, Priscilla, too."

"And Mary Alice Yoder." No one could step foot in Cherry Grove without meeting Mary Alice Yoder and never forgetting her name.

"When Arlen took me shopping the other day, she asked if we were courting. I think it embarrassed Arlen."

"Mary Alice speaks her thoughts more often than not. Daed pays her no mind."

"Who is Rhubarb? I find the name...rather...different, but I do like it."

LeEtta burst into laughter, her hand pausing in mixing confectioner's sugar, vanilla, and peanut butter. "That is a funny story about birthday twins, who happen to have sparks for each other."

"I've heard all about a Rhubarb having a birthday and have yet to meet him or her, not sure which." Oneida wrinkled her nose adorably. LeEtta loved how innocent and kind she was.

"Rhubarb is a him and a her." LeEtta went on to explain all about the young couple, who would soon wed. They would be forever known as Rhubarb to all their friends. When was the last time she could talk away a day without anyone reminding her she was the late-bloomer, the terrible cook, or the reluctant seamstress?

"Ach, now why did Arlen not tell me that?" Oneida fussed, shoving both floured hands to her narrow hips. "I knew it was a strange name, but folks use all kinds of strange names these days instead of naming their kinner after mamms and daeds as it has always been. I was trying to figure out whose birthday I missed."

LeEtta's laughter continued. She couldn't help herself.

"Well, now, it is good to hear your laughter. If you want a better laugh, I bet Ben could tell you about the time I fell on mei bottom in front of the whole church."

That wasn't funny at all. LeEtta collected herself. "You did?"

"Ask him about it. After all, he was the one who spouted the first laugh that got the whole community going."

"Ben doesn't share things with me," LeEtta said, biting her lip, all laughter gone from her heart.

"Ach, mei nephew has difficulty with putting the past behind him. I've tried helping him see life is better looking ahead, that we all fall short at times."

"I try to help too, but he only grows more distant when I do."

"Now, dear," Oneida said, coming to her side. "Those we care for the most are often the ones we are hardest on. Ben is hurt. He put a lot of hope in the farm he thought would be his one day, and when John offered it to Sam, it pierced him."

"Why did Ben's daed give everything to Sam? Did he not want

Ben to have any future, or his dochters?" LeEtta knew many families where, once the parents were ready to retire, they split farms equally between the kinner left at home. It wasn't strange that the youngest would inherit everything, but only because they were the last at home.

"Mary and Lisa will soon wed, but Ben has given his folks a reason to be concerned about his choices."

"Because of me?" LeEtta clasped a hand to her chest.

"Nee, my dear. You are a blessing to all of us."

"But his past is in the past. How can he forget it if no one else does? Ben's not like that anymore," LeEtta quickly defended. "Ben is married now, and he has made so many good choices for us."

"Has he?" Oneida sounded skeptical. "Then why did I find him sleeping in a chair last night?"

LeEtta felt the wind go out of her. What would Oneida think if she knew they were merely partners in keeping the farm running but strangers in a marriage?

"I did not question why he married so soon after coming here to stay with Eber and Mary, but now I fear he made a choice to prove something to his parents, and you are having to pay the cost."

"Nee, it's not like that. Ben didn't even want to get married!" LeEtta clamped a hand over her mouth but not quickly enough to keep the words from escaping. She didn't want Oneida to think Ben had used her or that he was the same boy who made a few bad choices.

"Let me put these in the oven and fix us some tea. I have much to hear yet."

A soft rap at the tack-room door drew Ben straight to his feet. LeEtta clearly wasn't going to let his last words pass. He deserved the chastising, but if she only knew what it did to him knowing someone had left flowers for her, she'd understand better.

"Oneida," he said, not masking his surprise when he opened the wooden door.

"I knew it! Don't tell me you sleep here." Her gaze searched the small space. "I bet Arlen knows it too. That stubborn man." She pushed her way inside, giving his makeshift home a grimace.

Ben had become so accustomed to sleeping in the tack room that he hadn't considered what his aenti might think. She may have known about his estranged relationship with Sam or how Daed thought him too immature to take over their family farm, but she didn't need to know he was determined not to trust another person who could easily hurt him again.

Her raised brow indicated she wasn't sure she wanted an answer. "You sleep in a dirty barn or sitting in a chair," she continued in her frustration. Ben lowered his gaze. He hadn't meant to fall asleep in the sitting room last night, but he was so tired, the chair comfortable and the fire warming, he drifted off with hardly a thought in his head.

"I'm sure you have some explanation, but don't you be putting blame on Sam for this," she wagged a finger at him. "You told me you left to earn your own land."

"I did, and things. . .happened."

"Jah, I know things happened. Gott tends to see that they do. LeEtta told me everything, or at least I think everything." Oneida crossed her arms over her chest and stared angrily at him. "You asked me to kumm to help her, the poor thing having no mamm or instruction, but now I feel you hoped I'd keep her attention busy so she didn't see what a lousy husband you are. Why are you not sleeping in your own home? I don't care how you came to be here, but I do care about LeEtta, and I know she loves you."

He knew how it looked. It looked like he married for land. "I don't deserve her," Ben said in an exasperated breath.

"Ach, this is why I never married," she muttered harshly and plopped down on the quilt on the floor. "Kumm," she patted a spot beside her, and he sat down too. "I know you have been through much."

"Much, because I let myself be," he admitted.

"Jah, but God is giving you a second chance. Not everyone gets that, Benuel." She never did waste words to make a point.

"I'm afraid." Ben felt like that little boy again, admitting fear to an aenti who insisted he feed animals as opposed to pulling weeds.

"Fear is not of God. You have been given a life that many would be happy to have."

Ben felt like the worst kind of man knowing she herself would be happy with what he had. "I'm working on it."

"Not from where I'm sitting. Benuel, I know Miriam has fretted over you living far from home and that you needed to leave because you and John didn't agree on things, but this is not the answer. You have so many people who care about you."

"People who'd just as easily betray you as love you." Need he remind her how true that was?

"Whatever," she rolled her eyes at him mockingly. "Folks make mistakes. It's never intentional. Your bruder misses you. Do you not know this? I talk to Miriam nearly every day." Ben was aware of how often she visited the phone shanty at the end of the drive and how she lingered there. "She says Sam has not been himself since you left. You two are very different, jah, but you have always been close. Your bruder needs you."

"He wrote to me," Ben admitted. "I think he's wanting to wed soon."

"That is what Miriam believes as well," she said, tilting her head to gaze up at him. "Did you write him back?"

"You know I didn't."

"Benuel David, how is this river between you ever going to mend if you don't start building your side of the bridge?"

"I have no interest in building any bridges," he said quickly but regretted the hurried remark as soon as it left his lips. "I do know I'm not angry with him anymore. Sam did the right thing. I would have done the same if it were me."

"So you have swallowed your pride. Glad to hear it."

Ben often wondered if Aenti Oneida knew how much she and Mamm were alike. Both cared deeply for others, and neither held back from speaking their minds when they felt it was necessary.

"He sent me a check." Ben told his aunt about the letter and the money he'd been carrying around that had been eating at him. Was it selfish not to use it? It was his money, after all. Arlen needed his arm working again, and Ben could think of a dozen things LeEtta could use to make her daily chores easier. The wages he earned working for Shep were only keeping them above water.

"Cash the check, Benuel. So much is needed here, and you know this. I don't know why you make a simple thing into a hard one," Aenti Oneida scoffed.

"I gave this to the farm. The farm I planned on running one day."

"And yet, Gott has seen to it that you had a farm, and Sam too. What is so wrong with both of you being happy?"

The truth stung. God had given him and Sam what they both wanted. "I don't know." He dropped his head in his hands. What was wrong with him?

"You cannot hold on to a sore spot. You have to let it heal. I know my bruder-in-law, but I also know you gave him too much to worry about with so many foolish decisions ever since you were big enough to break Deacon Byler's window with a baseball. Have you prayed about all that is troubling you?"

"Gott is a little busy answering everyone else's prayers to care for any of mine."

"Nonsense." She turned to him and shoved a hand on her hip as she quoted from the Bible, " 'A new heart also will I give you, and a new spirit will I put within you.' He can take away your stony heart and give you a heart of thankfulness."

Ben wanted that, but his heart clung to resentment and spiteful thoughts toward so many who had betrayed his trust and his love for them. "I don't know how to let go of it."

"You just let go." Her arms spread slowly as if releasing sparrows to take their first flight. If only it were that easy.

"I'll leave you with this, Benuel," she said as she got to her feet.

"Cash that check and start building a family of your own. Be a humble man and a worthy husband, and if Gott blesses you further, a devoted father." She reached for the door handle and then added. "I suggest you also buy LeEtta a Christmas present." She winked. "Women like knowing they are loved even if men are too stupid to tell them outright." She pointed a finger toward him. "Now I'm going to bed, but when I wake, I expect to see you lumbering down the stairs and into the kitchen for waffles and my best blueberry syrup and not entering from the back door!"

Ben nodded and watched her slip back out into the cold. Oneida was right about so many things. The only thing holding him back was himself. He also had been missing her waffles.

Taking his time, Ben gathered his things and waited until he couldn't see a single shred of light before making his way back to the house.

As quietly as he could, he crept up the narrow stairs, careful not to step on the creaking edges. He hoped LeEtta was sleeping but knew there was a chance she was up reading. From the tack-room window, he often saw her light on late into the night.

Opening the door to her room, he froze in his tracks. She stood in her gown at the window.

"Ben," LeEtta hiccuped in surprise.

Moonlight revealed her tender shape and brightened her lovely long hair hanging damp over her shoulder. In her hand was an open book, with her thumb holding its place in reading.

"What are you doing here?" She drew her voice to a whisper as she noticed the quilt and pillow in his arms. The sound of movement in the next room hurried him inside, closing the door.

"My aenti was never slow at unmasking secrets."

"That's your fault." She turned, ignoring his plight. "I told you to sleep in the haus since Daed moved out."

He had refused. It wasn't like she was asking him to share her bed. "I thought it was best to keep. . .a distance."

"From your fraa," she added with equal pluck. "Well, I'm glad Oneida helped you come to your senses. It's too cold out there, and"—one side of her mouth hinted at a smirk—"you can take care of the stove, and I can have a sleep without worrying over it now."

She should be furious at him, yet she was trying to make him laugh. Oh, how his heart wanted to love her. Ben reached up and yanked at her kapp strings. "I'll keep the fire, but don't you snore. I need sleep too," he replied with equal playfulness and went to spread out his quilt.

"Does this mean you're sorry?" LeEtta positioned his pillow nearest the wall, where the moonlight wouldn't be on his face. When he stood, she was close—too close. Reality slammed into him with another punch.

"LeEtta," his voice was low as he took in the way her eyes widened at their nearness. Ben reached out, taking her hand. It was a dumb move. He needed to practice patience. He didn't need to win her heart. Nee, not hers, which loved freely without condition. He needed to earn her respect and trust. He traced the small calluses, and his heart lurched in his chest. She worked just as hard as he did for the life they had. So why was he so afraid of what she could do to him?

"I'm sorry for a lot of things but not for marrying you." Ben felt her pulse quicken under his hand.

"I'm not sorry either," she said, ducking her head. "I wish you didn't have to sleep on the hard, cold floor."

Ben wished he didn't either. All of him wanted to love her, and yet fear still had a tight hold on him. When those you've known the longest become people who can let you down the quickest, trust is broken, and a man's vulnerabilities have to be protected. Even if at times, he could forget it all and let himself be caught up in a moment, it didn't mean he could easily forget how she could break him. At any given moment, her feelings could change too, just like his daed's did and just like his best friends' did. People changed. They broke your heart, but one thing Ben was discovering about LeEtta was that she didn't change.

"It's hard to—" He didn't finish. There was no real way to explain how much he cared for her or how much he feared what she could do to him. She loved him. He loved her.

"Benuel. . ." Her voice was barely a whisper. "This is the first time you have held my hand." She looked down at their connected fingers, her nerves just as shaken as his.

"There is much I don't know about. . ." She gave her bottom lip some consideration while she searched for the words he already knew. "I'm willing to learn, familiarity."

A fire, both comforting and burning, ignited in his chest. He no longer wanted a loveless marriage but to learn with her, but not when his mind wasn't thinking straight. "There are many firsts we will soon get at." Letting go, Ben took a step back and immediately felt a waft of cool air slip between them. "Gut nacht, LeEtta."

"But I thought you were sleeping in here so your aenti doesn't suspect." He hated how her voice pleaded with him.

"I need a shower first. A cold one. Go to sleep, LeEtta." Ben hurried out the door before he surrendered.

CHAPTER TWENTY-FOUR

Snow fell in heavy, damp clumps outside the large kitchen window, vanishing quickly as it touched the earth. The world was painted a dreary shade of gray and blue, but LeEtta couldn't help but smile. Snow, sticking or not, always made her do that.

Turning her focus back to the task before her, LeEtta watched the thermometer reach one hundred eighty-five degrees and then quickly removed the heavy pot of fresh milk from the burner. Next, it was time to add a fourth of a cup of vinegar. She had been waiting for a chance to make cheese, and Oneida said farmers' cheese was the best for anyone to start with.

"Do you know how to make mozzarella?" LeEtta asked, thinking of Ben. She imagined that he would surely like pizza with thick slices of salami and lots of cheese. Last night had been strange, but having Ben so close had certainly given her the best sleep she'd had in weeks.

She continued stirring in the vinegar. Behind her, Oneida and Mammi Iola sat at the table, kapps touching, reading the newest *Budget*.

"I do," Oneida replied. "My eldest schwester owns a lot of cows, and Margaret taught me years ago how to make it. I'll be happy to teach you that soon enough." LeEtta smiled, thankful that Oneida never minded sharing anything with her. She never made LeEtta feel like a burden or foolish for not having already learned simple skills.

Not only had she taught LeEtta how best to remove stains and how adding a little flour and sugar to peaches before putting them in a cobbler improved the flavor, she and Mammi were helping her make Ben a quilt—once they finished reading the paper, that was. Quilting was far less daunting when shared with others.

Glancing over her shoulder once more, she watched both of them scour the pages with gripping interest. Whatever they were reading had captured their full attention. LeEtta smiled, happy to see both had made fast friends despite the fifteen-year age difference. Then again, LeEtta was much younger than Oneida, and they were tightly knit in just a few short days. This had to be what it felt like to be surrounded by generations.

She gave Oneida careful consideration. How many times had she imagined her mother and how she looked? Did she walk with her chin up, or did she stare at her feet? Did she have a narrow waist like Oneida's? Did she like reading the paper or eating taco salads? In a simple blue dress and matching apron, Oneida looked the part: a mother doting over her elder. Oneida had brought light into their home, and LeEtta couldn't ignore how it felt to have someone bestow such kindness on her orphaned heart.

LeEtta glanced toward the large, north-facing window. Greenery lay in the wooden frame and smelled as fresh as it did yesterday when she and Ben fetched boughs of greenery for the house. Christmas was upon them, and for the first time in all her years, it felt special. No longer a season drained and emptied by reminders of Daed grieving a fraa lost to him long ago. Daed smiled more, she measured. He'd also been wonderfully kind to Oneida, seeing she knew her way around Cherry Grove; and never once had he fussed if she had a craving, taking her right away to fetch whatever she needed.

The whole community had enjoyed getting to know her better. Why the woman had never married and had kinner of her own was beyond LeEtta. Her patience and willingness to help others would have made her a wonderful mamm.

Turning back to the stove, she watched the separation of curds begin. What a beautiful process. It struck her as funny. Milk held under heat; it nourished and filled the body with everything it needed, and adding acid and souring it created something even greater than itself. Change wasn't so bad, she considered now. For all the bad, sorrowful, and terrible that came into a life, it molded, prepared, and encouraged brighter days.

"Here's one!" Oneida shouted, causing LeEtta to flinch. *What were those two reading?*

"And she was your age." Mammi Iola scanned the typed-up words Oneida pointed out.

LeEtta rolled her eyes. How had her grandmother convinced a perfectly sensible woman into such a waste of time? "I cannot believe she has pulled you into her search for a husband," LeEtta quipped. "And those widows are from Ohio! I don't figure Mammi plans on moving."

"They are not all from Ohio, dear," Mammi Iola informed. "And love knows no distance." Mammi scanned the page and perked.

"It doesn't matter. Whomever you meet, you always find a flaw with him." It was true. Mammi would spend countless hours searching and would even go as far as talking with eligible men her age, but in the end, none compared to the husband she lost.

"Ach *vell,* your dawdi was an upright man. Oh, and this poor young maed is your age, Oneida." Mammi Iola continued her foolish endeavors. "It wonders me why you never married. You certainly have a knack for running a home and a heart any man would be happy to take up a place in."

LeEtta had been curious about that herself, but she didn't find it proper to ask such personal questions the way Mammi Iola did. Oneida's shoulders slumped. LeEtta knew there was a story there. LeEtta continued to spoon curds into a colander lined with cheesecloth. Once that was finished, she squeezed out more of the liquid whey. Oneida had a great list of uses for it instead of pouring it down the drain. Whey was a great acidity booster for tomatoes and hydrangeas. Added to the feed, it was good for chickens and pigs. It was even included in soup stocks.

LeEtta was learning so many things that she barely had time to read anymore. Once that was done, she tied the cheesecloth with a string, gathered the edges securely, and let the curds hang over the colander and pot of whey like Oneida had instructed her to do. Then she turned quickly, waiting to see if Oneida had a reply to Mammi's probing question.

"I had a chance once, but that has gone away," Oneida said, suddenly more concerned with adding a new kapp string to LeEtta's kapp. How the last one just disappeared was further proof that LeEtta had no skill for sewing.

"Nonsense. If you thought that, you'd not be helping me," Mammi Iola debated. "Love has no time limit."

"My heart belonged to someone," Oneida said somberly pushing thread through the hole of the needle. "He was lost in a terrible winter storm."

"I'm so sorry, Aenti Oneida." LeEtta quickly went to her side and placed a hand on her shoulder in comfort. "I hate to admit it, but I do agree with Mammi Iola."

"Danke, dear," Mammi Iola said, lifting her chin.

"Gott has given you a big heart. You care for others, and I would be lost if you didn't care so much about me."

"Ach, you are such a sweet child. I never had kinner of my own, but I do enjoy sharing what I know with you. I am content with life as it is. That's all I really know."

"But we are never too old to learn, as you keep telling me." LeEtta smiled. How many times had Oneida spoken those words to her over the last two weeks? LeEtta leaned closer. "And Ben no longer sleeps in the cold barn because of you either."

"I'm glad to hear it," Oneida grinned.

"No one is content alone. I know plenty menner who'd think courting you a blessing. Why, Jake Delegrange is a widower. Do you like horses, dear?" Mammi leaned in close.

"I—I—" Oneida stuttered, sitting down the work at hand..

"Ach! Nelson Beechy would make you a fine match, and those kinner could sure use some help after Alan done jumped the fence."

"Lester Milford isn't wed," LeEtta put in.

"He's but a youngie yet. Nee, Oneida needs a man who knows what he wants in life. Not one known to straddle the fence," Mammi scolded.

The sound of Daed clearing his throat silenced the room. LeEtta didn't miss Oneida quickly stiffening, as if she'd been caught stealing the last slice of pecan pie on the plate. Daed cast a glance around the room before his gaze settled on her. Had he heard about Oneida's lost sweetheart? Did he not like any of Mammi's suggestions?

"I'm heading to town to fetch more mineral spirits. They're calling for snow in the next few days. I just wanted to see if anyone needed anything."

"Jah. . .I need. . .a few things if you don't mind the company." Oneida was already reaching for her cloak and bonnet, clearly hoping to escape talking any more about love and husbands. She'd certainly find a quiet ride to town with her father.

Daed flinched, casting a wide-eyed glance at Mammi.

"Well, that's gut. Oneida can help ready the buggy for ya." Mammi Iola shot him a cunning grin as he motioned Oneida out. Before he closed the door, Daed replied, "I don't need help."

"Hearts that know the same hurts tend to heal just as quick," Mammi Iola muttered before turning back to her search for a husband.

CHAPTER TWENTY-FIVE

The wind howled outside. A clatter against metal came from somewhere in the distance. How was a man supposed to get any sleep on such a disagreeable night? Clambering out of bed, Arlen shrugged into his clothes. After months of wearing the bulky, cumbersome cast, he had learned well how to manage simple tasks, but it wasn't a full recovery. His current freedom, having to only wear the simple wrap that allowed ample movement, still proved a challenge. He was eager to work again. A body didn't stay strong without using it. Nelson Beechy was a prime example of that.

Slipping into his boots, Arlen shoved away the care. What business was it of his if Nelson made eyes at Oneida during the last gathering? *None.*

He didn't want to think about Nelson or Jake or any other widowers in the community. He wanted to sleep, but nature seemed to have other plans for him.

Fetching a flashlight and his heavier coat, he lumbered out to see if all was well. Hopefully, it wasn't the barn door trying to rip off its hinges. The wind took his breath the moment he stepped outside, but the coat was warm and winter-ready now that Oneida and Letty had sewn in fresh woolen material.

Another bang and he aimed his light toward the shed. The culprit—a trash can lid that Letty had tied to the can so it wouldn't blow away—was thrashing against the shed. He tucked the can inside for safekeeping and aimed for the house.

His house. For a time. Empty, save he and his dochter, until now.

He reached for the door handle. Letty always left the front door open in case he needed anything. Some of Oneida's sugar pie wasn't what he needed, but he was up, fully awake. He might as well eat a slice and drink a glass of milk before going back to bed.

He gingerly closed the door and made his way to the kitchen. Straight beams of light separated the darkness, and that's where he found her. Head down, praying. Arlen paused, a memory evoked. How many early mornings had he found Laura sitting at their table, praying. He swallowed back the tingle forming in his throat. He still missed his fraa. The years had made it harder and harder to pull her face out of memory, but the empty space was still there.

He should turn and leave, but his feet remained planted. She wasn't praying, he realized, but thinking. Hopefully not about Nelson Beechy.

Didn't she know too much thinking could rob a person of sleep? She wore a white kerchief, revealing more of her brown hair than he had already seen. He shouldn't even have noticed at all. She was much too fine a woman for gawking at.

A scent of pine filled his nostrils. Despite himself, he had to admit her little touches, the greenery draping window sills and the scents of cloves in the air, distracted him from his normal blue mood this time of year. The woman was a distraction, he measured.

She liked to talk too. He grinned thinking on their last ride into town. Who knew she had been to so many places? He had only traveled a few times back home to Indiana but had never seen mountains or oceans as she recounted them so descriptively. Did she know her plain brown eyes flickered with excitement when she told him how she waded in salt water up to her knees? He blinked back the thought.

He loved his fraa and shouldn't be thinking about another wading ocean waters. A man had to stand firm. Problem was, he couldn't stop thinking. Oneida was nothing like the women he knew. Nothing like the woman he had loved for twenty-two years beyond the grave. He liked the way she laughed when he complimented her. Her cheeks warmed, and she had a habit of adjusting her glasses. He tried to recall if Laura blushed like that. Too many years had robbed him of the visual memory, but he was certain she had. Sweet Laura, his one true love.

"Ach, I'm sorry." Oneida got to her feet in surprise at finding him lurking in the doorway.

"For what?" As far as he knew, the woman hadn't done anything but make his daughter happier than he had seen her in years. If he were being honest, she had filled his house with light and love and laughter that it had long ago lost.

"I—I—" She stuttered. "Is something wrong?" She adjusted her glasses and gave him a concerned look.

"Nee, I couldn't sleep." He clicked off the flashlight. "Figure a piece of sugar pie and milk might do the trick." He smiled, hoping it didn't look unnatural on him, and when she put a hand to her lips to quiet her giggle, he reckoned he still knew how.

"Not sure that's a remedy for insomnia, but I'll fetch us a plate."

Us, he mused as she went to the cabinet and fetched two small plates. "It's a transparent pie. Ever since LeEtta insisted I try one of the Miller's Bakery small tarts, I had to have the recipe."

Arlen took a seat as Oneida cut them two slices of pie and poured two glasses of milk. Once seated, they bowed their heads. Arlen prayed that pie cured insomnia and that Oneida Eicher didn't think him disabled or clumsy. She tended to fuss over him more than necessary, even when he insisted he could do things himself.

When he opened his eyes, their gazes locked. Surely she found his uncombed hair amusing, as told by her smile, but she quickly put her fork to work. He was too old to try to impress a woman.

"Are you enjoying your visit here so far?"

"I am," she said, dreamily. "Cherry Grove reminds me of home, but without all the chores." She laughed low, an enchanting sound that tended to send the hairs on the back of his neck tickling.

God had blessed her with a nice voice, he reckoned. "You're a guest and do plenty already," Arlen replied. From his perspective, Oneida was always choring, baking, or teaching Letty how to sew. "It's not like wading in oceans," he replied, quickly filling his mouth with a larger-than-necessary bite so he didn't say anything else stupid.

"Nee, it's not. It has its own charms. I can see why Ben is so happy here in your house."

"Not my house now." He took another bite and chewed slower. He hoped he didn't sound bitter, but bitterness had crept under his skin. He hated to admit he liked the dawdi haus with the smell of new paint and floors that didn't have a creak in them. A place where old haunts couldn't find him. But he and Laura had built this house together. What a shame she never had much time to enjoy it.

"Ben's not so happy here," he admitted. Arlen blamed himself for that. He hadn't been the most welcoming toward the young man.

"Well, he will be once he stops being stubborn and realizes what a fine dochter you raised." Now it was Arlen's turn to blush. "You did well, Arlen, raising her all on your own. In case no one ever told you, I thought you should know."

Her words stunned him momentarily. Men didn't take compliments and turn them into sentiments, but he did like knowing someone noticed how he had taken a newborn, fed her, bathed her, and hadn't fumbled too badly over the years. Arlen appreciated her observation. Would she still feel that way if she knew that he had taken Bishop Schwartz up on his wisdom?

"She's all I got left. I can't imagine losing her."

"She is a married woman now, Arlen." Oneida reached across the table and placed a hand on his. "You must see that. You have a life to live too, you know." She removed her hand, perhaps feeling the same warmth as he had.

"I'm an old man. I have lived plenty." He had lived his life to the fullest, for a time. How could he think to live such a life again without Laura?

"Nee, we are only as old as we think we are. I'm still twenty, didn't ya know?"

She did have a youthful spirit and barely a wrinkle, except for the ones earned from smiling like she did. How had no man ever seen her and not fallen head over feet? "Is that why you never married?"

"Nee, I came close." Her tone grew solemn. "He is gone now, and my heart never really moved past it. Was that what it was like for you?"

Arlen didn't like to talk about Laura. It was too painful, which is why he was just as surprised with himself as Oneida was when his heart opened and his mouth began to spill out his thoughts. "Laura was a fine woman. She used to sing when she was in the garden." He smiled at the memory. "She liked the color yellow." Why had that stuck with him? He'd yet to know.

"Yellow is a happy color."

He looked up at the woman across from him. She knew what ate at his heart and why he sheltered LeEtta so. She had suffered the same loss, and yet she woke up each morning with a purpose. He admired her for that. The ability to move on.

Arlen took another bite of the transparent pie that he could clearly see and let his mind drift twenty-five years back. The first time he and Laura walked together. She had been with friends. He had been visiting cousins. Arlen somehow was blessed enough to talk to her. One talk turned into twenty. He smiled at the memory and gave his sore shoulder a rub.

"Laura wanted lots of kinner," he said dully.

"Reuben was nineteen and had a laugh that made everyone wish to be next to him." She didn't pity him but had her own scars. So often, it was pity he found from others. Then again, Oneida wasn't like...others.

"What happened to him?"

"Winter came early, as it is now." She set down her fork. "I think that's why I was happy Ben called for me to come visit. It's hard not to think of him this time of year the most."

"It is the same for me with Laura. She died after having LeEtta. December tenth."

"Reuben went to fetch a horse that had wandered off during a blizzard. We don't have many of those in Ohio, you know." They didn't have them often in Kentucky either, he thought, but he remained quiet, letting her share. Perhaps it would be a balm for her to share, as he was discovering it was for him too.

"He never came back. His daed found him the next morning. He had fallen down a bank and into a creek. They say he hit his head."

This time, it was Arlen's turn to reach out and offer some comfort. "I'm sorry, Oneida. That must have been hard on you."

"It was, but we cannot know Gott's plan. Which is why it's so hard to know what is best for us. We can only hope to always do the right thing and follow where He sends us."

"Jah, and He sent you here." She met his gaze once more. "I'm glad for it."

"I am too, Arlen." There came that blush again. Arlen didn't realize he was still holding her hand until he looked down. It wasn't right, feeling something for this woman he barely knew. He pulled back as guilt riddled over him.

"I think we should help them."

"Who?"

"Ben and LeEtta. Did you know he'd been sleeping in the barn?"

Arlen had and liked knowing someone was near the livestock in case there was a need. "That is their business." It was best to finish his pie and be on his way. Talk of Ben and Letty just made him itchy.

"Don't you want them to be happy?"

Arlen put down his fork, his appetite now gone. Just seconds ago, he was looking at the woman across from him, feeling his rusty heart flutter. He knew the trappings of love and the joys of marriage, and although LeEtta knew nothing, she had married a man who worked hard and, when he thought no one was looking, watched her with eyes of affection.

"It's my fault they are forever yoked. I did something."

"What did you do, Arlen Miller?" Pushing her glasses up on her face, her lips tightened into a tight little bow of fury. He might as well tell the truth. Perhaps then she'd stop fussing over him so, and his mind could stay focused on what was, not what could be. He told her about his talk with the bishop. How he worried over the farm and finances. Oneida's blank expression didn't waver once when he admitted he thought the neighboring bishop's idea was a good one. After all, the fella had shown up when Arlen needed help the most. He spared her how he felt the day of the wedding, but it did sour his stomach recalling how ill Letty looked.

"I reckon one could look at it as if I meddled, but a decision had to be made."

"You should not take credit for what Gott has done." Oneida laughed.

Arlen tilted his head and narrowed his gaze at her. He had expected a few harsh reminders that match-meddling was for women and that marriages of convenience were a thing of the past. Instead, she laughed.

"Gott would have never let them marry if it wasn't meant to be. I see the way she looks at him and how hard she tries to please her husband. I know Ben. He has troubles of his own that need healing. You may have agreed to the foolish idea, but the fact is, you could not keep this farm with your arm like it is, and Ben couldn't move past losing the farm he worked his whole life for. LeEtta is the one thing you both have in common. The one thing you both love more than land."

Arlen didn't like to admit it, but Oneida was right. He too saw how Ben watched her, and Letty did have stars in her eyes when she looked at him.

"I say we plan a birthday supper for her and find new ways to help two lonely people express their love."

"New ways? Love doesn't need improvement. It's love, and it's easy if your heart is open to it." Now if he could only take his own advice. "Why is this called transparent pie?" He tried changing the subject.

"Because it's so transparent that it disappears!" She pointed at his empty plate and smiled. Gone. He had eaten the whole thing without even realizing it.

"Arlen, I think it's time to open our hearts. I mean, help them open theirs." Oneida corrected herself and pushed up her glasses in readiness.

"I agree."

CHAPTER TWENTY-SIX

Rubbing her eyes to rein in her focus, LeEtta lumbered into the early morning kitchen. Despite wool socks, her feet felt the chill of the morning. First things first. She added a few sticks of kindling to the fire. Ben kept his promise, seeing wood was added at some point last night. Flames licked at the fresh wood. She smiled as she went to shut the door but misjudged where her hand could safely grip the handle, and the immediate contact singed her flesh.

"Ouch! Ouch! Ouch!" She jerked her hand back quickly. The sound of footsteps in the next room instantly startled her. Before a scream burst out of her, Ben was there. He quickly shut the stove door before any crackling sparks shot out.

"Let me see," he said in a husky voice. His dark hair needed combing, his shirt was wrinkled, and his feet were sockless. Had he slept on the couch, she wondered?

LeEtta pulled her hand to her chest and inhaled a deep breath. No wonder he didn't want a traditional marriage with one as clumsy as her. "I'm gut," she said unconvincingly. "I thought I was alone."

"So I gathered." He turned on the gas lighting over the table and reached for her arm. "How bad is it?" His brows narrowed in concern.

"Not bad." A lie he quickly discovered.

"Kumm," he pulled her toward the sink. "Let's run cold water over it. Now open your palm."

"Nee, Ben. I can see to it. You should get some rest." She didn't want to see if there was another mark there, and she certainly didn't want Ben to think she was unable to shut a stove door without an accident.

"Open your palm, LeEtta."

"I'm not a child, Ben. I will see to it myself. I've been taking care of scrapes, cuts, and burns since long before you came about."

"You are not a child, but you are my wife. Please let me see to this for you." With that, LeEtta opened her palm and let him gently run cold water over her fingers and palm. "It's already blistering."

She'd take his word on it but noted his hair needed a trim. A twinge of pain shot through her, forcing her attention to her palm under the flow of water. He was as tender as she knew he would be, though his furrowed brows and tight lips denoted contempt for her foolishly misjudging the handle.

"I wasn't paying attention," she tried to explain. "I didn't sleep well. Don't tell Daed. It doesn't hurt. Really, it doesn't."

"You don't have to pretend with me," he said, locking eyes with her. "I know you're strong, and. . ." He looked at her hand again, his thumb caressing her wrist as cold water trickled over her palm and fingers. "You are still soft."

Waves of lightheadedness overcame her. Whether by his touch or his words, she hadn't a clue.

"You know you don't have to try so hard to prove yourself to him." He gave her a sidelong smirk.

But she did. Daed would never think of her as more than a helpless child if she didn't work hard each day to show him differently. "Like you, I imagine. You came here to prove something also, did you not?"

"It's not the same, LeEtta. Arlen only has you and fears losing you."

"He's lost so much because of me too."

"Is that what you think?" Ben turned off the water and reached for the burn ointment in the nearest cabinet overhead. He guided her to the nearest chair, and LeEtta sat while he worked the ointment over her palm and fingers.

"Gott does not make mistakes," he shrugged. "Or so I'm told, and you were wonderfully made and created by Him. What happened to your mother is terrible, but I assure you neither Arlen nor your mother would think her death was your fault."

LeEtta knew she was but a newborn, incapable of taking a life, but if she hadn't been born, her mother might not have died. "He has grieved over twenty years for her. She was the love of his life!"

"Jah, but life goes on, LeEtta. I think Arlen is learning that."

LeEtta tilted her head to get a better look at him. The man *ferhoodled* her to no end. "Do you believe that, Ben? That even when bad things happen, we must go on?" LeEtta ached for Ben to find his own kind of peace, to mend the threads between him and his own family.

His eyes never left hers, and in them, LeEtta could see he was contemplating his own words.

"I do now." He stood, twisted the B&W Ointment bottle closed, and brushed her cheek with his knuckles. "I'm learning one cannot hold on to the past, not when they have so much to live for." With that, Ben leaned down, kissed her forehead then aimed for the stairs to ready for the day, leaving LeEtta with a hope in her heart that change was finally blowing her way. Love kissed in such a way, the heart knew.

"Danke, Lord," LeEtta whispered.

Ben stepped into the barn just as he did each Saturday morning. Between his job at Shep's and his duties on the farm, he set aside Saturday mornings for cleaning the stalls and ensuring all the animals had fresh bedding. If all went right, he'd see to giving the generator a good cleaning and then plug all the holes that were letting cold air seep into the phone shanty. He had taken his aenti's advice and called home.

Lisa had bent his ear talking about her newest beau and how much she disliked dairy farming. Ben laughed picturing her helping Sam with morning milkings as Daed insisted she do. His smile widened knowing Mary would complain less but make those dramatic noises of displeasure the whole time. He pitied Sam. His brother would have his hands full with those two now that Ben didn't serve as buffer between sibling quarrels.

He thought of Mamm and how her voice quivered while they talked about weather and nonsensical things. Oneida was right. She missed her eldest, and if Ben was being honest, he missed her too.

Ben paused in his steps when he noticed Arlen brushing down Posey. "Gut mariye," he said.

"Thought I'd see her cleaned up before services tomorrow," Arlen said.

Ben liked knowing there were still chores Arlen was capable of doing. "Want me to finish up for ya?"

"Nee, you go on about your choring. Me and her are old friends."

Something else Ben had noticed recently was how his father-in-law seemed more content. His words held less vinegar than before, and he no longer hovered over LeEtta's comings and goings so much. Oneida's recent remarks filled his thoughts as he reached for a pitchfork leaning against the wall. What would his father-in-law say if he offered to help him get that new elbow, as Arlen called it?

"Been meaning to tell ya." Arlen cleared his throat. "I found footprints outside the house. I don't know who's been coming around, but they still are."

"Anything missing?" Ben lifted a brow. So far, their visitor had merely stolen a dress and perhaps a few eggs.

"Nee, but I don't much care to think someone is looking in windows and watching Letty."

"Me either. I don't like to point fingers, but. . ." Ben wanted to share his thoughts about Jonas Hostetetler, but blaming others was the old Ben. Still, Jonas was the only person Ben suspected capable of such mischief.

"Go on," Arlen encouraged.

"Jonas Hostetetler lives just over the hill. We both know he only went to the bishop in hopes of getting rid of me. I think he had more than a crush on her." Ben watched his father-in-law consider his words. His one good arm continued to brush Posey in long, dedicated strokes.

"I can have a word with Marcus," Arlen said.

Clearly, he knew it wasn't innocent play but a more troublesome habit that might lead to something more serious. Ben didn't know what he would do if Jonas continued stalking LeEtta. Nee, it was best to put an end to it all soon. "You've been neighbors for a while," Ben considered. "Perhaps it would be best if I have that word with him and Jonas."

Before Arlen could disagree, Ruby's van came racing into the driveway. "Did you hire a driver today?" He looked at Arlen.

"Nee," Arlen replied as they both went out to greet her. The sun lazily peeked over Bishop's Hill, leaving an eerie orange cast over the farm. The van pulled up to the barn doors, and Leo stepped out.

"Gut mariye," Leo said with a grim look and two large bags in his hands. Ben liked their friendship and had come to learn Leo wasn't one for grim looks.

"Whatcha got there?" Arlen pointed.

"I've come to return a few things." Leo offered Ben both bags. "I'm sorry about this, Ben."

Ben accepted the bags and glanced inside each one. Arlen leaned over his shoulder, eager to see what all the fuss was about. Inside was a pair of boots. "My shoes," Ben said, handing Arlen the bag. When he opened the second bag, Ben's heart stilled. It was not a prank or an angry kid hoping to let everyone know he was upset. It was. . .obsessive.

"LeEtta's dress," Arlen said angrily.

"And," Ben dug deeper and produced two round hair holders, a red comb LeEtta had thought she misplaced, and one white missing kapp string. Ben saw red. Such personal items, belonging to his fraa. How the kid even managed to take them right out from under their nose, he hadn't a clue.

"He should be here apologizing, not his bruder!" Arlen demanded.

Ben said nothing, because he too felt that Jonas should have returned the items himself and confessed to taking them.

"Daed hauled him over to the bishop's, or he would be." Leo tried to assure them that Jonas was not being let off with a warning. The severity of the situation would be taken seriously.

"I had no idea. I mean, we all knew he had a crush on her. Jerm and I even teased him." Leo ducked his head. "I never thought he'd..."

"It's all right, Leo." Ben reached out and touched his shoulder. "As much as I'd like to wallop your little bruder for this, I do know how quickly we can become obsessed with something." It didn't mean Ben would easily forgive Jonas and his behavior, but Ben knew obsession. For as long as he could remember, he'd obsessed over the day the family farm would be his. It consumed him to the point that he had alienated himself from his family when he didn't get what he wanted.

"So you aren't angry?"

"I'm plenty angry, but Mamm always said let the water cool before putting both hands in it." Ben shrugged. "And pretty maedels do tend to make us do dumb things."

"Don't I know it. I'm off to do a little shopping now. I have no idea what to buy a woman who loves stars, makes pottery, and would rather beat me at basketball than marry me."

"Let me know when you figure it out," Ben jested.

"I think I will ride over to the bishop's and see all is done," Arlen said flatly and aimed back inside to fetch Posey.

"He's not happy, and I don't blame him."

"Nee, he's not, but he's taken care of her so long that it might do him good to speak to Jonas."

"To be honest"—Leo grinned—"I kinda worried how'd you react. That's why I came. If that was Mandy, I'd wallop the kid too."

"I probably would if I went with him. Best I stay here. Arlen will see he regrets ever stepping out of line."

"And the bishop will see he confesses for it. I don't know what he

was thinking, but now he'll think before he acts, for sure and certain."
Ben hoped so.

"I should go on in and see that she gets this," Ben said, lifting the
dress bag. "Thanks for coming by and clearing things up. I hope you
figure out what to buy Mandy. I've yet to even think about what to
get LeEtta."

"That's easy. Everyone knows she's always wanted lambs for this
farm, and I'd suspect anything would make her happy. Mandy, on the
other hand. . ." Leo said as he rubbed the back of his neck. "I've paid
up for the afternoon. I reckon you can tag along. Help me, and I'll
help you. I won't look so stupid shopping for pretty things with you
next to me." Leo smirked.

Ben gave Leo's invitation much thought. He could help a friend
out and, in turn, see LeEtta have something too. In fact, he was eager
to do something for her. She'd not be too happy to find out Jonas had
been behind all their missing items and been lurking about. Ben wanted
her to feel safe. He wanted to shelter her from such things.

"I can do that, but. . ." Ben wanted to do more than buy a few
fanciful things. If he knew his fraa, what would really make her happy
was seeing those around her happy too. That would take more than a
few bills. "Can we drop by the bank first?"

CHAPTER TWENTY-SEVEN

LeEtta tried to pay no mind to what day it was. Ben's words helped her remain positive all through the long three-hour church service, but still she couldn't help but feel hurt that she had yet to offer a single thank you to anyone wishing her happy twenty-third birthday.

In fact, no one remembered at all. She tried not to let it trouble her as she sat in the buggy next to Ben. The truth was, she had never told him, and he never asked, but she had hoped Daed would have at least mentioned it over breakfast.

Letting out a sigh, she pulled the heavy vinyl buggy covering over her legs to block out the cold. It wasn't like she was accustomed to her birthday being of importance. Not even Mammi had considered her by making her favorite triple-chocolate kuche. Instead, her grandmother left earlier than usual from the gathering, and she wasn't the only one.

"I hope your aenti is feeling all right," LeEtta commented as Ben veered his new horse, Clover, off of Farrows Creek and onto Cherry Grove. The Shetlers had been the hosting family this week, and despite the snow falling in slow, meandering flakes, the large home had been wonderfully toasty against the weather outside.

"I'm sure she's fine," Ben said, not at all troubled by Oneida's abrupt exit today. Hopefully, it wasn't something she ate.

"It was kind of Arlen to offer to take her home," he remarked, holding the reins firmly. Clover was a beautiful painted horse but still shied every time a car passed by.

"Daed is kind," LeEtta reminded him. "Of course, he was happy to see her home safely. After all, she knows so few folks here." She stared at the changing landscape once more.

"It wonders me if the flu ain't going around again. Ellen left early too, and did you see Jerry leave as soon as he finished one plate? I've known him all my life and never knew him not to take seconds."

"I'm sure it isn't the flu."

He couldn't know that, LeEtta silently quipped. People could be only starting to feel ill, showing no signs yet.

"Jerry was probably just eager to pick up Eunice now that they are in separate districts. Leo thinks he's going to talk to her daed soon."

"That's wonderful!" LeEtta squirmed in the seat happily. Eunice had been head over heels for Jerry for a long time. Many wondered when he would finally ask. "Eunice will be so glad, considering she's been waiting for him for what she says is forever," LeEtta added.

Yet LeEtta couldn't help but worry about Ellen. She always stayed behind, helping the hosting family tidy up until most had gone home. No sooner had the second round of menner sat to eat, and then Mammi Iola was nowhere to be found. Why would she hurry away before sharing her latest news about answering a letter in the *Budget* for a widower in Michigan? News like that usually had Mammi Iola excited to share. Since when would her grandmother miss a chance to induce surprised looks on Gemma and the rest of the women?

"Mammi left early too," LeEtta shared the thought out loud.

"Maybe she had somewhere important to be." Ben grinned cunningly. If LeEtta wasn't mistaken, her husband looked as if he was holding on to a secret.

"What are you smiling at?" LeEtta gave Ben a curious smile.

"It's a fine day," he replied as they pulled onto the single gravel lane leading home. Before she could inquire more out of him, LeEtta noted five buggies parked in front of the house.

"Ben, something's wrong." LeEtta's heart dropped. "I knew everyone didn't leave early for no reason at all!" She could barely contain her worry as he brought Clover to a halt in front of the barn, but before LeEtta could leap out and see what happened, Ben stopped her.

"Ben, don't. Daed could be hurt, or maybe Oneida is sicker than we thought!"

"No one is *krank* or hurt, my dear," Ben said, continuing to wear a grin.

Confusion flittered over her—and was that Jerry's horse next to Mammi's old mare?

"It's just a few folks hoping to wish you a happy birthday." His smile was gentle. "Happy birthday, LeEtta Ropp."

It was the surprise that made her speechless, not Ben speaking her married name. *They remembered.* Her eyes watered immediately.

"Don't be crying. This is a happy day, is it not?" Ben leaned forward and kissed her cheek, a sweet gesture that warmed her from the inside out.

"They're here for *my* birthday?"

Ben chuckled, helping her down from the buggy. "They are here for *your* birthday. Go on while I take care of Clover, but please act surprised. Oneida and Arlen put a lot into making this day special for you."

"Daed?" LeEtta choked out. Her father had never once, in all her years, put forth any extra effort on her birthday. In fact, he avoided each one, but LeEtta always knew he would make up for it during Christmas, making sure she had a few presents to open. Knowing her father had been a part of this, the tears came in abundance now.

"Jah, Oneida insisted it was his idea," Ben added. "Don't cry." His brows furrowed. "It's a happy day, LeEtta."

"I can't help it," she told him. "It's hard for him. I can't believe he wanted to spend today with others and with me."

"He's putting the past behind him, Letty." He brushed her cold cheek. "Step inside the barn until I get the buggy unhitched. I'll give you a minute, then we will walk in together."

Thankful for his consideration of her unbidden emotions, LeEtta stepped into the barn and worked to contain her wild inner nature. She had never had a birthday supper before, or someone who considered her as Ben was right now. As he said he would, Ben gave her all the time she needed to cry happy and sad tears. The past was now behind them, and today was fresh and new. No birthday had ever been so sweet. LeEtta pressed a hand to her cheek again, where Ben's lips had touched her, and stepped out.

He stood patiently waiting with his gaze facing the house and his back to her. "Danke, Ben." LeEtta wrapped both arms around him and hid her face in the warmth of his heavy, long coat. His arms squeezed her softly. They stood there holding each other until the side kitchen door opened, and Jerry Hostelter appeared.

"You two coming?"

"Guess we better get in there before he eats all your kuche." Ben urged her into the house.

Overwhelmed, she did her best to hold back any more pesky tears from falling and set her bonnet on a nearby table. Little Bethie and Laverna were the first to greet her, fighting over who would give her their birthday gift first.

LeEtta didn't have the heart to tell them Ben had beaten them to that, and her face warmed at the thought as she smiled up at her husband. Like Daed, he too had changed. Slower than a tarpon heading uphill, but change had come. LeEtta turned to Oneida, offering her a grateful look. She was the reason for all the blessings that had been brought to their home.

"Happy birthday, Letty," Daed said, giving her a long hug.

"Danke, Daed," she said, hugging him a little tighter.

"Oneida here made all your favorites," Mammi Iola said. "But I made kuche!"

Her favorite kuche! LeEtta's heart swelled in unmeasurable joy as she sat at the table filled with family, friends, kinner, and food. Who knew a single day could mean more than any other.

After a meal of baked spaghetti and fresh garlic bread, LeEtta watched her friends tidy up as she opened a small package from Anna Jay's daughters.

"I drew the horse," six-year-old Anna Mary insisted.

"Me too! Me too!" Bethie bounced to be sure not to go unnoticed.

"Danke, girls. You are all so sweet." Another round of warm hugs commenced. LeEtta's heart tugged as little arms held her. How she ached for kinner of her own.

As the men strolled into the next room, LeEtta cut herself a second slice of triple chocolate kuche.

"I can't believe Jerry didn't tell me he was going to speak to Daed," Eunice said, still mooning over the prospect of marriage soon.

"I'm so happy for you."

"Now we need to get Ellen married."

"I'm in no hurry." Ellen carried a stack of paper plates to the trash can.

"True love takes its time. It's not the same for each of us," Mammi Iola defended, earning her a timid smile from Ellen.

"It's really coming down out there," Eunice remarked glancing out the window. Snow fell in fast-moving, heavy flakes, covering the ground quickly.

"Can we go play in it?" Laverna asked with wide brown eyes. Even at four, she had no fear any longer about playing outdoors, even with a snowstorm threatening.

LeEtta bent to her level, "It's not the kind of snow one plays in, dear, but once it stops, I'm sure your daed will enjoy taking you girls for a sleigh ride." Giggles and giddiness filled the room. LeEtta loved how much each of them had changed in recent weeks.

"I think sleighing and snowman building will be awaiting us

tomorrow, but for now"—Dan swooped up little Bethie causing her to squeal—"we need to get you home before the roads are covered."

"I best be heading home before this gets any worse too. Ol' Nana isn't as sure on her feet as she used to be," Mammi Iola announced.

"Best I take ya," Daed said stepping into the kitchen. He reached for his hat and the new green scarf Oneida had knitted for him recently. LeEtta wished she knew how to knit but was thankful Oneida didn't mind seeing Daed had the extra warmth he needed.

"Save me a slice, will ya?" He winked at Oneida.

"Jah, we should see to getting home too," Jerry announced. "We can drop Ellen off on the way. I know you don't have proper shoes on that horse." Jerry gave Ellen a pointed look.

"Mei bruder was to do it, but. . ." Ellen ducked her head.

"Don't worry. I know Val and Ham have been busy of late on the new house."

LeEtta agreed. There was no sense in Ellen traveling in this, and Jerry knew well how to handle such weather. One by one, everyone said their so longs. LeEtta prayed God would watch over each of them. Even if a horse was properly shoed to travel in snow, there was still the matter of cars and drivers who were not.

"Oneida," LeEtta said, once the quiet came again. "Danke." LeEtta wrapped both arms around her and felt love flow through her very being as Oneida hugged her back. "I know this was your doing, but you have no idea how much today meant to me."

"I know how much it meant to both of you, dear. You daed has struggled a long time over losing your mamm. It's hard to let go sometimes, but healing comes eventually." Oneida smiled motherly. "I pray healing is coming to you both."

"I'm going to see to the milking." Oneida wrapped her head in a shawl and slipped into her coat. "I do hope he returns soon." Her voice held a hint of worry before slipping out the door.

"She's worried about Mammi and Daed out there," LeEtta remarked. Oneida had grown so close to all of them, it was understandable.

"She worries anytime the weather turns. She always did. Now you sit and eat your kuche. I'll see to the rest of the dishes." Ben helped clear the table and refused to let LeEtta wash even a fork. It felt strange to sit at the table and eat while he tidied up, but she didn't mind having this little bit of time alone with her husband.

CHAPTER TWENTY-EIGHT

Ben had seen to the extra horses before returning to the house. Neither mare was happy to be sharing a stall, but he was confident once they settled, they'd be grateful for the warm shelter and extra feed this evening.

Inside, he watched his aenti pace the floor, pretending to tidy things, but he knew she was struggling between trusting all was well and fretting over Arlen Miller. LeEtta seemed not to notice, her own feel-good day still fresh in her smile. Then again, as far as he could tell, LeEtta hadn't noticed how close her daed and his aenti had become in such a few short weeks.

Despite that troubling thought, he too was beginning to worry as the clock chimed a second time and still Arlen hadn't returned.

LeEtta stood, staring out the large kitchen window next to Oneida. "I've never seen snow fall so quickly." Flakes the size of cotton balls rained down. The world outside had grown darker, but one could easily make out the world of white burying everything in its path.

"How long does it take to drive to Iola's?" Oneida's voice wavered as she asked for a second time. For someone who was always the epitome of calm, Ben didn't like seeing her ill at ease.

"Don't fret. Mammi will be fine. Daed could find his way blind-folded," LeEtta answered. "Mammi Iola has weathered worse storms than this one. Did you not hear her talk all afternoon about the blizzard of '78?"

"LeEtta's right. Arlen can see himself home sure enough." Ben hoped their assurances helped.

"But even though he no longer wears his cast, he still only has use of one arm. He doesn't show it, but he struggles," Oneida informed them both. Jah, feelings were growing between the older pair, Ben was sure of it.

"It won't be much longer, Aenti Oneida," Ben assured her. "LeEtta, how about hot chocolate?" Ben said as he gave her a glance, and she quickly noted the need to distract Oneida until Arlen's return.

"Of course. Hot chocolate on an evening such as this would be nice."

"He thinks I've never seen snow," Oneida scoffed. "But you can barely see out there," she said, looking out the long, north-facing window. "What if Arlen—?"

"Oneida, are you worried about Mammi...or my daed?" Suddenly, it hit her. Ben watched as reality dawned on LeEtta. All those quiet words passing between them, and how Oneida always made Arlen's favorite sweets. How many times had he quickly offered her a ride into town?

"Ach, LeEtta. I'm worried for both of them. Don't be *deerich*."

"I'm not being foolish at all. I see how much you encourage him to do things, without pushing him too hard. You have been a gut freinden to him, and me, but I see how important you have become to us both." LeEtta tilted her head to face Oneida directly. "Daed has never smiled once in December, and now he smiles all the time. You are clearly more than a little concerned. You look like you may burst!"

Ben leaned against the counter, itchy. He wasn't one for sentimental chatter, but he did want to know if his aenti and father-in-law were secretly courting. Perhaps he should have never sent for her.

"I'm sorry if I worried you. I never meant for any of this," Oneida blurted out before grasping her middle. "I just wanted to help, but I didn't realize that I needed things too. Arlen has been so understanding.

Now he could be. . ." She sucked back a whimper.

"All is well, Oneida," Ben tried to reassure her once more.

"Nee, Ben, it isn't." Oneida looked up to him with damp eyes. "You don't know, but I lost someone special once in a storm like this. It's hard to think. . ."

"He'll be fine, and if he isn't back in another half hour, I'll go find him myself," Ben promised.

"Then I'll have both of you to worry about," Oneida said, nearly sobbing.

"Then we must trust Gott to see him home safely," LeEtta replied. "Our faith is all we ever have. Things. . .people, can come and go, but our faith teaches us to trust in Gott's will. Trust Gott will see Daed home safely."

Ben and Oneida both looked to LeEtta with profound admiration. The love Ben felt for her was unmeasurable. Despite whatever life tossed her way, LeEtta always took one day to the next and faced it.

"Jah, we must trust," Ben seconded. "I say we don't stand here watching snow fall but put our minds on something else."

"Like what?" Oneida wiped at her cheeks.

"Let's play checkers while we wait." LeEtta announced. "The winner has to play Daed," she said on a confident grin.

"I know you both are only trying to help, but I think I'll go see to waiting in the sitting room if you don't mind." They watched Oneida stroll into the next room.

"I'm sure Daed only saw to it that Mammi had a fire and plenty of wood in the house before he left, but I hope he returns soon, or else I will have to convince her to teach me to knit," LeEtta said, turning to him.

"I'm sure you'd be a quick learner, but if she wants to wait out there for him, we should let her." LeEtta nodded in agreement. "So you wanna play?" He tilted her a look.

"If you feel like losing," LeEtta returned with that challenging grin that had his heart flipping in his chest.

"I might let you win one game," he said as he held up one finger. "It is your birthday and all, but only one."

"How kind of you, husband."

The clock chimed while the wind howled outside. LeEtta slid another black chip into place. "King me!"

Ben couldn't help but laugh at her eagerness to see him lose again. Oh well, it was her special day after all, he mused.

"I don't see you winning this game either."

Ben added another black chip to her first one. "That's what I get for challenging you. I should know by now that there isn't much you can't best me at."

"I'm sure there's something you're better at." She giggled.

Ben blushed at her comment. He liked to think he was pretty good at kissing her, and it wasn't the first time this evening that thought had come to him.

Suddenly, the side kitchen door opened, a burst of cold air blowing in.

"Is that Arlen?" Oneida appeared immediately. "It's so terrible out there that I didn't even see you pull in." She rushed to Arlen's side, brushing snow off of him and helping him out of his heavy coat. "You gave us all a fright, Arlen Miller," she continued.

"It's coming down hard and was mighty hard to see, but Posey knows her way home sure enough," Arlen replied.

Ben watched Oneida continue to fuss over Arlen. The endearment made him glance at LeEtta as she smiled at the two. Love had bloomed here, and now it was blooming even more so in his own heart.

"Iola could have slept here tonight. You had no business going out in this." Oneida hugged his damp coat to her chest as she bent to help him out of his boots. Snow sprinkled the floor, but Ben could see it melting quickly under Oneida's temper. "I will surely have a word with her."

"All is fine, Oneida. I didn't mean to make you worry. I just wanted to be certain she had plenty of wood packed in. Iola shouldn't be out in this."

"And neither should you!" Oneida's rant continued.

With wide eyes and amazement, Ben and LeEtta remained planted in their seats as they watched the two elders battle it out.

Arlen placed a hand on Oneida's arm, assuringly. "I was fine. I'm sorry. I should have considered how leaving in such a storm might worry you," Arlen said softly as he stared down at her.

Oneida pushed up her glasses and studied him. "You could have—" She put a hand over her mouth and pushed back a sob.

Ben reached across the table, tapped LeEtta's arm to get her attention, and then nodded for her to follow him. Quietly, the two slipped out of the room to leave the two elders to talk—but not before Ben heard Arlen's promise.

"I'm not going anywhere, Oneida. I'm not leaving you."

CHAPTER TWENTY-NINE

A child was missing, a mother was distraught, and every soul in Cherry Grove had collected at the Schwartz home.

The snowstorm had only lasted a night, but its effects the following day had made even the simplest of chores a hard task. LeEtta was just readying leftover meat loaf when word reached the farm that Dan and Anna Jay's young child was missing. With her heart in her throat, LeEtta dressed heavily and joined volunteers in the search for four-year-old little Laverna.

Inside the Schwartz home, women crowded together with heavy concern, while outside, men gathered to decide who would search where. LeEtta shivered against the sound of a mother's desperate tears.

"She wanted to sleigh ride, but. . ." Anna Jay fell into another run of sobs.

Guilt plunged into LeEtta's chest. Had not she been the one to mention sleighing after the storm? She had to find Laverna. Rushing out of the house, LeEtta was met with a strong waft of wood smoke and cold evening air. Ben insisted she remain inside with the rest of the women, but how could she after seeing Anna Jay beside herself and knowing she was partly to blame? One more set of eyes was surely needed.

LeEtta reached into her deep coat pocket and pulled out her flashlight. She checked it was still in good working condition before tucking it under her arm and fetching a second pair of gloves. She shouldn't have mentioned sleighing, getting the kinner's hopes up. Dan had been so busy at work that, of course, he hadn't had time to take the girls on sleigh rides. *Foolish, foolish Letty*, she chided herself as she added a second pair of gloves over her hands.

"Best take my coat if you have a mind to go out helping them search," Ruby insisted.

LeEtta stared at the long blue puffy coat. "It's not that cold. I have on plenty of layers." She had on her thermal underpants under her dress, and Oneida had recently sewn an extra layer into her coat. Despite temperatures reaching only to the upper thirties, she was plenty warm.

"I guess you're used to it," Ruby said, slipping her coat back on. "I'll go in and see if there's something I can do, though in a time like this, I reckon just being here is all I can offer."

LeEtta watched the driver move inside the house. Sometimes, just being there was plenty, she thought as she flipped on her flashlight and scanned the landscape.

All they knew so far was that Laverna had taken her little sled with her. LeEtta peered up the hill to her right. Men were already combing the area in a long line, no more than twenty feet apart, and working upward. The moon sat at its peak, giving them extra ability to spot the little black coat and the child wearing it.

However, something in her gut pulled LeEtta to follow the flow of the creek. She couldn't imagine Laverna aiming this way with her sleigh in tow, but following that internal tug had been helpful in other times. A couple of lights flickered in the distance, proof she wasn't the only one searching along the creek.

Northern winds blew gently, but their bitterness stung her cheeks. LeEtta scanned the virgin snow for evidence of small feet as she made her way to the creek. Aiming her light downstream, she saw thick saplings and dormant brambles that would make a chore for a small child to enter. She aimed upstream, moving slowly, carefully, looking for any signs, listening for any sounds. Voices called out, and LeEtta paused in hopes Laverna called out in return. Darkness was moving in faster at this section of the farm. A chill ran over her, prompting her to move more swiftly through snow drifts collected along the banks. No way could a small child last long in a night such as this one.

A rhythm of a slow trickle of water moved just below the surface of the ice. LeEtta crossed at a narrowing and was greeted by an old fence line too cumbersome for a child Laverna's size to pass through or over.

"Laverna!" LeEtta called out a handful of times as she followed the fence line up a small grade. From here, the house was no longer in view. She prayed Laverna hadn't wandered this far. How terribly scared and cold she must be.

Trees became denser as a small field came into view, and crystal-like snowflakes twinkled in the beam of her light as she trudged through snow now reaching the tops of her boots. Tracks here indicated searchers had passed through. Her heart sank. For every minute Laverna wasn't found, closer came the worry of the cold or a possible accident.

"Gott, please help us find Laverna. She is so very small. Help us return her home to her mamm, I beg of You in Jesus' name. Amen."

With fresh determination, LeEtta ignored the burning in her legs as she hurried along the landscape, her eyes trained for anything out of place—evidence Laverna had been here—as her flashlight scoured the area.

Tracks from a large horse led her toward a pond. Someone had been coming here, brushing the snow from the ice to help it harden for harvesting. The ice had to be swept often during snow and usually wasn't harvested until January or February, once winter had set in a spell, but as an early winter was upon them, LeEtta could see someone was making the extra effort to help fill more family icehouses.

A small imprint caught her eye. "Laverna," she muttered. Snow had shifted here, making the track hard to make out. It could have been a small animal, but hope filled her heart that she was on the right path.

Across the pond, two men were searching the edges. Did they see the tracks too? LeEtta stepped onto the ice. It was solid, just as she suspected it would be.

If the men were already searching this area and moving on to another, perhaps she'd be better off heading back and searching the barn. Then again, she did recall seeing Rob Glick and his sons head in there with Dan just before she had strolled off into the snow. For sure and certain, they'd be scouring the rafters and dark corners for little Laverna.

Pausing every so often to listen, LeEtta continued around the water's edges—or at least her best idea of where the edges were, considering all the snow. Just when she felt as if all hope was lost, she heard it. Faint and hoarse from cold air and trembling in fear, a small voice. Whipping her head to the right, she pointed her light in that direction, and there she was—the one they had all been out searching for.

"LeEtta!" Laverna called out again, her voice almost stolen by a gust of wind. Arms outreached, Laverna immediately stepped onto the ice in a desperate attempt to reach LeEtta, and then suddenly disappeared.

"Laverna!" LeEtta screamed. No longer caring if the ice could hold her weight or not, she raced straight to her. Her boots were terribly hard to run in, and her extra layers of clothes made it difficult to move as swiftly as she knew herself capable of. Inches from the small hole, LeEtta dropped her flashlight and dropped to her belly. She quickly reached out for the small hand reaching for hers.

Behind her, voices called out, "She found her!"

"Hurry! She's in the pond!"

"Bring blankets," another voice thought to call out.

"I've got you, Laverna. Hold tight." LeEtta pulled the child free and brought her straight to her chest. Her lips were blue, but her dark headcovering was dry. Thankfully, she was only in the water for a few seconds, but for a child, LeEtta still feared it was long enough that hypothermia might overcome her.

"I heard Daed call me, and I came running. I saw you and fell,"

Laverna cried in a raspy, weakened voice that was almost LeEtta's undoing.

"Now, now, all is well now. Gott kept you safe and sent me right to you," LeEtta soothed as she quickly worked the child's coat and shoes off of her.

"Ach, Vernie." Dan Schwartz scooped his daughter up into his arms. Another dark shadow appeared. Jerry Hostetler, and he quickly wrapped Laverna in a blanket.

"Let's get you to the house. Your mudder and the dok have made something warm to drink just for you," Dan said, racing to get the small child into the house where fires would be burning hot and hearts would be lifted in praise.

LeEtta felt the air push out of her. The whole ordeal had only lasted a few seconds, but it had felt like a decade knowing the child had almost been lost to them. God had answered her prayers, again. It never ceased to amaze her how He never forgot His children. He comforted them when they were lost in the wilderness, and He sheltered them from every storm.

"You gut?" Jerry asked, helping her to her feet.

"Jah, but my heart is pounding so hard. When I saw her fall, I feared I wouldn't get there in time." LeEtta looked up. At the other end of the pond stood a few men, their lights glowing through the evening night air. Her eyes locked onto a familiar sillouette among them. Did Ben know how much God loved him even though his faith was struggling? Did he know how much she did?

"But you did, LeEtta. You got her just in time." Jerry's words brought her back to attention.

"She might be kault, but she will warm up quickly. We are blessed. It could have been worse. God's will helped us find her. I sure hope there will be something warm for us too." LeEtta smiled as a shiver ran over her.

A shift underneath them forced both their hands to fling out from their sides. LeEtta glanced down, suddenly realizing the ice had been weakened here.

"LeEtta, run!"

Those were the last words Jerry Hostetler said just before they buckled into the frigid waters.

On instinct, LeEtta reached out to catch herself on the nearby ice, but unfortunately, her weight and Jerry's created a hole too wide for such safety. It was the shock of impact, she figured, that made the sting of the cold water delay in overcoming her. Panic filled her as the water pulled heavily on all the extra clothing she wore. Her boots filled quickly, making it hard to keep her head above the water. She fought desperately, but the added weight only pulled at her harder.

Her nostrils burned as icy water intruded them. She reached the surface, coughing, gasping in as much air as her lungs would allow her, before slipping down again.

A second attempt for the surface, and she inhaled a longer breath. Through blurred vision, LeEtta could see Jerry climbing out onto the nearby bank. Jerry was safe, she thought as she went under once more. Jerry's cries for help were the last sound she heard before going deeper. Using every muscle, LeEtta fought to reach the top again, but this time it was too far. At least she knew Jerry would not perish with her.

"Help!" she wanted to scream—but not down here, where water stole her air. In one last effort, LeEtta strained against the cold death awaiting her, reaching out of the water for something—anything to grab on to. Opening her eyes, she saw him. Ben was there, in the water, pulling her back into the world.

LeEtta tried helping him, knowing he too was struggling to get them both to the shore, but it was no use. She had used up all her energy on that last surface.

Soon, many hands were on her, pulling and dragging her onto the shore. LeEtta turned to see Ben get to his feet. They'd made it. She breathed in a blessed breath of life. Laverna, Jerry, Ben, and her. They were all safe, and suddenly she was cold.

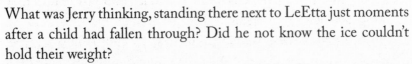

What was Jerry thinking, standing there next to LeEtta just moments after a child had fallen through? Did he not know the ice couldn't hold their weight?

Ben tried not to think about what could have happened. LeEtta was safe now, or so Dok Stella insisted she was. He shivered, recalling the quick sting of icy water when he'd jumped into the lake without thought of his own life, but of hers. "Danke, Lord," he silently whispered as he held both hands tightly around the cup of hot tea Oneida had poured him, his heart still shaken by all the events of the evening.

"I can't be thankful enough for you, Ben," Arlen offered a second time as he nursed his own cup at the other end of the kitchen table.

"I'm thankful Gott put you right there when you were needed most," Oneida added, draping a warm towel over his shoulders. The warmth enveloped him. Laverna was safe. LeEtta was safe. All was well.

God *had* indeed put him right there, right then. Ben was supposed to return with the others to the house after searching the high hill. When he saw lights down toward the foot of the hill, he deviated off course. For what reason, he hadn't a clue. He had carried LeEtta in his arms back to the Schwartz haus. Ruby immediately drove them home, despite being soaked to the bone. No matter how cold Ben thought he was, he knew LeEtta was colder.

With emotions still tugging in various directions, he quietly sipped on his tea, the bitter roots and sweet honey a delicate mix of his inner being. LeEtta had scared the life out of him. That's what she'd done. He set down his cup and glanced toward Arlen, his head in his hands as they awaited the dok to emerge with further assurances that LeEtta was well.

"I told you long ago, God puts us where he needs us most, even if we don't understand it. We are all very grateful for you today, Ben." Bishop Graber squeezed his shoulder.

Ben felt ashamed as he was continually praised. He couldn't help but think about how close he'd come to losing his fraa. That moment when he'd heard Jerry call out, Ben felt as if every unspoken word, every new hope he had for their future would fall away without LeEtta knowing how much he loved her. He hadn't been the man she deserved, his pride and bitterness holding him back. By choice, he failed her more often than not. Yet she still loved him, despite his flaws. She never gave up or quit as he did. She was light and air and hope, and he hadn't even told her.

The sound of footsteps brought Ben quickly to his feet. The bishop's fraa emerged into the kitchen. "Will she be all right, Dok?"

"She'll be fine. Just keep having her drink the tea I gave Oneida, and rest. She needs to rest." The dok looked to Ben and smiled. "She is more worried about you. I think you should go up and let her see for herself you are well."

Ben didn't need any further encouragement and rushed up the stairs and into the room he once dreaded. In a lamplit corner, she lay in a sea of quilts, her head barely peeping out from the covers.

"Ben?"

"It's me." He closed the door and went to her. "If you think you will be warmer downstairs by the fire, I can help you down and set things up for you there."

"Nee, I'm happier in here. It's the one place I've spent most of my life, really. Are you okay?"

"Of course." He smiled despite how his stomach knotted seeing how pale she looked.

"But you jumped in. Why did you jump in? You could have drowned or frozen to death!" She narrowed him a look and sat up in the bed.

"Don't you know?" He gently urged her back onto the pillow. His beautiful, loving fraa and her big heart. How grateful he was Gott was always in control. "The hero always saves the girl."

"Ach, now you are being *gegisch.*"

"I love you, LeEtta." He'd held back the words long enough. Ben had known soon after their wedding his heart was hers, but once more his foolish, stubborn pride stood in the way. When she opened her mouth, Ben lifted a hand. He wasn't finished. "I'm sorry it took me this long to tell you. I'm sorry I've been so stubborn and selfish and…"

She reached up and touched his face. "Angry. Bitter. Are you also sorry you pretended not to like my cooking?"

"Jah, terribly sorry for that. I love everything you cook, but no more cheese, please." He cocked his head and offered her a timid grin. In return, her smile bloomed. He didn't have the full effect of the light that often wafted from her. Her eyes glassy, her skin ashen, but his heart tripped up again, as it had that first time.

"You should get your rest. Dok Stella says you need plenty of it."

"I'm not sure I can now. You just told me you loved me, Benuel Ropp."

Ben slid into the bed beside her, lifting his arm invitingly. LeEtta needed no encouragement to rest her head there. "Just sleep, dear. I'm not leaving your side, and I'll still love you when you wake up." He leaned down and kissed her lips gently then pulled her close to him.

"Are you warm enough?"

"I am now," she said.

CHAPTER THIRTY

"Onei?" Arlen called out in a low voice before stepping all the way into the house. Surely Oneida was awake. Arlen suspected she was already cooking up something hearty for LeEtta this morning.

Arlen on the other hand hadn't slept a wink all night. He'd almost lost the only person in his life. LeEtta was the world to him, and all he had after losing Laura. He'd tossed and turned, thanking God upon every breath for keeping Letty safe. Then Arlen realized something he had been avoiding for some time. LeEtta wasn't the only one his heart cared for.

Oneida was right. Life was a gift, and he still had plenty of life in him yet. A person could be cut short of it at any given moment. Arlen was no youngie, and he still ached for love. The kind of love he remembered having all those years ago. He'd had only a short time with Laura. Those blessed beautiful first years, and he had spent a lifetime living them out in his mind, over and over and over. It had been enough, until now.

"Arlen." Oneida appeared in the doorway. Her wrinkled dress and crooked kapp evidence she had obviously stayed up all night seeing over Letty.

"If you've kumm to see in on LeEtta, they're still sleeping," Oneida said, removing her glasses and rubbing her eyes before putting them back on and floating him a half smile. "I must have dozed off."

"I'm sure you needed some rest too," Arlen replied feeling all of a sudden tongue-tied.

"If you give me a few minutes, I can ready breakfast."

"I'm not here for breakfast," Arlen admitted. "Well, I'm never going to turn down anything you cook." Her face turned a pretty shade of warm pink, causing his hands to tremble. Since when did he tremble at anything life tossed at him?

"I'd like to talk to you before they wake." *Because no man wants an audience when he's about to make a fool of himself.* He had to be touched in the head to think she'd even consider his thoughts.

"Oh." Her mouth made a pretty little O shape. Arlen liked the sound of surprise in her raspy voice. "Let me at least get us some kaffi first."

Arlen removed his coat and hat while she put water on to boil. He didn't need anything to make him any more nervous, but perhaps it was best Oneida was fully awake to hear him out.

She fetched them both a cup, then added sugar, a splash of milk, and enough of that healthy instant kaffi stuff that he was beginning to take a liking to.

She set down a cup at his seat and then her own. He gave her time to take a few sips, in no rush to end being near her. Truth be told, once revealing his true feelings, this might be the last time they spent alone together.

"What did you want to talk about?" Oneida inquired as she sat gingerly before him, sipping on her cup. Arlen stared at her longer than he should have. She was nothing like Laura, but then again, after twenty-four years, a man did some changing.

"What happened to Letty got me thinking." He looked down into his kaffi, the creamy mix such a perfect contrast of Oneida's eyes. He lifted his gaze once more and felt his heart kicking at him to get on with it.

"Ach, I know. I still can't believe how close we came to losing her!"

Her head shook as she stared into her cup, lost on the fact she said *we.* Arlen's heart swelled, knowing she cared for his dochter as much as he did. "I know how much you care for her, and I want you to know how much I appreciate you for being here for her."

"Nee, I'm so happy to be here. Your dochter is such a fine person, Arlen. Watching her and Ben find love and healing together is just wonderful." She sighed, a soft sound that made him get all trembly again.

"Jah, we all needed healing, I think. Me especially, and I want to thank you for that too."

Oneida ducked her head again, her innocence on display. He rather liked the woman who didn't take no for an answer, but her tender side appealed to him too.

"You're wilkum, but you helped me too, Arlen. I have held on to something that was taken from me long ago. If not for you, I would have never realized I could have what they do."

"We both can." He pushed his cup aside and reached for her hand. It was cool to the touch and as soft as a new pillow. Arlen inhaled a breath and let it out slowly. This was so much easier when he was twenty-three and eager. "Will you want to return back to Ohio soon?"

"Ach," she said, her thin brows lifting in surprise. "I can't very well keep on here. Those two don't need me in the way while they are getting started. But I will admit, I don't look forward to going back one bit."

"Then don't." It was a simple plea, yet filled with the desperations in his heart.

"What do you mean?"

"You know what I mean, Onei." She smiled at the nickname. "I don't want you to go. In fact, I very much would like it if you stayed . . .here. . .with me."

"Are you asking me to marry you?" Her brows lifted in surprise as her lower jaw hung open in the reality of what he was asking her. She hadn't a clue how beautiful she was when something took her by surprise.

"Jah, I am. I never thought my heart could love another; Laura meant so much to me. But you came, and it opened right up. I've enjoyed our talks together and look forward to many more with you. I've been falling a little more in love with you each time I see you. I know we aren't youngies anymore with big plans, but whatever future I have is yours."

"Arlen Miller." She stood, tears falling like snowflakes, but the smile hinted that she might actually consider his proposal. He stood, held his breath, and hoped God had delivered more to his life than a son-in-law who made his farm and daughter happy.

"I would love that!"

"You would?" Arlen was taken back, and yet, the sudden urge to kiss her propelled him forward. Maybe Letty was more like him than he thought.

LeEtta smiled as she stirred pancake batter in the large bowl. The love between a man and a woman were indeed very different than the love between a husband and wife. Her heart fluttered, recalling how Ben had held her last night.

Laughter filled the kitchen, pulling LeEtta back to the present. "Don't be taking all day. The pan is hot," Mammi Iola reminded her. She'd arrived bright and early to check on LeEtta. What she got instead was hearing Daed's announcement that he and Oneida would marry kumm spring. Oneida had always thought spring was the perfect season to wed, the beginning of the seasons.

LeEtta poured batter into the hot skillet while Oneida flipped bacon to crisp next to her.

"I can't wait to send word to mei family," Oneida whispered. "Clay and Liz will be more surprised than I was." She giggled.

Of that LeEtta was certain. Daed too was all smiles. How LeEtta's heart filled seeing him so happy!

They all sat to enjoy breakfast together on this fresh day of new beginnings. While Ben and Daed talked of spring crops, Mammi Iola and Oneida swapped recipes for lemon custard. LeEtta soaked it all in as she devoured pancakes drenched in maple syrup. Love had returned to the farm, and it filled the tiny house all the way to the rafters. Her heart silently sang in the waft of hope, love, and tomorrows.

Chewing slowly, LeEtta considered each member with immense love and hope for all their futures. When her gaze landed on Mammi Iola, her heart skidded over a few beats.

In all her baking and searching for a new husband, Mammi Iola was still alone. LeEtta watched as she chewed on a slice of bacon, listening to Oneida, and wished there was someone out there who could bring Mammi as much joy as Ben had her. Someone like Dawdi, who always made an extra light shine in Mammi's eyes.

Silently, LeEtta prayed God would see over even the least of them if it be His will.

"Why don't you go rest in the next room while we tidy up," Oneida urged, getting up from the table.

"I'll make you a cup of kaffi and bring it in soon enough," Ben urged as well. "You still look a little pale, my dear."

LeEtta didn't know how she looked, but she had never felt more fussed over in all her life. Near-death experiences to love's gentle awakenings. She didn't mind getting out of doing dishes, so she happily slipped into the sitting room.

Standing at the front window, she watched a pair of cardinals hop from one snowy mound to another, their beautiful red coats standing out in the white world around them.

Contentment washed over her. She couldn't be happier for her father, and for herself. Praying since she was but a toddler for a mamm, she'd not let the fact she was now grown and married discourage her sweet blessings. *God's timing*, she measured, and smiled.

"I'm happy for them," Ben said stepping behind her. He offered her a cup and carefully wrapped his arms around her.

"Oneida has waited a long time for love, and I'm so happy for her, for them. Even Mammi Iola can't wait until they marry."

"Oneida always did have a way of making shadows disappear and smiles...appear," Ben told her.

"I will soon have a mudder," she said wiping a happy tear from her eye.

"Jah, and I can't think of a better mamm for you than someone just like her." He squeezed her gently. "It looks kault out there. We should go back to bed and stay there all day," Ben replied. Carefully, he took the cup from her hand, setting it on a nearby end table. In each other's arms, they watched crystals blink in the sunrise across the wide ocean of white.

"What of the milking?" LeEtta asked.

"Arlen is feeling young again." Ben chuckled in her ears. "Let's fake illness and go back to bed," he whispered as he nuzzled her neck.

LeEtta liked that idea. "Shh, or Mammi will hear you." LeEtta giggled as he tickled her tender flesh. LeEtta would have loved to pretend an illness that would force them back upstairs, but she had promised Oneida and Mammi Iola that she would help them plan for a wedding.

"Is that Ruby?" LeEtta noted the blue van with the maroon fender speeding up the drive. She had yet to know the woman to drive at a respectful rate.

"Jah. I wonder who she's bringing." The Englisch driver tended to leave the best of folks at LeEtta's door. She couldn't wait to see who was here.

LeEtta and Ben watched an older man step out and give the house a quick look before speaking to Ruby, who was probably staying until he found where he was heading. When he turned around again, he held a bouquet of flowers in his hands.

"Ach, do you know him?" LeEtta asked her husband.

"Nee, I have no idea who it is." Ben went to the door, LeEtta right behind him. Before the stranger could knock, Ben opened the door to greet him.

The stranger was not as tall as Ben. His coat looked new, but someone must have missed clipping a loose thread dangling from the bottom. His beard was full, the color of the snow shadowing his frame. His eyes were sunken with age as wrinkles creased every corner.

"Wilkum." LeEtta spoke first.

"Hello. I'm looking for Iola Graber. Her neighbor, Frannie, said she would be here." He voice was terribly deep, his stance determined.

"Jake Delegrange! What are you doing here?"

LeEtta flinched at the sound of Mammi Iola strolling up behind her. Over her shoulder, a dishcloth. Her perplexed look was evidence she wasn't expecting him.

Ben and LeEtta stepped back, giving the two elders room to speak. "You know him?" LeEtta whispered to her grandmother.

"Iola and I grew up together," Jake informed them, his grinning eyes never leaving Mammi's.

"Jah, but then you had to go break horses out west"—she flung an arm in the air—"and forgot to come back!"

"I didn't forget." Jake moved up to the porch and offered her the flowers. "I just took a spell to get back." Mammi didn't look amused as she crossed her arms stubbornly. It was all LeEtta could do not to burst into laughter. Mammi had spent three long years searching for a husband, and this one. . .was searching for her.

"I stopped by the bakery. Hazel hasn't changed a bit." He scratched his cheek and smirked.

"I should have figured she'd put her nose in my business. She always did."

"Well, if you'd listened to her back then, I wouldn't have had to ride in that van all the way here." He lifted a brow. "You still know how to make a decent cup of kaffi?"

LeEtta snickered. Mammi's kaffi was legendary for its stiffness, but right off she quieted, noting the elderly man at her door looked as if he might not mind strong kaffi at all but rather preferred it.

"Of course I do. Think I'm too old to remember?" Mammi scoffed, holding her ground. Whatever the history here between them, LeEtta ached to know.

"I hope you're not too old to remember everything," he said more softly, lowering his gaze.

"Well, kumm inside before you catch your death of cold out there. You're probably gonna want me to make taco soup too." Mamm turned and marched toward the kitchen, flowers in hand.

"Jake." Daed reached out and shook the elderly man's hand. "I hope you will join us for the noon meal, and perhaps supper later on. I'm eager to hear how you know Iola anyhow."

"Danke, I'd be happy too, if she don't toss me out the back door."

"Mammi Iola would never do that," LeEtta quickly put in. "You must be old friends," she prodded curiously.

"She taught me how to tie my shoes when I was just a boy, and I taught her how to ride a horse." Jake smiled. His wrinkles and tan flesh spoke of a man who hadn't set out to retire anytime soon.

"Can you still tie your own shoes?" Mammi Iola asked from the doorway.

"I can tie my own shoes and have gotten plenty good in the kitchen since we last spoke."

"Then you can stay for supper, I reckon."

LeEtta's Homemade Tartar Sauce

1 cup mayonnaise or Miracle Whip
2 to 3 tablespoons sweet pickle relish, drained
1 tablespoon minced onion
1 tablespoon lemon juice
⅛ teaspoon black pepper, or to taste
¼ teaspoon salt, or to taste
½ teaspoon dried dill weed

Mix ingredients until well blended. Keep refrigerated.

Iola Graber's Taco Soup

2 pounds hamburger
1 package taco seasoning
½ cup chopped onions
2 tablespoons flour
2 quarts tomato juice
½ cup brown sugar
1 can of pork and beans
1 small can of corn
1 cup salsa
Salt and black pepper to taste

Fry hamburger until no longer pink. Drain. Add onions during last several minutes of frying to saute lightly. Sprinkle with flour and stir well. Add remaining ingredients and heat to boiling. Serve with corn chips, cheese, sour cream, or ranch dressing.

Bestselling and award-winning author **Mindy Steele** is a welcomed addition to the Amish genre. Not only are her novels uplifting and her characters relatable, they touch all the senses. Her storyteller heart shines within her pages. Research for her is just a fence jump away, and she aims to accurately portray the Amish way of life. Her relationship with the Amish credits her ability to understand boundaries and customs, giving her readers an inside view of the Plain life. Mindy and her husband, Mike, have been blessed with five grown children, ten wonderful grandchildren, and many great neighbors.

THE HEART OF THE AMISH

Full of faith, hope, and romance, this series takes
you into the Heart of Amish country.

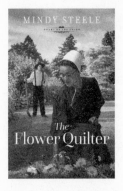

The Flower Quilter
By Mindy Steele

Barbara Schwartz struggles to find what brings
her joy amidst traditional expectations. But while
staying with her grandmother in Indiana, a chance
to help landscaper Melvin Bontrager may lead to
a unique expression of her artistry—and romance.

Paperback / 978-1-63609-642-1

Ruth's Ginger Snap Surprise
By Anne Blackburne

Ruth Helmuth learns that being independent
doesn't necessarily mean you can't accept help—
especially if it means saving what's most important
to you and maybe realizing your dreams in the
bargain!

Paperback / 978-1-63609-689-6

The Quilt Room Secret
By Lisa Jones Baker

Trini seems to have her life all lined up, owning
her own quilt store before the age of thirty—but
secret dreams pull her, despite falling for a handsome farmer. And soon she will be faced with an
agonizing choice for her future.

Paperback / 978-1-63609-775-6

Courting an Amish Bishop
By Mindy Steele

Simon, a dedicated bishop, and Stella, an herbalist, each have been so busy serving others that they have neglected romance—until now. Brought together to help the sick of the community, is it possible for them to have a second chance at love?

Paperback / 978-1-63609-815-9

Mary's Calico Hope
By Anne Blackburne

Mary Yoder is happy with her life despite her disability from a childhood accident, but then a Mennonite doctor comes into her life, challenging everything. Can Mary risk hoping for a future free of pain and a love outside the faith she has already been baptized into?

Paperback / 978-1-63609-855-5

Serenity's Secret
By Lisa Jones Baker

Serenity Miller, the flower shop owner of Arthur, Illinois, is content with her path in life. But a brush with danger and a taste of romance make her question the secrets she has always held close.

Paperback / 978-1-63609-958-3

JOIN US ONLINE!

Christian Fiction for Women

Christian Fiction for Women is your online home for the latest in Christian fiction.

Check us out online for:

- Giveaways
- Recipes
- Info about Upcoming Releases
- Book Trailers
- News and More!

Find Christian Fiction for Women at Your Favorite Social Media Site:

 Search "Christian Fiction for Women"

 @fictionforwomen